DARKNESS RISING

Volume Five: Black Shroud of Fear

Books by L.H. Maynard & M.P.N. Sims

Shadows at Midnight
Echoes of Darkness
Incantations
The Hidden Language of Demons
Moths
The Secret Geography of Nightmare
Selling Dark Miracles

As editors

Darkness Rising
Enigmatic Tales volumes 1-10
Enigmatic Novellas volumes 1-6
Enigmatic Variations volumes 1-5
Enigmatic Electronic online
Best Of Enigmatic Tales
F20

DARKNESS RISING

Volume Five: Black Shroud of Fear

L.H. Maynard & M.P.N. Sims

PRIME ○
Canton, Ohio

Contents

LOOKS
Mark Siegel

Jagger despised the homeless people who panhandled in front of the courthouse. He had no less sympathy for them than the dotcom executives he'd just put out of business, and no more. But there was something disquieting about them, something less real and yet more substantial, as when you happened to look in a mirror that revealed an unsuspected wart on your backside.

Even at five o'clock it was stifling out on the street, well over a hundred degrees, and not well suited to his two thousand dollar Armani three-piece. The month-long trial had taken it out of him, and the elation of his victory had left him light-headed. The setting sun blinded him with its glare. He actually stopped on the sidewalk, momentarily disoriented, forcing passers-by into the street to avoid him. Christ, what a mistake, pausing here. The bums would be on him like flies. As it was, he'd be hit up five or six times just walking to the parking lot, making him feel like a fool if he gave to each of them, arbitrary if he gave to some and not others, and ungrateful for his own good fortune if he gave to none. What in God's name was he supposed to do? He tried not to look at them, tried to move his legs toward the underground parking. If you looked and one of them was looking back, he had you. What the hell did that mean? The thought struck him as if it had come out of the ether rather than his own head. So it was only natural that he looked around.

The homeless man was sitting on a brick border of the elevated bushes that surrounded the courthouse. He swam into focus as Jagger's head finally cleared, and they were staring right at each other. The homeless man was filthy, bearded, layers of largely unidentifiable, wildly unmatched clothing ending in worn black army boots, a real trash heap harlequin. That he endured like that in this heat was a testament to misguided evolution, Jagger thought. Jagger thought about reaching into his pocket for change as a strategy to co-opt any request for dollar bills, but years of practice kept his hand from betraying the inclination. Jagger turned his head and started to move off down the sidewalk, but couldn't resist one reflexive look back. The look, so characteristically Jagger, denatured his curiosity with dismissiveness. It was a chilling, anaesthetizing look that said his best defense was this overwhelming offense. If Jagger's soul owned a vehicle, it was that look. And here was a bum, pulling him over for speeding through shit town. Because, when they locked eyes, Jagger found he couldn't pull away. Neither man spoke, yet, unmistakably, a transaction occurred.

When Jagger finally fell into the front seat of his Lexus, a few bucks lighter, he couldn't help stealing a glance at himself in the rear-view mirror. Whatever he had expected wasn't there. The engine roared to life at the twist of his key, and he realized he was surprised and relieved that it worked.

*

As it turned out, the car was one of the few things that still did work. When Jagger turned up at eight sharp in his office the following morning, the cheers and hearty congratulations of his colleagues and staff turned to puzzled frowns. Their looks stuck to him like dirty soap film. He closed his office door and tried to busy himself, but Morgan showed up almost immediately. His partner froze his hand in mid-shake and stared at him. 'Michael? What's the matter?'

'What do you mean?'

'You look . . . strange. I mean,' he added, 'you look, well, not fat or old or anything, but if I didn't know it was you, I'd swear someone was wearing your skin for a Halloween costume.'

'Just tired. Trial is like running a marathon. Takes a few days to re-hydrate.' In truth, Jagger didn't feel tired at all. He just felt . . . wrong.

He realized, after screwing up pretty much every meeting he had that day, that he was, to say the least, distracted. Distracted: that was the word. And detached, as if he were outside of his life, as if the work he'd done for the past fifteen years had nothing to do with him. And it went on like that for the next week, and the one after that.

*

Jagger began to experiment with being someone . . . different. He tried picking up women in bars. He tried going to the opera, to movies, to the racetrack. All of it was outside of him, not his life. Only when he was wandering the streets, alone at any hour of the day, did he have some sense of rightness, but it wasn't a pleasure, wasn't even a long-term possibility. His intellect was too restless; his values too related to the person he knew he had been for his entire adult life. He was wasting his time, achieving nothing.

That is, nothing except a gradual sense of awareness about what was missing. It was his complicated arrogance, the I-could-own-you-but-I-don't-want-you-near-me quality of his personality. He stared across the grubby bar he was trying out, through the bartender and into the mirror behind him, with what should have been that patented Jagger look. A slack-faced potato-head stared back at him. But then he did see the homeless man from the courthouse enter the bar.

He looked different too. He would have had to, to even get into this place without causing bouncers to heave to their size thirteen feet. He was a bit cleaner, sure, but he had a confidence, a sense of control that he hadn't had that afternoon a few weeks earlier. He didn't sit down, but not because he seemed uncomfortable. It seemed more as if he disdained the company. Well, what's wrong with that? Jagger thought. I disdain them too. Only I'm sitting here with them for some reason, while you're buying a bottle of Jim Beam to take back to the park, or the sewer, or whatever penthouse you apply your makeup in.

Jagger paid and followed the man out. From behind him, it was easy to observe the unselfconscious swagger, the way other people just as unselfconsciously moved around him, gave him a foot more on either side than they gave the other pedestrians on the sidewalk. Homeless people, thought Jagger, aren't just me without a home, without money. They're aware of living always in enemy territory, remaining hidden except to forage among those who fear and despise them. They live without possessions, while civilized people define themselves by their possessions, are defined by their possessions. He wondered if those homeless he saw still carrying their meager, filthy things around in plastic garbage bags were carrying vestigial organs, or trying for turtle-hood by carrying their homes on their back, or were like the dead waiting by the river for a boat to cross over into their new, true world. Their filth, he thought also, had to bother even them, so that they wound up retreating even from their own skins, further into themselves, trying to find a protected internal cave or space, peering out like turtles at the world hurtling past. They were alone, without family or lovers, without hope of love, or at best some kind of turtle-love, briefly banging the hardened shells of their outer-beings into each other.

The harlequin man entered a small ungated park near the courthouse, and walked up to the bandstand, drinking thoughtfully from the bottle, looking somehow like a politician about to take his place on stage.

'Hey! I want it back!' Jagger surprised himself with the outburst, an old pitcher finding he had one more good inning in him.

The bum spun around, raising his bottle like Diogenes's lantern. Just when Jagger thought he'd been insane for shouting, the man gave him one of Jagger's own quintessential looks.

'You son of a bitch,' Jagger gasped. 'You did steal my look. How the hell. . . '

'Fuck off.' The bum mounted the stage and headed for the back of the bandstand, but Jagger followed him.

'I'm serious. I don't know how you did it,' Jagger protested, hopping up on stage himself, 'but I want it back. I'll pay you. Look.' He pulled a wad of money out of his pocket.

The bum, glancing arrogantly back over his shoulder, paused and turned around. He eyed the wad suspiciously, though not without a calculating interest. 'You make a lot of money, huh? I could tell by your suit.'

'Yeah. So what?'

'So, you think you need whatever I've got to keep making a lot of money, huh?'

Jagger started, fumbled for a response, and the man laughed. 'If I gave a shit about a lot of money, why would I sell off the . . . thing that makes it?'

Jagger stared at him. The man laughed again, then held out the fifth of Jim Beam, offering Jagger a drink. He was offering Jagger charity, but it was only going to be loose change.

Jagger took a swig from the bottle, and then suddenly swung it with all his might at the man's head, connecting in an explosion of prismatic refractions and crystal sound. Then Jagger knelt on his chest and began to strangle the man, repeating only, 'I want it back. I want it back.'

Finally, a look of resignation seeped into the other man's eyes, an acceptance that he was going to die anyway. Jagger kept squeezing, and kept staring. 'Give it back!' Just as the man's eyes rolled up and a noise that wasn't a gasp escaped his lips, Jagger felt it, felt something, experienced a momentary blinding that did not come from light. He rolled on his back in exhaustion, eyes shut tight, as if to capture the thing fluttering around inside his eyes until it calmed enough to stay put. He lay next to the bum, a fallen brother or sleeping comrade, finally opening his eyes to the starry night.

Jagger found he wanted to keep lying there. But as the moon rose over the bandstand, he forced himself to his feet. There was his career to think of, a career he could finally get back to, now that . . . he was himself again. He didn't bother to look around the park for possible witnesses. That was a good sign, he thought, threading his way through the nodding and stooping bodies, restless on the lower benches and grassy knolls of the park. As long as you don't meet their eyes, they'll never really look at you, never be able to identify you, to get you. Yet something tugged at him as he was regaining the sidewalk, and he cast a look back, seeing . . . something. Ghosts? Victims? People who should have been invisible to him, who would be again, soon.

He found his car in the underground parking, fished the key into the ignition while the automatic interior light was still on, but then couldn't stop himself from looking up into the rear-view mirror. What stared back at him was a face furtive and confused with guilt, anxiety, a nameless fear, the face of a haunted turtle. As the interior light suddenly blinked out, he realized he'd stolen the wrong look.

TOAD
Geza Csath

Toads I detest. Other animals I like. I realize they're all equally magnificent creations of nature, but the toad disgusts me horribly.

I'll tell you why, friends. Just the thought of it and I shudder; my stomach turns over with a frightful aversion; damp, cold toads shuffle before my eyes and crawl into my throat; a toad's spittle croaks reeking in my ears; icy spasms strike my spine. I don't get to sleep tonight. Still, I have to tell you why the little toad disgusts me so, why my muscles stiffen in mortal alarm when I glimpse a pair of rotten, flickering toad's eyes shining into my mind out of the past.

The toad is the creature that brought me the most significant hours of my life, hours of horror, to say the least. Of course, you think that what I'm saying is spoken by a poor, miserable man whose eyes were confused. My friends, I know you may find mine an interesting case at best. But think again, I ask you, and don't be so inhumane. Because I suffered in behalf of thousands of others—I suffered a fear that crazed me, a fear thousands never meet with in their whole lives. You'll probably never come across it. So try to realize that and bear with me—don't just stare at me.

One April night I am shaken out of my dreams. It's raining. I turn over and try to get back to sleep. I toss, I turn; I remake my pillow; but I can't sleep. A kind of fever shakes me there in the quiet, in the dark; a nervy, peculiar fearfulness holds me. Outside the April shower's pouring down. Beside me my wife is breathing.

I feel that dread overcoming me. No hiding from it anywhere.

At first I try. I read to myself. I do addition and multiplication in my head. I go down the old list of classmates' names in my head. Nothing works. The fear grows and spreads into every drop of blood in my body. My heart is jumping. I feel a pressure in my skull. I am freezing all over and my forehead's sweating.

Then a sound strikes my ears. A sound like a crying child, the moaning of a tortured beast. The sound paralyzes the brain in my head. A cramping shivering leaps up and down my spine.

I listen.

The sound repeats itself louder, stronger. I listen, and every nervous fiber stiffens with the horrible torture of it. A gripping howl, challenging, threatening me at first from a great distance, and then right around me as though it poured out of the furniture in the room, the very wood of our bed.

The sound of an infant whimpering, being tortured to death. The sound of an ancient owl with torn wings, crying its destruction out to the night.

And it never stops. It pauses at whiles. Then steadily grows stronger, more painful, horrifying.

I am bathed in sweat. I jump from our bed, light a candle, listen. Again the sound comes from far off, and then emanates from around me. Shivering, holding my hands over my ears I go from room to room. Now it seems to be coming from the kitchen. As I approach, this ghastly, whimpering moaning and croaking seems to fill the entire kitchen.

I am desperate to locate it. It seems to be coming from one corner, where the washtub is. I tear the tub away. It's an animal the size of a cat. It's curled up in a ball, and now it's sluggishly unfolding itself towards me.

It's a toad. But what a toad! I've never seen anything like it. It's got hair all over it. A nightmarish green flickers in its eyes. A miasmic stench blossoms from it. And the sound is streaming, pouring, flooding from its gaping mouth. The ghastly song is uttered as though directed by some great force.

And the instant I'd seen him, a thought came that seized me by the heart.

In our district they believe that someone must die in the house where a hairy toad appears in the night. I'd even heard of several such deaths myself. One of our neighbors, a rich farmer, had recently told me he'd seen the cursed thing with his own eyes—and his beautiful daughter Agnes had died soon after, at eighteen.

Not for a minute had I believed him. One doesn't after all believe in fairytales. Besides, a toad like that's unknown by the scientists; so why should I have believed him?

But now, standing face to face with the toad, I believed its horrible portent with all the blood in my being! I dropped like a bolt on it, and I knelt tight on its cold, repulsive body.

And it burst out with a roar so powerfully deep that it seemed the neighing of a stallion. I was scared that it would waken my wife. I seized the beast and hurled it with all my strength against the tiles of the kitchen floor. It clanked like a cannonball and got up, bounding back to its corner in one jump. In my helpless rage I kicked at it and kept it from landing on its feet. A green fluid, oozed from it, a sticky, smelly secretion that marked its trail. While I was trying to gain time to think what to do, I spotted the hatchet and decided to destroy the monstrosity. I drove it to the corner where the hatchet was standing and grabbed it to make a swift end to the beast. Whether I fumbled or missed or whatever—but the toad got to its hind legs, jumped up at me, and bit me right in my neck.

It had teeth.

I shook it off me and held it down, kneeling on it again. It neighed strongly, as it had earlier. Then I smashed at its head with the butt of my hatchet. Green blood spurted in my face, and I realized what an incredible strength this animal exerts to escape when it's trapped. I bashed at it and battered it again and again. Then I chopped it to pieces, cutting off its legs and its head, until only a shapeless, slimy and foul green mass remained.

I finished this terrible job, sighing with relief. I felt that I'd succeeded, perhaps, in saving my nearest and dearest from the threat of death. Trembling, shivering yet peaceful too, I went back to our bedroom. My wife still slept, breathing evenly. A smile passed over her pale face. I went up to her and kissed her. She sighed faintly. For a long while I gazed anxiously at her, and then, exhausted, fell heavily asleep.

I wake early the next morning—I'm an early riser—and it comes to me that I never cleared the toad's remains away, or the bloody hatchet and the traces of the struggle. I slip out of bed, dash towards the kitchen to prevent—if it's at all possible—the servants or the children from seeing anything, or wondering what had gone on in there.

And I *am* surprised—not a trace visible. The hatchet leans in its corner.

The kitchen floor is spotless, and the maid not yet in from her room.

Now, my friends, naturally you say I dreamt it all. I'd like you to know therefore that exactly two weeks after that night my wife was laid out in her coffin.

JACKIE
Gene O'Neill

Dr. Alexander Cato waited for his old friend, Shane McCarthy, at the top of the steep flight of steps up to the San Francisco Hall of Justice on Bryant Street, feeling more than a little apprehensive.

Last night he'd readily agreed to meet Mac, an attorney with the San Francisco Public Defender's Office, at 9:45 A.M. to conduct a psychiatric interview with the notorious Jack Dumont.

Now, Alex had second thoughts. After all, in the last six months since moving north to Marin County, he'd built up a pretty solid private practice. What did he have to gain getting involved with this case? From everything he'd read about the accused, it was pretty cut and dried. Dumont, a transvestite, had picked up and brutally killed five men during the last year or so. But a week ago in a lot south of Market, four teenage squatters had witnessed him murder and mutilate his fifth victim. The cops caught him still in drag, knife in hand, and hands stained with his victim's blood.

Surprisingly, last night on the phone Mac swore that Dumont was innocent and he would convince Alex if only he'd meet with the accused. It was ridiculous—the man was obviously a sociopath, probably fit the FBI profile of a serial killer—

'Hey, pal!' Mac shouted, puffing up the steps, then hugging Alex, as he caught his breath. 'Sorry I'm late. C'mon.'

Alex's old friend led them through the noisy crowd loitering in the lobby and past the security station with the metal detectors, directing Alex into the elevator, finally leaving the din behind them. On the fourth floor they found the appropriate defendant's room: a small, depressing cubicle, dimly-lit, furnished with a heavy wooden table—scarred with scratched-out graffiti, mostly initials—and four matching chairs.

McCarthy sat his thin briefcase on the table, and nodded at Alex's huge, beat-up brown case still on the floor. 'Planning on staying overnight?'

Alex laughed. It was indeed as large as a small suitcase, but he found it was just right for everything he needed when away from the office on assignment—a battery of psychological tests, a small recorder, notepads, pens, pencils, several large reference texts, and the usual medical diagnostic instruments.

The attorney took on a serious expression as he flipped open his briefcase, withdrawing a thin manila folder.

'Here's what I have so far,' he said, opening the file on Dumont. 'He has no record, never been in any kind of trouble, except for a DUI in the distant past, nothing juvenile, at least that's accessible. He's never been in jail before. And never in a mental institution.' McCarthy paused and glanced at Alex. 'Our boy is clean, except for a possible drinking problem, which I'll come back to later. He grew up on the Peninsula, raised by a single mother. They lived in the same trailer park in San Mateo during most of his school years. After high school graduation, he spent four years in the military, a bus driver at Kadena Air Force Base on Okinawa most of that time. No problems in the service. Got out and drifted for about ten years, doing various kinds of work, but always employed. Only problem was with alcohol. About six years ago he settled down in the City, began going to regular AA meetings, and was on the wagon, until two years ago, when he started drinking again.' He glanced at Alex. 'That's the highlights, pal.'

'Any problems as a kid?' Alex asked. 'Channel 5 mentioned something about a history of abuse. And later, you know, torturing animals, being mean to other kids, that kind of thing?'

'I've got no details there, but I could have someone check the trailer park in San Mateo, see if anyone remembers him. Maybe check police complaint records there.'

'What kind of work did Dumont do in the City?'

'He's been a veterinarian's assistant for five years. Let's see, Haig's Small Animal Hospital in the Marina. Dr. Haig has nothing but praise for his work.'

'How about checking his co-workers, see how he actually treated the animals, anything else they want to say about him?'

There was a rap on the door, then a corrections officer led Jack Dumont in by the arm, seating him at the table and saying, 'I'll be just outside the door, Mr. McCarthy.'

'Thanks, Gavin.'

Dumont's physical presence surprised Alex. Of course the man wore an orange jump suit, like all San Francisco jail inmates, and he was shackled, both hands chained together to a waist belt and his ankles too. No, it wasn't that. It was his general demeanor.

Jack Dumont was older than he appeared on TV—forty at least. Alex had thought he appeared prematurely bald, but his blonde hair was just very thin on top and receding—you could see the pink of his skull—and combed straight back. His cheeks were rosy, which contributed to the youthful appearance. He wore a slight, pleasant smile, his gaze steady, his flat bluish-green eyes wide with a kind of childlike curiosity. He was neat and appeared to be very alert.

'Jack,' McCarthy began, 'this is my old friend, Dr. Alex Cato, a psychiatrist. He's here to help us with your defense. He may want to talk to you a number of times, give you some tests, whatever. Essentially, Dr. Cato is here to determine if you are the type of person who could have committed any of the five murders.'

'I'm not crazy, doctor,' Dumont stated bluntly, looking directly at Alex.

'No, Jack,' McCarthy said emphatically. 'That's not why he's here, to determine insanity . . . ' The attorney paused, then added, 'I know you're innocent, *not* crazy.'

Dumont shifted his gaze to McCarthy, then nodded, his smile broadening slightly. 'Thank you,' he whispered gratefully, almost shyly.

'You're up, Doctor,' McCarthy said, pushing back slightly from the table.

Alex took the recorder from his fat briefcase. 'I like to tape my interviews, Jack, so I can listen to them again, perhaps jotting down additional questions I didn't ask and so forth. Do you mind?'

Dumont shook his head. 'I don't have a problem with that, Doctor.' His gentle voice matched his appearance.

For a moment, Alex forgot he might be talking to a murderer, and a very brutal one at that. He cleared his throat and began, 'Jack, as I'm sure you might guess, I'd like to start back a few years.'

But before he started the background questions, Alex slipped a pack of *Marlboros* and a lighter from his jacket pocket and put them down on the table just within Jack's reach, even with his hands shackled. Dumont didn't make a move toward the cigarettes, nor did he ask for one.

'Smoke, Jack?' Alex finally asked, pushing the pack a little closer.

'Thanks, Doctor,' Jack replied, managing to clumsily slip a cigarette from the pack. Alex lit it for him, smiling to himself. It was a rough measure of impulse control that Dr. Michael Jennings had often used back at L.A. County Hospital psychiatric unit when Alex was still an intern. 'Okay, let's begin with your family . . . '

About an hour or so later, Alex and McCarthy were still in the room, but the guard had taken Jack Dumont away.

The attorney made an anxious shrugging gesture with his hands, shoulders, and eyes, as if asking his friend: *What do you think?*

'Well, he doesn't fit the typical profile,' Alex said. 'There may have been some childhood abuse from several of his mother's boyfriends, but she was usually the victim. He doesn't indicate any early problems with animals or other kids—no latent hostility. In fact, he seems to really like animals, wants to breed dogs some day. He's older than the serial murderer profile indicates. Of course there have been older serial killers, but their grisly work was delayed by being institutionalized. You say there is no record of that. The excessive drinking may indicate some kind of problem—I'm not sure if it's sexual or not. He did have a girlfriend until two years ago. And he doesn't really fit the sociopath pattern either. His speech is very measured and precise, thoughtful, almost painstakingly so, not the least impulsive. His behavior doesn't seem impulsive either. He appears to know right and wrong and have a conscience. Able to give and receive affection. There's lots of other stuff. I'll need to do extensive testing *if* I decide to get involved. But I want to listen to the tape tonight, before I give you a final decision on that, okay?'

'Well, take this home, too, pal,' the attorney said, pulling a long sheet from his briefcase that resembled a seismograph with its squiggly lines. 'This is a lie detector test, given two days ago by one of the City's best. The attached report unequivably states: Jack Dumont does not *believe* he killed anyone, ever. My client is innocent, Alex.'

'Then how do you explain the eyewitnesses and other evidence?'

McCarthy grinned wryly. 'The eyewitnesses are all wrong. That wasn't Jack Dumont. If you decide to get involved, I'll show you the real killer.'

Show me?

They stood up at the same time, Alex more than a little confused. His initial findings? A lie detector confirmation that Jack Dumont was innocent? And his friend's promise to reveal the real killer?

'Call me when you decide to climb aboard, Alex,' McCarthy said, as they parted at the bottom of the steps to the Hall of Justice.

Alex Cato called Shane McCarthy later that night and agreed to work with him on the Jack Dumont defense. He was almost positive that Dumont was not a sociopath and didn't fit the typical serial killer profile either; but it was curiosity that really hooked him. Curiosity and a chance to do something more exciting, perhaps be in the public limelight. Even though McCarthy enthusiastically welcomed him aboard, Alex couldn't get the attorney to say anything more about the *real* killer. They agreed to meet again with Jack Dumont at the Hall of Justice, the next day at 3:00 p.m.

Tuesday afternoon, the attorney read additional information his staff had uncovered as they waited for Dumont in the defendant's room. 'The old couple managing the trailer park remembers Jack as a good kid. No problems, except with a couple of his Mom's boyfriends. Loud arguments, that type of thing. His co-workers at the vet say he likes animals, period; and they are shocked that he is accused of any crime of violence.' McCarthy glanced at his notes. 'Oh, and no formal police complaints in San Mateo, except for one assault complaint against a boyfriend, when they first moved to the park. That's all I have.'

The door opened and the same guard ushered Dumont in. Shackled, the defendant sat on the other side of the table after first saying hello to both of them.

'Jack, Dr. Cato wants to do a number of tests,' McCarthy explained. 'But maybe he can do those tomorrow or sometime later in the week. I'd like to . . . Oh, I brought you something.' He opened his briefcase, taking out what looked like a pair of binoculars; then, unscrewing one of the lenses, he turned to Alex. 'You need to forget what you're seeing here, Doctor.' He extended the binoculars to Dumont, who tipped the opened lens to his lips and greedily gulped down the contents from the disguised flask. 'Jack gets pretty dry, and this will help lubricate his vocal cords,' McCarthy added by way of explanation, actually winking conspiratorially at Alex.

Jack Dumont sighed, and handed back the binoculars. The attorney screwed the lens on and put the disguised flask back in his briefcase. 'Just an ounce of good bourbon.' Then he pointed at Dumont, who was slumping down in a very relaxed posture, chin against his chest, eyes closed.

McCarthy turned to his friend, explaining, 'I first discovered this after another lawyer back at the office, Trey Ellroy, suggested that maybe booze tipped off something in Jack. As you recall, Dumont fell off the wagon about the same time as the first killing. So, I took a chance, smuggled in a small drink. Boy, was Trey right. Watch this!'

After a moment or two, Dumont, who appeared to be asleep or in a trance, suddenly sat up and visibly shuddered, as if experiencing a nightmare. Then, he gasped in a deep breath, and his eyes snapped open. His facial features had been dramatically transformed. Hardened, more streetwise, more cunning; the eyes less childlike and deepening in tone, actually glittering with an emerald fire of malevolence; the lower lip was pushed out slightly in a kind of seductive pout.

'Jackie, are you here?' McCarthy whispered, peering intently into the bright gaze.

The eyes blinked, focused on the attorney. 'Yeah, man, I'm right here in front of you.' It was not Jack Dumont's gentle, shy voice. It sounded like a woman's . . . kind of loud, hoarse, and sexy.

Then the light bulb went on over Alex's head. *Jesus.* He was looking at a multiple personality alter-opposite gender.

'Jackie, this is Dr. Cato. He's here to help Jack beat this thing.'

The crooked smile was actually kind of attractive and reminded Cato a little of the actress, Ellen Barkin.

'Hey, a shrink, all right, and not a bad lookin' dude, either,' Jackie said, staring into Alex's face, licking her lips in a provocative manner. Then she laughed deeply. 'Don't worry, Doc, I ain't puttin' no moves on ya.' She shook her head. 'I usually go for a little rougher trade, if you know what I mean.'

'Tell Dr. Cato about that, Jackie. Getting all tricked out and cruising the bars,' McCarthy suggested.

She glanced over at the attorney, giving him a hard look, before shrugging and nodding, as if saying: *Okay, why not?*

'Yeah, been doin' it for the last two years, ever since numbnuts let me out—'

'Let you out, Jackie?' Alex interrupted, after clearing his throat. 'How'd he do that?'

She smiled slyly, then whispered, 'The booze triggers it, man. The more he drinks, the longer I'm out.'

'Does he know about you, Jackie?' asked Alex, putting the pack of

Marlboros down in front of himself on the table, barely within her shackled reach.

'Nah, he doesn't have a clue,' Jackie explained in a kind of bored tone. 'He wakes up, everything blacked out—' Suddenly she reached out and deftly snaked a cigarette from the pack. 'Ya got a light, Doc?'

Alex took out the lighter and lit the *Marlboro* for her.

Jackie took a deep drag, turned slightly and blew the smoke in the attorney's direction, who she knew did not smoke. She grinned mischievously, then turned back to Alex and said, 'Yeah, I used to get out in the old days, but not for very long, and never dressed *to kill* . . . ' She giggled. 'If ya'll forgive the expression.'

'So, you been with Jack for a long time?' Alex asked.

'Nah, not really,' she replied, sucking in another deep drag from the cigarette, watching the smoke drift up toward the air intake screen. ''Bout six years or so, I think. Caught me just before he quit drinking.'

Caught me? Alex repeated to himself, thinking the expression odd but keeping quiet, hoping Jackie would continue. But she said no more and eventually reached over and snubbed out the half-smoked *Marlboro* in the ashtray. Then she closed her eyes and leaned back, her face gradually softening . . .

Now it was Jack Dumont again slumped in the chair.

'That was the real murderer,' McCarthy whispered, reaching over and pushing the ashtray away from him to the far side of the table. 'But we can't keep her out long. I bring in any more than an ounce of booze, and we're risking getting caught by the guard.'

Jesus. Alex had never seen an alter in person, even though he'd read about a number of cases, and seen some film at USC. He shook his head, then murmured as if refreshing his own memory, 'Multiple Personality Syndrome . . . one of the five Dissociative Reactions, characterized by separation of self and some kind of memory loss.' He turned to the attorney, who grinned back broadly.

'Hey, pal, we got something here or what?' McCarthy asked.

Alex nodded at his friend: *We got something here.*

'Okay, I have some precedent research to do,' the attorney said, standing up. 'From your side, I want to know more about this Multiple Personality Syndrome thing. Everything you can dig up, especially how valid it is considered within the psychiatric community. And how about this sociopath deal? If he's not one, do we need some extensive testing for support?'

'I'll take care of my end,' Alex said, picking up his suitcase. 'I'll want to do more testing, first . . . ah, set me up an afternoon block of time on Friday,' he said, after checking his patient calendar.

On Friday, Alex met Dumont alone and administered a pair of projective tests, the Rorschach and the Thematic Apperception Test, then the Minnesota Multi-phasic Personality Inventory, which had a built-in key to detect subject lying. He also conducted a structured interview, using the recently published Sociopathic Serial Murderer Profile Inventory developed by the FBI.

Over the weekend, Alex scored the tests; and he began his survey of the medical literature on MPS.

Early Monday afternoon, Alex called McCarthy and discussed his progress. 'Yeah, Mac, I'm one hundred percent convinced that Jack Dumont is not a sociopath, nor does he fit the FBI serial murderer profile. And I've got some test back up now, including one with a key that he's definitely telling the truth.'

'That's great, pal,' McCarthy answered. 'And you could testify to all that in court?'

'Sure, no problem,' Alex replied confidently, wondering about the restrained nature of his friend's tone. 'What's the matter, Mac?'

His friend sighed deeply. 'Oh, I've researched several cases where attorneys tried to introduce MPS as a defense in a criminal trial,' McCarthy answered slowly. 'So far though, I haven't found *one* where the California courts allowed it as a defense. No precedent for what we want to do.'

'Other states?'

'Yeah, I have a clerk checking.' Then, McCarthy chuckled, his enthusiasm picking up slightly. 'Man, can you see us introducing Jackie during the trial?'

Alex smiled and nodded to himself. But he knew that was unlikely unless they could get MPS allowed in court as an accepted legal concept, and the thought dampened his spirits.

'What else you got on your end, pal?'

'Well, it kind of fits what you say about non-acceptance in court,' Alex answered. 'There was a lot of excitement years ago, when the first cases of MPS were published, but the enthusiasm in the psychiatric community died down. In treatment, the alter or alters were usually called up by the therapist during hypnosis and *that* was the problem. All the subjects were highly suggestible, and there was some controversy that alters were the result of some kind of subtle suggestion by therapists, actually originating with the psychiatrists—'

'You mean they thought the patient actually caught MPS from the therapist?'

'In a way that's right,' Alex responded, smiling wryly at the way his friend characterized MPS as a contagious disease, making him recall Jackie's expression: *Caught me.*

Alex continued, 'And up until recently, there has been an absence in the literature of very many cases; but in the last four years there has been a major swing, again a growing acceptance of MPS within the psychiatric community, especially in spousal abuse treatment. The direction of therapy has changed radically, too. Now, there is an attempt at fusion of the alters into one personality, a unification of the dissociative reaction. Hypnosis is still the major accessing tool to the alters. No doorways opened with booze.'

'What about psychiatrists successfully testifying in court about the existence of MPS?'

'The medical literature doesn't mention anything about that.'

'Wait, maybe *I* can find something under Spousal Abuse, one of the recent murder cases where MPS might've been used as a self defense,' McCarthy interrupted, enthusiasm returning to his voice. 'Yeah, I'll check it out. What's next with you, pal?'

'I'd like to run a few tests on Jackie, if we can keep her out longer—then compare similar test results with Jack's.'

'Whoa, that's a good idea but really dangerous,' McCarthy said, pausing. Reluctantly, he agreed, 'Well, maybe another ounce in the binoculars. But we're out on the edge doing that, you understand?'

'I know,' Alex agreed, 'but the results might justify it. Do you think she'll cooperate?'

'I don't know,' McCarthy said, his tone again restrained.

They set up Wednesday afternoon, when Alex had only one late appointment, followed by an evening group.

On Wednesday, Jackie emphatically declared, 'No friggin' tests, period. I ain't the goofy one, Doc.'

She preferred to talk about the case, smoking one *Marlboro* after another, growing exceedingly restless as she interrogated both McCarthy and Alex, gradually realizing that so far the defense didn't look too strong.

'Well, I ain't hangin' 'round and goin' down the tubes with ole numbnuts,' she said with a sense of finality. 'Nope.' She shook her head, frowning deeply. 'You boys don't get him off, he'll be by his ownself on death row, maybe *sooner.*'

McCarthy cut a laugh short when Jackie glared at him, her green eyes flashing. 'Hey, man, I mean it!'

'What exactly do you mean, Jackie?' Alex asked. 'You have plans on leaving?' The discussion had shaken his confidence about the wisdom of staying involved in the case.

Jackie stared at him for a moment in silence. Then she kissed her fingertips, and leaned across the table, stretching to the end of her shackles, and patted Alex's right hand, as if she were reassuring a small boy. 'Yeah, I got plans, Doc,' she whispered hoarsely then winked lewdly.

'What are you saying, Jackie?' McCarthy said. 'You aren't going anywhere.'

For a moment she just let her wet fingertips rest on Alex's hand, looking him squarely in the eye. Then she straightened, leaned back in her chair, and laughed humorlessly. 'Yeah, I guess you're right, counselor,' she said, glancing first at McCarthy, then at her shackles. 'I'm pretty well stuck, ain't I, now?'

After meeting with his late afternoon patient at his office in San Rafael, and returning to an empty home before group, Alex felt restless and at odds with himself—trying to think of a way to gracefully bail out on his commitment to his friend. Jaimie was gone, still teaching one of her Lit classes at Marin Community College. His throat felt dry and sore.

Alex still had over an hour before group. Not interested in watching TV or reading, he wandered the house, still feeling unsettled. Then, reacting to a strong impulse, he got back in his car and drove through town, stopping at a seedy-looking saloon just off Highway 101, *The Black Knight.* A place he'd never visited.

Inside the bar, Alex paused, letting his eyes adjust to the dark, recognizing Merle Haggard's husky voice coming from the jukebox, singing, 'Tulare Dust.' Two men dressed in work clothes were shooting pool, and paid him no mind. Alex crossed the room and slipped onto a stool at the bar, setting his briefcase down beside him, wondering why he'd brought the damn thing in here. Just a stupid habit, he told himself, grinning sheepishly and glancing around. No potential paying customers here.

The bartender, a beefy, red-faced man, wiped the already spotless counter, slid a basket of shell peanuts in front of Alex, and asked, 'What will it be, friend?'

'Ah, Jack Daniels and water,' Alex said, then added, 'make that a double, please.' He surprised himself with the order, not usually drinking hard liquor.

'You got it,' the bartender replied, grabbing a bottle of black label from behind him on the counter and pouring the whiskey. He hesitated a moment after giving Alex his drink, then moved down bar as one of the pool shooters came over and ordered two more Buds.

Alex took a couple of sips, the drink actually soothing his sore throat, and relaxed, enjoying the cool air in the bar. He intentionally kept his mind off the Dumont case. Behind him the pool balls clicked as the two men continued shooting. He finished his drink, already feeling the alcohol hitting his system. The bartender shuffled back and pointed at his empty glass.

Alex glanced at his watch, shook his head, and asked, 'Bathroom?'

'Down the hall past the jukebox,' the bartender answered, pointing in the general direction with the bottle of Jack.

Alex slipped off the stool, picked up his briefcase, and walked down the hall to the men's head. Inside the restroom, he set the case by the mirror, then paused to glance at himself. His face felt funny . . . hot, kind of numb. Suddenly, his vision tunneled and he was overwhelmed with a shortness of breath; gasping, he slumped, leaning against the cool mirror—

—She was smiling crookedly into the mirror, her emerald gaze glittering mischievously. She kneeled, slipped a cosmetics case from underneath her clothes in the briefcase, then, after carefully applying lipstick, eye shadow, and some liner, she winked and announced in her sex-husky voice, 'Showtime, folks!'

YOU PAY FOR THE ROOM
H. Dusendschon

Walking through the wall into the next room proved to be unnerving although simple enough. One just walked through as you would walk through an open door. An exact duplicate of the room she'd just left is what she found, but she stayed. The other room contained her dead body.

Evangeline worked the streets for five years and had a list of regular clients. She took extra business when things got slow. Her rates had increased to two hundred an hour, which rivaled the best girls out there. She was accomplished and beautiful.

She swallowed hard and returned to the room where she'd been killed. Her beauty had been snatched from her in death. Her face, blemish-free with lovely bone structure and creamy chocolate color, had turned purple and bloated. Her pretty, dark eyes bugged out, and her tongue filled her mouth. The cord used to strangle her still entangled her throat.

The guy appeared harmless. A mousy, little man with spectacles, not regular glasses but spectacles. Wearing an expensive suit, shoes, and speaking with dignity, he'd politely opened the door for her. He closed the door and struck from behind. It lasted for two minutes. He was surprisingly strong, and she couldn't scream. No rape, no sexual gratification, he just killed her. Pocketing the cord and dusting his hands, he left. He wore kidskin gloves.

He left her on the bed with her short skirt around her hips, arms and legs spread-eagled. She looked at her corpse. I have—had—nice legs, she thought.

They weren't chubby like most black women she'd seen. She walked back through the wall into the vacant room. She'd had enough.

Evangeline hoped somebody found her before she started to smell. She wondered how often these rooms were cleaned. Such a dump to die in, she thought. They rented the rooms by the hour here. She sat in a cheap wooden chair and cried. Surprised ghosts could cry, she looked at herself in the mirror. She looked the same as she did before she was killed, thank God. Her mascara ran. She wondered where one gets ghost makeup.

Not knowing what to do, she wandered around the hotel from room to room. Business was slow this time of morning. There were two couples in 405 and 407 going to it and a blowjob happening in 412. The girl looked fourteen. I can't stay here, she thought, and went down the stairs to the lobby. A young boy with a bejeweled old woman was registering as she went out to the street.

Standing on the steps, she saw the street as never before. People like her walked everywhere. Some of them walked around the living, others just passed right through them. Evangeline felt stifled and went around the corner of the building into the alley. The sun began to come up over the rooftops of the Combat Zone.

Three men stood in the rear of the alley; rather one sat and two stood. Two were white, one black and over seven feet tall. One had a baseball cap—New York Mets—and corduroy jeans with a turtleneck. The one sitting on a step had blond hair and bright blue eyes. He wore jeans, boots, a white shirt and wide belt, giving him the appearance of an out-of-place cowboy. He certainly looked scrumptious, she thought.

'Hi,' the baseball cap said. 'Hey look, Stretch, new blood and a real looker.'

'Be nice to the sister, Paddy,' the black man said. 'Looks like she's new to this condition. You must remember how you felt.'

She didn't know whether to shake or what to do. 'I'm Evangeline, but I'm called Angie. Some crazy john just strangled me in the hotel.' She wanted to cry again but held back.

'A lot of that going around,' the one called Paddy said. 'Along with shootings, knifings, poisonings, half the people in this city are dead.' He laughed at himself then and red hair fell out from under his cap. A smart-ass Irishman, Angie thought.

The cowboy, after listening to all this, stood up and spoke. His calm voice came through clear. 'Welcome, Angie, they call me Rafe.' He walked over to the Irishman. 'Are you ever going to get sick of the sound of your own voice? You're an idiot.'

Paddy shrunk back a little, and Stretch looked at his feet. She had no doubt who called the shots with this bunch. He turned to Angie. 'This guy's a serial killer. He's murdered eleven prostitutes in two months. I talked to some people about him last night.' He smiled at Angie for the first time. 'Yes, we're still considered people. We're between the two sides, between life and death. We can talk to and touch each other but not the living.'

'We should get her better clothes so she doesn't look like a whore,' Paddy said, with a cocky grin on his face.

'I am a prostitute and not ashamed of it.' Angie turned an angry face toward the Irishman. 'You probably gave us plenty of business.'

Paddy turned bright red, and Rafe laughed out loud. 'She's got you there, Paddy. You spent a lot of time in the Zone.'

Stretch spoke up. 'Isn't that where you bought it, Paddy? In a kind of barroom fight?'

The Irishman sulked now. 'At least my gang didn't shoot me.'

'It wasn't my gang. I never belonged to no gang.' Stretch turned to Angie. 'The cops said I got shot by accident in a drive-by. I just happened to live in the worst part of the city, and I'm a big target.' He showed her a wide grin.

Angie decided she liked the tall guy. He just accepted things as they came along. It made her feel guilty about her self-pity. 'How about you, Rafe, how'd you die?' she asked.

'I got involved in a battle,' he answered. Getting to his feet, he brushed himself off. 'Paddy's right, though. You should change clothes. We'd all be less distracted.'

She recognized the compliment, and it made her feel good. She even looked good dead. 'How do I change clothes?'

'Come on, we'll show you.' Paddy smiled and beckoned for her to follow. The four of them began walking up the street, toward the better part of town. They entered a large department store, and proceeded to the fashions. Angie felt uncomfortable there.

'Pick something out, whatever you like,' Rafe said.

She pointed at a purple sweater. It had a turtleneck but would show her shape. 'I can't just take it,' she said.

'Sure you can.' Rafe reached out and took the sweater off the rack. He held the sweater in his hand, but the original still hung there. 'You see? You have one and the other one is still there.'

'How . . . why . . . ' She couldn't come up with the question. Paddy and Stretch smiled at her.

'I'll try to explain,' Rafe said. 'Did you ever hear the term *doppelganger*?' She shook her head. 'It means ghostly double. It was meant for living people, but everything has one. Like your *doppelganger* is dead in a hotel room, but it still has its clothes on, right?'

She frowned a little but it made sense. Her dead body had on the same clothes she wore now. She could take clothes off the racks and there would be nothing missing. She'd gone to shopping heaven.

As if reading her mind, Rafe said, 'Don't get carried away. You don't need much stuff, and you have no place to put it. Your place is probably closed down, and we just pick vacant rooms in nice hotels to hang out in. You don't have to sleep, but you can. You don't need food, but you can eat or drink if you like just for the taste. Neither of those things are necessary now.'

She nodded and picked out a black pleated skirt, just short enough to show her legs. She also took a pair of black leather small heels, a leather jacket, and a jaunty red beret. She came from the dressing room looking classy.

'You didn't have to change in there.' Paddy offered some advice. 'Nobody could see you but us, and we're all naked before God.'

'God is one thing, but I'm not ready to get naked in front of you yet.' She smiled when she said it though. 'I'd like to find one of those hotel rooms for tonight if you guys don't mind. I want to make plans.'

'Remember, we don't know how long we're going to be In Between,' Stretch said. 'We could go to the other side any time.'

'I know, but I have to do this. I just thought you three would give me some advice.' Angie had a very serious look on her face.

'What's so important?' Paddy asked.

Angie raised her voice a little in anger. 'I need to figure a way to get the son-of-a-bitch that killed me before he gets another girl. I won't ask you to help, I just need some advice.'

'I'll help you, Angie,' Stretch volunteered, and Rafe nodded. They all looked at the Irishman.

'Okay, okay, I'll help too. Just thank the Lord he's provided you with the wisdom of the Irish.'

'There's very little we can do physically to stop this guy,' Rafe said, after he'd found them a nice room in a plush hotel. 'It takes a lot of practice and concentration to move an object in the living world.'

'But it can be done?' Angie asked.

'Yes, it can be done.' Rafe rose from the couch. 'Watch.'

He stood in the middle of the room, arms at his sides, staring at an empty beer can provided by the previous occupants. The can lifted from the table, floated to Angie, and returned. It had made a trip of almost ten feet. 'Now you try.'

Angie took up a position next to Rafe, staring at the can. She tried to narrow her mind to include nothing but the can, as if sighting a gun. Concentrating with all her might she moved it six inches in the air before it clattered down on the table.

Each took a turn. Paddy moved it the same distance as Rafe, but Stretch did the best. He had the can almost at hand, a distance of at least twenty feet, when it stopped and clattered to the floor. 'I started thinking about a ball game,' he said, and shuffled his feet. 'I always had lousy concentration. In school I stared out the window all the time. The teachers gave up on me.'

'Now you can all see how hard it is to do,' Rafe said, floating it easily back to the table. 'What if the can was full?'

Angie had been trying to pick the can up, but kept grabbing its ghostly counterpart. 'It's impossible,' she admitted. She thought for a minute then came up with an idea. 'Can we implant suggestions in the minds of the living?'

'That's easy in probably ninety percent of the people. You may have hit on something you can use.' Rafe smiled in approval, stroking her shoulder.

'You mean I could tell a lovely young thing to disrobe and she'd do it?' Paddy asked, grinning from ear to ear.

'*Suggestions*, she said. It doesn't mean the person is going to act on it unless it makes sense.' Rafe's voice showed a little impatience with Paddy's ludicrous question.

'I also think we should find this guy, see what makes him tick—find out where he lives and works.' Angie was on a roll now.

'Good idea,' Rafe agreed. 'There's one thing we can do. Angie's the only one who knows what our man looks like, but she can send us all an image. We have to make our minds receptive to her while she concentrates on his appearance. Form a circle and hold hands.'

Angie formed a picture of the man as she went to the hotel with him while the group concentrated on her. She tried to remember every little detail to convey to the rest, right down to his shoes.

'Everybody got it?' Rafe asked as the circle broke.

Paddy nodded. 'Harmless looking dude,' he said.

'*Spectacles*,' Stretch yelled. '*The bastard wears little spectacles like my granny.*'

'We start looking tomorrow at work time, if that's okay with you, Angie,'

Rafe said. 'You're in charge of this investigation.'

Angie had to smile. She'd never been in charge of anything during life, and even though she was dead it felt good. 'That makes sense. We'll split up and search everywhere. I'd suggest the high paying, professional places. You don't wear clothes like his if you're an everyday working stiff.'

'You, of course, mean blue collar,' Paddy said. 'We're the stiffs.' He popped a ghostly beer, and Angie laughed. Her first good laugh since her death.

They began first thing in the morning. Starting at the Common, they went in three directions with Rafe covering Cambridge. Their ability to move through obstacles, crossing streets without fear, and moving through live people, gave them amazing speed. Still, the first day, they came up empty.

At night they hung around the streets of the Zone where the killer picked Angie up. He had been on foot so she had no vehicle description. Chances are he parked clear of the area, came on the MTA, or by taxi. Just the same, there was no sign of him.

'Maybe it's too soon for him to be on the prowl again,' Paddy suggested when they met at the hotel. 'Angie made the paper, though.'

'In the back pages, I bet,' she added. 'Nobody cares when a hooker gets killed. The consensus is 'she had it coming.' I'm going to check the papers tomorrow to see if there's a time pattern.'

'Beat you to it,' Rafe said. 'The criminology class at Harvard is charting this guy. The murders are exactly four days apart. The guy is a creature of habit. They've worked up a profile.'

Angie poised on the bed like a cat ready to pounce. 'Give it up, Rafe. Quick, before my curiosity kills me—again.'

'He always kills by strangulation, suggesting he doesn't like a mess. All victims have been attacked from behind, with the exception of two who must have put up a struggle. He's neat and attentive to details—never leaving prints, broken glass, even spilled liquid. No one has ever seen him, or if they have he's attracted no attention.'

'Wait a minute,' Angie interrupted. 'When he took me to the room, the desk clerk saw him clearly. He paid for the room.'

'The desk clerk told the cops he was average size, wore a long, gray coat, and gloves. That was it and describes half the businessmen in Boston.' Rafe held up his hands in a gesture of futility. 'This guy has nothing out of the ordinary about him. He blends into the furniture. His speech is even common. The theory is he's a clerical employee perhaps in an accounting office, bank, or other position where he doesn't deal with people. The classes' best guess is a job involving numbers, explaining the devotion to detail.'

'We still have three days at the most,' Angie said. 'Should we concentrate on professional offices?'

'I think so,' Paddy spoke. 'And make sure we look in all the back rooms. Maybe he's a money counter for the mob.'

At noon the next day, after searching all morning, they met back at the Common. They heard yelling and screaming coming from the Garden and Stretch galloped across the grass as fast as his long legs could carry him. In between strides he took a couple of leaps.

'I found him. I found him,' Stretch yelled. *'I even got the name and address.'*

They gathered around him, faces brightened with wide-eyed disbelief. 'Bradshaw and O'Toole Accounting Office, two blocks from the IRS office.' It seemed as if Stretch took a leap with every word. Rafe put a hand on his arm.

'What is his name and address?' Rafe asked.

'Jonathan Carver, 1139 Charles Place, Apartment 14, we should check it out before he comes home.' Stretch stopped jumping while receiving a barrage of pats on the back including a hug from Angie.

Carver's apartment looked neat as a pin, as did the hidden room in the master bedroom. 'This is one sick son-of-a bitch,' Paddy said. If it bothered the Irishman it had to be bad.

Photos of girls covered a bulletin board. The pictures had been labeled and dated. The last photo was of Angie on the bed. 'Where does he get those?' she asked. 'I didn't see him take a picture.'

'You must have still been alive but unconscious,' Rafe answered. 'He takes a picture of all the victims right after he kills them. Look at these, the first was four years ago.'

'It reads 'Chicago',' Stretch said. 'There are some from New York and Providence.'

'This guy's been killing girls all over the country. Any clue as to where he'll head next?' Paddy starred down the line of pictures, intent on the group from Boston.

'I know most of these girls' territories and the hotels they use,' Angie said. 'They all worked in the Zone on different streets. We always had an arrangement with the desk clerks. We made sure the guy paid for the room and the clerk overcharged, pocketing the difference.'

'See if you can develop a pattern,' Rafe said. 'A man this organized has to have a definite plan.'

'Look here, Rafe.' Stretch slid the top of the dresser back, and underneath found a secret drawer. It contained eight different types of garrotes in a neat row. They, too, had numbers.

Paddy looked also. 'It doesn't make sense. Some are numbered in the teens when others, like the piano wire, only has a two.'

'The numbers are the girls killed with them,' Rafe said. 'I would say the piano wire is his least favorite, too messy. The favorite is the nylon cord.'

'Sick, this guy's not human,' Stretch said, and turned away.

'I think I've got a pattern,' Angie broke in. 'It looks like he started in the middle of the Zone and has been working his way out clockwise. If you figure the hotel where we went, his next move would be two blocks into the strip club area.'

'I don't see a map,' Paddy said.

Angie's eyes sparked. 'I don't need a map; I grew up there. My mom was a stripper.' She didn't bother to tell them that mom was also an addict and part-time hooker.

Who cares, she thought.

The die had been cast. One of them agreed to stay with Carver while the rest went to the Zone and waited. Paddy volunteered to stick to the killer. 'I think it would be best if a man stayed with the sicko, no offense, Angie.'

Angie just grinned. 'You're welcome to him. I should check out the area in the Zone anyway. Maybe I can come up with a plan.'

In the harsh environment of the Zone, the three waited. At first they checked all the surrounding hotels, watching their patrons. Angie could tell which ones the girls would use and the off limits spots. The girls themselves, from what she observed, weren't that different from her other colleagues.

'We won't be able to i.d. the part-timers,' she told Rafe, who had not contributed a whole lot. 'The strippers who turn tricks once in a while, I mean. Some will, some won't. Sometimes they'll do it just because they like a guy, but I don't think we have to worry. He picked me off the street. Going into a club would mean witnesses.'

'Angie, you should have been a detective,' Rafe said. 'By the way, somebody does care.'

She frowned, cocking her head to one side inquisitively. 'I don't know what you're talking about.'

'Someone does care that you lived a tough life growing up.'

'You read my mind?' Her eyes popped wide in wonder. 'Have you always done that?'

Rafe shook his head, smiled, and walked away.

On the fourth day, just as predicted, they heard Paddy's high-pitched voice yelling.

'Paddy's voice gets high when he's excited,' Stretch said. 'You can hear him in Cambridge.'

Angie still found it strange that he could yell like that and the living just kept walking, not hearing a thing. Paddy bounded down the street through lampposts, people, and cars, waving his arms. 'He's coming, he's dressed just like Angie said, and he's got the nylon rope. I came ahead to warn you. He's in a yellow cab.' They all faced the Common, spread out a little, and waited.

Rafe spotted him first and shouted for the others in a voice loud as a trumpet. By the time the other three reached him Carver was walking down the sidewalk. Dressed just as Angie remembered, he wore blacks and grays. A gray, snap-down cap rested on top of the spectacles, but the eyes could be seen darting to the sides, ogling the girls.

A lot of girls walked the streets this time of morning. Some walked to the end of the block and back, others made a round trip around the block. To stand still invited the cops. One of the group kept Carver in sight at all times.

'*Over here.*' They heard a loud call, and saw Stretch's long arm waving in the air. Carver had stopped to talk to a girl. She wore plenty of make up, but Angie could tell she was just a kid. Remembering when she started, she knew a fifteen-year-old could look twenty-five.

'She's not even out of her teens,' she told Rafe and Paddy. 'Let's try the suggestion.'

In unison they said, 'Turn him down. Don't go with him.' She turned and walked into the hotel anyway. They kept up their chant as Carver checked them in. He kept his eyes lowered when he paid for the room. The brim of his cap covered the leering eyes. This desk clerk could never I.D. him, Angie thought.

They entered an old-style, grated elevator. Carver guided her in before him with slight pressure on her back. She never turned and looked at him, and his hand fumbled in the coat pocket. Angie and her friends entered with them, chanting the same words. By the time the elevator stopped, on the seventeenth floor, their chant had become a shout.

She paused at the door of the elevator, pressing her fingertips against her temples. She stood there for a few seconds, then walked into the hallway. 'Damn, I thought we'd done it,' Angie said in frustration.

'You were close,' Rafe said.

'I'm not giving up,' Angie spoke in anger. She followed on Carver's heels, her face ferocious. The others followed the determined Angie.

Carver laid the resolved fee on top of a dresser so she could see it. The girl then turned her back to remove the coat. Her honey colored hair hung down to the center of her back, and through the make up Angie could see her youth. Although pretty, she had not achieved the full curves of maturity.

'*We have to stop him,*' Angie said, standing in the middle of the room, arms folded. '*Concentrate!*' She turned her mind on Carver who was pulling the nylon cord from his coat pocket.

The others joined her, staring at the murderer, with anger on their faces. None of them came this far to fail. The girl continued to take off her blouse as the cord got hung up in Carver's pocket. Paddy's face turned bright red with concentration and Stretch's was turning purple.

Angie drew on her childhood—all the names, references to her mother, men making lewd advances, the time she was raped by five boys. Her anger boiled up, and Carver stumbled to the left.

'*I moved him,*' she shouted. '*Did you see that, Rafe?*'

He put his arm around her shoulders. 'Yes, I did. Use Stretch, he was the strongest in the test.'

She remembered. Stretch had moved the can the farthest in the hotel room. He only failed when he lost concentration.

'*Help me, Stretch,*' she yelled. 'Remember all the kids that made fun of you. Remember how the girls laughed and wouldn't go out with you. Remember the tall lonesome boy at the dances, too clumsy to dance. The guy who was tall enough to play basketball but fell over his feet. They all laughed, didn't they?'

Stretch's face changed to anger, hate, and finally concentration. He stared at Carver as though his eyes could cut a hole in him. He put out his hands in a shoving motion and cried out. The scream was filled with anger and despair.

The killer had the cord out of his pocket when his feet betrayed him. They carried him sideways toward the half open window facing the alley. He tried in vain to gain balance but moved faster toward the window. The girl heard the clumsy steps and turned to see Carver crash through the window, breaking the sill. He tried to grab out but his own cord wound around his hands. The glass shattered and a second later came the sound of a crackling thump.

The young prostitute ran to the window, and the others joined her. She put her hand to her mouth and gasped. Carver's body lay on the bricks of the alley below. The arms and legs twisted in unnatural positions while a dark pool spread from his head. The spectacles lay broken next to him. The cord still bound his hands.

The girl, hands shaking, quickly dressed and ran from the room. She had the good sense not to use the elevator. She'd have time to get a good story before the cops came looking, Angie thought. The other girls would help her.

The four silently left and walked down the stairs. They kept strangely quiet until gaining the street. 'We did it,' Angie finally said. 'Thanks, guys. Thanks for all your help.'

Stretch spoke first. 'We couldn't have done it without you, Angie. You made us strong.' Paddy nodded in agreement. Rafe hung back. Angie thought suddenly: *Rafe has always hung back.*

A white light enveloped them for a second. 'It's time, guys,' Rafe said.

'Time for what, Rafe?' Stretch asked.

'Time to cross over to the other side. In other words, you've made it.' Rafe's face had a wide smile. 'That unselfish act put you on the team. I'm real proud of you.'

Another bright light appeared at the end of the alley. 'There's the door, walk through it,' Rafe said.

'Aren't you coming?' Angie asked. 'You're one of us.'

'I'll be along,' he said. 'I have other business yet, but mention my name when you get there. My full name is Raphael.'

PRISONERS BEFORE THE FIRST HORIZON
David Rawson

In July 1474, a stonemason turned seafarer named Joao Edison da Silva set sail from Lisbon and travelled west.

The following month, the sailors of da Silva's ship saw the sun set before what they thought to be an enormous storm.

The men turned to prayer or to their captain for reassurance. Those who did the latter were duly calmed by the facility with which da Silva explained the phenomenon before them—a facility that was born (though this he kept secret) of his having been forewarned of such a thing.

Curiously, far from being obscured by the storm, the setting sun appeared white against it, and da Silva told his crew that the white was the light of the Holy Ghost and the colour of goodness. Provided they sailed for the light they would come to no harm, though they would be greatly tested. He explained that the secret of their survival and ultimate triumph didn't lie in their bodily strength, or their seamanship, but in their faith.

The next day the sun dawned red in the east. To the west though, there only lay darkness. Even at midday this was so, moreover, the portion of the sky that lay in shadow had grown during the morning. As the ship drew closer to the storm the unease of the crew grew, though none wished to voice dissent after da Silva's speech of the previous night. Yet even in their fear, some were able to quietly appreciate the beauty of the coming darkness. It carried at its edges a purple lustre that yielded, via the richest blue, to the pale, familiar sky.

Unspoken too, was the belief that those lustrous jaws were fast closing around them, and that they might be swallowed up before the sun had made its rendevous with them in the west.

At the key moment, when he judged the temper of his crew to be about to give way, da Silva strode about the ship reminding them that faith alone could move mountains. He stated that the speed of the sun was the measure of their fidelity, and that if the bright goal were no longer to lay on their course they would have proved themselves unworthy of it.

The winds rose as the jaws closed in on the ship. The sea grew as black beneath them as the sky was above. They were driven west at a hitherto unimaginable speed.

Ahead lay what appeared to be a silver ingot jammed between sea and sky. With each minute that passed its provenance became clearer and clear to the sailors; its meaning firmer and firmer. This, they exclaimed over the noise of the wind, was the light of the white sun coming up to them from beneath the waves. And what man could drown beneath those waves and not be carried to the Lord? Its real domain was beneath the sea and it was fitting that they, pious men of Portugal and the sons of fishermen, should discover that it was such.

Only da Silva didn't shout and shake his neighbour. From the outside at least, he appeared as quiet and composed as could be. To his men he'd become a figure of courage and unimaginable resolve in the face of the unknown. Their estimation of him wasn't so wrong, yet the real reason why he held himself aloof from them wasn't holy courage, or the demands of station, but fear. He knew that the light of the white sun that they had seen earlier wasn't that which they saw now. Only one body, whether it dwelt in the heavens above or in the depths below, shone with such a silvery grey light. Now that enticing light shone upwards from a locus to the west of the ship, like some immensely bright torch in some immeasurably deep well.

The well of light grew until a great crescent of it spread out in their path. It seemed to lie before them and under them. At this new panorama, the men were blissfully happy and sang and danced upon the deck as though it was a stage—the eerie light casting them like marionettes before a black curtain. None of them though, asked why this light failed to dispel the darkness about them.

Soon the sound of the wind was joined by another lower and far more ominous noise—it too growing louder with every furlong they made to the west. With it, the sea grew more turbid and white foam began to envelope the ship, till with a violent jolt the bow dipped down into it. The sailors hung on for their lives, their earlier proclamations of holy invulnerability forgotten as the instinct to live took hold of them. The ship ploughed down at extraordinary speed, each man struggling to breathe as the foam was forced into his face and lungs. To drown seemed inevitable—yet soon there was no more water enveloping them, little air even, and no more noise.

They had sailed clean over the edge of the world.

A man walked across a surface composed of the finest dust. Yet though he walked briskly, he didn't kick up any clouds of that dust. If, however, he'd looked behind, he would have seen as a consolation that he left no foot-prints—a useful attribute, one would have thought, in the domain of the Devil. But he didn't look. The Devil didn't creep up behind the inhabitants of this dull and near forgotten annex of his infernal empire. Besides, a ghost rarely needed to look over his shoulder.

Yet today, ibn Halifa walked with more purpose than he had in the five centuries since he'd sailed west through the Pillars of Hercules—carried away on the moist tongue that lapped so invitingly at the edge of the known world.

Rumours had abounded for some time—for there are rumours (especially rumours) in the antechambers of Hell—that a ship had beached itself in one of the shallow and appallingly tranquil seas.

For once, ibn Halifa didn't torment himself with thoughts of the gardens he'd long left behind, with their shaded cloisters and more particularly, their troughs of cool, slowly running water. He merely prayed that the rumour was true and fought to suppress the possibility that demons were playing on his near infinite capacity for hope. For a few moments he imagined these crea-tures crouched in tunnels beneath his feet, gazing up at him through this desert so dusty that it might have been made of the finely ground bones of men such as he. He fought hard against these imaginings—such was the strength that had kept him sane through the centuries of waiting.

It occurred to him that if the seas of the moon had been the deserts of Ara-bia and North Africa, he could have walked a thousand times to Mecca by now. For a moment he dwelt upon the vulgarity, even blasphemy, of such a thought. He shrugged though—those who worried about committing blas-phemy were worried about their destiny. Once one had been dead five hundred years, one became more phlegmatic about such things. On the moon one had time to think—whereas in Heaven one had no need to, and in Hell, little opportunity. Five centuries on the moon made a clever man very cunning indeed. Cunning enough to realise that for all the gods there was only one currency—souls. With the prospect of souls to bargain with, he could regain his garden, whether it be on earth or in heaven. Of his own abilities he'd no doubt, however his plan depended on two other beings—the Devil's lunar governor and a mortal man.

Nearly twenty years earlier, he'd contacted a party of spirit seekers gathered around a planchette in one of the darkened rooms of Cordoba. Via the medium, he'd spoken to a young and adventurous stonemason named Joao Edison da Silva. Three times since, da Silva had spoken to him by the same means; the first as a renowned master mason; the second as the son-in-law of a wealthy Lisbon merchant; the third as the most able lieutenant of one of the most respected seafarers in the whole of Iberia.

Da Silva had vowed to act as the body that ibn Halifa didn't have. The Arab had spent much time pondering upon the possible reasons for the Portuguese agreeing to do this. Only one seemed credible: that for the man who has made adventure his art, to see death—moreover, to see a satellite of Hell—and then return, had to be one of the greatest of challenges.

Though ibn Halifa had great faith in his plan he was acutely conscious that the lunar governor, Ahrimabaal, was a sensualist—a creature not to be impressed by ideas alone. When he'd watched the governor touch things with his fat but tactile fingers, he'd meditated upon the beliefs of the Cathars, and in particular, their tenant that all matter was inherently evil. The corruptly appreciative hands of the chief lunatic would be his conduits to the ear of that creature's infernal master—as long as da Silva brought with him his precious cargo.

A disturbing noise broke the Arab from his reverie. His head was filled with the sound of snickering imps, though as yet he was unable to discern their forms in the monochrome landscape. The little winged prentices of the governor would be busy reducing to stock the bodies of the newest prisoners of the moon; the stream from whom created the miasma that passed for an atmosphere on this outstation of death. It was ibn Halifa's least favourite sound, but nevertheless, this high excitement amongst the imps meant new arrivals that couldn't be far off.

Captain da Silva stood on the deck of his ship, close to the starboard side.

The ship listed a little to port and thus he was raised quite considerably above the level of the lunar 'sea' that stretched ahead of him. For a while, he watched the imps at work. The spectacle had a certain irony for him, for he'd carved such as these on his travels as a master mason. In the bleaching lunar light these imps even had the quality of stone.

Though he could, in part at least, detach himself from the horror beneath, da Silva was touched (a little) by guilt, for though he'd come knowingly to this place, his men had given up their lives—perhaps even their souls—having placed their faith not only in their religion but in their captain. As he contemplated what he'd led his men to, their ghosts sat in the hold of the ship. They cowered in total despair, unable to shut out the sound of the imps scuttling across the deck above, dragging their corpses behind them. The poor sailors didn't realise that beneath them, concealed within the stony ballast of the ship, there lay the one thing that might save them.

Da Silva did—indeed his whole mission had been with the purpose of bringing this cargo to the moon: a cargo that could only be fashioned by the hands of corporeal men. At that moment though, he didn't know which was worse: to languish in abject despair like his crew, or to have hope, but a hope based entirely on an extraordinary plan that might be doomed through his own slackness of thought.

It was as well then, that he was soon distracted by a solitary figure moving towards the ship from somewhere away to his left. Though too far away for him to be certain, it looked too upright in its gait to be another imp.

He didn't dwell in it though, because he was again distracted—this time by a change in tempo of the impish activities going on below.Far away to his right, a dust cloud had been kicked up. Most certainly kicked up, for as far as he'd been able to discern, this god-forsaken world had no weather.

The cloud appeared, like the lone figure, to be heading for the ship.

Away to his left, ibn Halifa could also see the cloud but unlike da Silva he knew precisely what was making it—the train of Ahrimabaal himself. In its van were the ubiquitous imps, but here marshalled by various minor demons that formed the officer corps of this annex to the underworld. Behind them, and carried in a black and red bedecked palanquin was Ahrimabaal. He was kept aloft by a group of especially tall Vikings.

Like ibn Halifa, the Vikings had sailed beyond the world many centuries before. The story of how some had come to be carrying Ahrimabaal's palanquin had always amused the Arab. The Vikings had found the loss of their corporeal selves particularly hard to bear. Not that this had bothered

Ahrimabaal; it was just that the imps found it difficult to carry the governor, he being so monstrously large. Ahrimabaal was also irritated by the imps' ill discipline and had long harboured the desire to be carried in a more stately fashion. Thus the Vikings came to perform the task, which, of course, had necessitated the restitution of their former selves. They were subsequently granted certain privileges—some of which brought up the rear of the train. These were what ibn Halifa had termed the 'anti-houris'; their voluptuous bodies forever out of the reach of all the ghostly seafarers—save those mentioned above.

Ibn Halifa knew that he'd be able to reach the ship first. Nothing was quite as fleet of foot as a ghost and besides the hangers-on that clustered around Ahrimabaal inevitably slowed him down. It was important to the Arab that he did so, because he now felt certain that the ship was indeed da Silva's, and he wished to check that the imps hadn't disturbed the Portuguese's precious cargo.

By the time da Silva could discern individual figures in the caravan of Ahrimabaal, ibn Halifa did indeed stand before him. They didn't speak for fear of being overheard by the imps, but one nod of the head from da Silva was all that ibn Halifa needed.

Indeed, before the Arab could join the captain on the deck of his ship, the imps of Ahrimabaal's unholy vanguard had arrived and begun squabbling with those who'd first discovered the ship—overturning some of the cauldrons of human soup that they'd been preparing. The demonic officers struggled to keep order, even devouring several of the diminutive fiends in the process. All this was only brought to a halt by a rumble of displeasure from within the palanquin, which the Vikings had in the meantime placed close to the ship.

Da Silva was tempted to stay above it all on the deck, but decided to make his way down to be beside ibn Halifa. Once order of a kind had been achieved, Ahrimabaal began to speak, his form remaining invisible, but his deep voice rippling the veils that covered the sides of the palanquin.

'You're most unusual for a newcomer, Captain da Silva. I've heard that you don't carry the usual marks of fear and ill fortune upon you—intelligence that I can now see was correct. And the magician Halifa, here so punctually—hardly an Arab trait. I believe you've come here quite knowingly, captain. Am I not correct?'

'Yes,' affirmed the captain.

'Why?' asked Ahrimabaal, with genuine curiosity rather than his usual superciliousness.

'To bring home the knights of the known world: the noble and the brave who have languished in your domain,' he replied, as though he'd thoroughly rehearsed the line—which of course he had.

There were squeals from the imps, half in delight, half in astonishment at this perceived affront to their master.

'Does the King of Portugal seek to conquer the moon?' asked Ahrimabaal in a similarly theatrical vein.

'The captain has come as a merchant—a dealer in souls, your Infernal Highness,' said ibn Halifa before da Silva could continue.

'Captain—a merchant has something to offer and I see nothing before me—except you. And everything you are I now possess, do you understand? That is the business of souls.'

'I bring one thing with me,' said da Silva, gathering his courage.

'And this thing is but a manifestation of an idea—the greatest of ideas,' added ibnHalifa.

Those surrounding the palanquin began to whisper to one another. Far from hushing them, Ahrimabaal indulged himself of this gossip. It was clear that he was excited by the prospect of some plaything brought all the way from the earth for him.

'Well—let me see it, and quickly then,' he ordered like a spoilt child—which is, after all, the model of all-evil.

Da Silva asked a number of Ahrimabaal's Vikings to follow him into the hold of the ship. They cleared an area of ballast and there, buried beneath it, was a very large barrel, the width of three Vikings and nearly as tall. With great difficulty they carried it out of the hold and presented it to their master, whose red eyes peered intently at it through a gap in the palanquin's veils.

Da Silva gestured to the Vikings to lay waste to the barrel with their axes. The resulting debris was removed to reveal a large stone ball whose surface was most intricately carved. An irregularly shaped area stood a little proud of the mass of stone, which had been carved in elaborate swirling patterns. The raised area was fringed in gold such that it was further delineated from its finely chiselled surround.

The governor of the lunarians ordered that the veils be cleared so that he could inspect it more closely. He tilted his bald, gleaming head as close to the ball as he dared without risk of toppling forward. Then, with his pudgy, ring covered fingers he caressed a particularly attractive boot shaped prominence of the gilt-edged carving.

'The known world, your Infernal Highness,' said ibn Halifa, stepping forward and sweeping his hand across from Hibernia to Cathay.

'I didn't question the meaning,' said Ahrimabaal sharply. A cynical smile crossed his face. 'I questioned the conceit—that you, a Mohammedan should arrange to have carved the likeness of the world presided over by our betters. The grand conceit too, of seeking to improve that world by warping it upon the face of a ball.'

'The Greeks proved that the world is indeed a sphere,' said ibn Halifa undaunted.

'Then why are you here?' asked Ahrimabaal, pointing to the Arab and the Portuguese in turn. The imps began snickering.

'Because, your Infernal Highness, insufficient men believe it to be such,' replied ibn Halifa with his usual suaveness.

'But this situation will not prevail for much longer,' added da Silva, fixing his gaze upon Ahrimabaal. 'The harvest of errant souls will not be there for you to reap—your master will grow impatient.'

'I cannot see how you've arrived at such a conclusion,' said Ahrimabaal coldly.

The alchemist and the adventurer glanced at one another, knowing that the next few minutes would be critical.

'If your Infernal Highness will allow me to be so bold,' said ibn Halifa with a flourish, 'you will doubtless have noticed that the span of the known world takes up but a fraction of the circumference of the globe. Already, as my friend the captain has told me, there are many men readying to make the arduous voyage across the giant sea they believe separates east from west.'

The Portuguese took over from the Arab.

'They're obsessed with the idea that they can find another route to the riches of the east. And when great riches beckon, men suppress their fear and the ideas that went with that fear no longer hold good.'

Ibn Halifa addressed the governor with gravitas.

'It's all very simple your Infernal Highness—when the world changes, the world changes.'

'And you will be the loser,' added da Silva bluntly.

Ahrimabaal said nothing.

Ibn Halifa walked round to the side of the globe that was invisible to the governor.

'If your Infernal Highness would care to look at this,' he said, hands extended towards da Silva's handiwork.

The Vikings made ready to move the palanquin, but Ahrimabaal stilled them with an impatient gesture. Then something extraordinary happened. With surprising agility for such a corpulent beast, he levered himself out of the heavily padded seat and in a trice was atop the north pole of the globe—perched there like a giant toad. For some moments there was a great commotion and the excitable imps had to be stilled. Superficially at least, ibn Halifa remained unperturbed—over the centuries he'd grown used to Ahrimabaal's gaucheries.

Ahrimabaal himself appeared not the least concerned with what the others thought. With head tilted and chins squeezed against his chest, he was looking down at the golden shape that lay between his legs. Carved in relief, were two roughly triangular areas connected by a sliver of stone, the whole not merely edged in gold but entirely covered by it.

Ibn Halifa coughed.

'The New World, your Infernal Majesty.'

'And a new franchise for the conveying of souls?' asked Ahrimabaal, without looking up.

'Precisely,' said ibn Halifa, 'though not all to the one destination, I must add. May I explain?'

The Arab drew closer to the globe.

'The gold isn't merely to catch the eye. These will truly be two golden lands—yet in rather different ways.'

Like a psychic surgeon, he pushed a ghostly hand into South America.

'To the south, will be a land of unspeakable beauty; of cities of gold and mines of silver; a magnet to adventurers; a place to tempt the damned and more importantly to you, the would-be-wicked—yet a land that might also separate the truly virtuous from those already so through the accident of fortune.'

He made as if to caress the great bay that lay between the two landmasses and then swept his hand up as far it would go towards Ahrimabaal's groin.

'And to the north, a land rich in promise for the multiplication of souls; a land of merchants and mammon; a land of—how shall I put it?—Opportunities for all.'

Ahrimabaal's red eyes glinted and his legs trembled with excitement as they straddled the globe—the earth appearing like a nut in a nutcracker.

'A most ingenious conceit, my magician friend.'

'You're most kind, your Infernal Highness, but the conceit will be yours, not ours. His Infernal Majesty, we feel sure, would approve your holding in thrall the errant souls of the New World.'

Visions of a major seat in the underworld flashed through Ahrimabaal's mind. He imagined exchanging the trickle of souls who'd crossed the boundaries of the earth, for a torrent of those who'd transgressed the laws of propriety. However, his self-satisfied expression soon gave way to a sourer one. Something unpalatable had come to mind.

'For all your talents, ibn Halifa, I do however see a great problem in this scheme,' said Ahrimabaal, slowly shaking his head as though he were pondering upon some terrible misdemeanour. 'I might give up this lunar fiefdom and yet fail to see the transformation of the world in men's minds that you believe will happen. Men might continue to drop from the edge of the world, but not into my lap, but that of some upstart. I'd be left with nothing.'

Ibn Halifa countered with the broadest smile that Ahrimabaal, or indeed any of his prisoners or flunkies had ever seen.

'Ah! My dear Infernal Potentate! Now comes the very beauty of the scheme—that which ties the knot upon the bargain and allays all fears. You'll release the brave seafarers of the moon, such as my friend the captain. They'll go back to the Old World and spread the idea of that New World, such that it takes as firm a hold as can be in the minds of men.'

'And why should they do that?' asked Ahrimabaal, sitting up stiffly and putting his hands on his knees.

'Because no man can keep a world a secret, even if—and some might say especially if—he wishes to plunder it himself. Man is the most promiscuous of beasts,' said ibn Halifa, sensing that his plan neared fruition.

Ahrimabaal nodded, though this time he contained his excitement with the thought of what lay ahead—namely an interview with his superior.

'Ibn Halifa, you're a dangerous man. One suspects, however, that you'll be found too wicked for Heaven and the magic garden that you crave.'

Captain da Silva walked up to the globe, the globe he didn't need to touch because he'd carved every square inch of it. Though the real one would now hold as little mystery as that before him, he knew he'd return and carry out his part of the bargain. With a wry grin on his face, he looked across at the magician from Mauritania—the man who'd dared to square the circle, or rather, to have it inflated to its full and rightful proportions.

'He'll have his magic garden—somehow,' said the adventurer from Lisbon. 'For though I don't know how, I do know this—he may be too wicked for Heaven, but he's most certainly too clever ever to be allowed into Hell.'

'Or too far from its sight,' added Ahrimabaal, before clapping his hands.

At this signal a beast appeared who was as hirsute as his master was hairless.

'Prepare the catapults,' ordered the governor.

As night fell across the known world, volleys of shooting stars conveyed in code the details of a certain proposal to the agents of an underworld empire.

The reader will have gathered that there is no need to pursue this story any further.

However, some rumours are worth reporting.

Captain da Silva returned with his crew to the Old World, and is believed to have lived out the rest of his life in Genoa.

The god of the Mohammedans and Christians doesn't keep lists, but it is said that ibn Halifa's name is to be found on no other. It would seem a fair assumption that at this very moment, by either his own, or by divine making, he reclines in the arms of dusky maidens beside the most gently flowing of streams.

Of course, his infernal master accepted 'Ahrimabaal's' proposition. However, it is said that the latter added a single proviso—it being that the underling could have only one of the New World lands as his fiefdom, but was allowed to chose which.

Ahrimabaal is purported to have chosen the southern one, such that the fallen souls of this land of 'gold, glory and God' would be his to disport with. That left his master with equivalent rights over the north.

One wonders who had the best of this arrangement?

Only one thing though, is certain—the Devil rarely gets the worst part of any bargain he makes.

WHERE THE BODIES ARE BURIED
Peter Tennant

'Geoffrey, so good of you to come.'

'Not at all, old chap,' said Sir Geoffrey Colling as he stepped into the tiny flat that was the humble abode of his oldest friend. 'But what on earth can have got you in such a state? On the phone you made it sound like a matter of life and death.'

'Life and death?' Herbert Goodchild repeated the hyperbole in an interrogative tone and nodded, finding it entirely appropriate to the situation. 'Yes, that's exactly what it is. A matter of life and death.'

'All very cryptic,' said Sir Geoffrey. 'And a touch melodramatic too, if you don't mind my saying.'

Herbert frowned, then turned and led the way down the short hallway to his living room. He walked with the aid of a stick, arthritic fingers knotted around the wood, and his back bent almost double. The two of them were contemporaries, but Sir Geoffrey looked thirty years younger and moved with a grace and vitality that belied his age.

'Whisky?' asked Herbert, moving to the antique drinks cabinet that stood against the far wall, one of the few family heirlooms that he hadn't as yet been forced to sell.

'Bit early in the day for me,' said Sir Geoffrey, and cast a critical eye at the half empty bottle of Glenfiddich that was the entire complement of his friend's drinks cabinet, then looked all around him at the unmistakable signs of moral and economic decline. He shook his head and sighed, depressed as ever at the sight of Herbert's reduced circumstances. It was too much a reminder of how his own life might have turned out.

At Cambridge the two of them had been considered the cream of the nation's youth, the brightest and best of all a proud empire had to offer. Herbert, if anything, had been judged the more promising, but after heady days in academia it had all gone wrong for him, the anticipated pursuit of the glittering prizes left in ruins as a result of too many disastrous errors of judgement, while for Geoffrey the opposite had been the case. All the good things in life, wealth and power, prestige and honours, had simply fallen into Geoffrey's lap, seemingly without any great effort on his part. Fifty years on the difference in their fortunes could not have been more marked, and all that remained to them of the past was the still cherished bond of friendship. Geoffrey had offered financial assistance, but Herbert had always declined, preferring to eke out a living from his dwindling family inheritance and retain the small measure of pride this self-sufficiency allowed him.

'Please be seated,' said Herbert, pouring whisky into a greasy tumbler and then draining it in one go.

Feeling uneasy for no particular reason, Sir Geoffrey brushed grey powder of unknown provenance off the sagging settee and gently lowered himself down onto it, shifting slightly as a spring with a mind of its own and a long standing grudge against human flesh gouged his left buttock cheek.

'Look, Herbert, I have an appointment with the Minister at . . . '

'Yes, Geoffrey, I appreciate that you're a busy and important man,' said Herbert, his voice such that his old friend couldn't help but detect the note of bitterness. 'It's good of you to make time for an old fogey like me.'

'Don't get maudlin, Herbert. It doesn't suit you. You're my oldest friend and I'll always have time for you. Now are you going to tell me what this is all about or must we sit here until the cows come home?'

Herbert eased himself down into the chair opposite Sir Geoffrey, face momentarily creased with pain as the arthritis made its presence felt in some extremity.

'It's about that young man my god daughter is seeing.'

'Ashley Mortimer?'

'That's the one,' said Herbert, pulling a sneer as if the mere sound of the name repelled him. 'I want you to get Caroline to break it off.'

Sir Geoffrey stared at him in amazement. 'You can't be serious?'

'Never more serious in my life.'

'But what on earth makes you think Caroline pays the slightest bit of attention to anything I say? Besides, what's the matter with Ashley Mortimer? The times that I've met him he seems agreeable enough. Good family. Good career prospects. I'll admit the age difference worried me a bit at first, but people don't bother about that sort of thing nowadays. A few snipes about toy boys in the tabloid press, but . . . '

'This is not about age.' Herbert leaned forward, his face seeming even older and more haggard in the early morning sunlight that filtered through a dust-ridden pane of glass. Absent-mindedly Sir Geoffrey noted that he hadn't shaved yet, and the collar of his shirt was frayed. The observation made him feel sad. Herbert had once been so dapper, and the merest hint of any neglect or oversight in personal grooming would have left him mortified.

'Geoffrey, you have to listen to me. I believe that if Caroline continues seeing this man she's placing her life in jeopardy.'

Sir Geoffrey opened his mouth to laugh, but caught himself when he saw the earnest look on his friend's face. 'My God, you *are* serious.'

Herbert nodded and gave a small, self-deprecating smile, satisfied that at last he'd got Sir Geoffrey's full attention. 'You'll do it then?'

'How can I? Herbert, if you know something damning about young Mortimer you have to tell me.'

The other man sighed. 'Geoffrey, what do you suppose happens to the bodies of murderers, all the truly evil men and women who have walked the earth, people like Sutcliffe and Hindley and Brady?'

Sir Geoffrey looked at him aghast, thrown by the conversation's sudden change of direction and wondering if his old friend had finally lost his mind. 'Herbert, I . . . '

'Please, Geoffrey, just humour me.'

'I've no idea,' said Sir Geoffrey, not bothering to disguise the exasperation in his voice. 'It's not something I've given any thought to. I suppose they're buried in the prison grounds in unmarked graves or something of that sort.'

'What would you say if I told you that they were all buried together in a secret graveyard?'

'I'd say that you'd been drinking too much of that Glenfiddich you're so fond of,' said Sir Geoffrey, and forced a smile to soften the barbed comment.

'But it's the truth, Geoffrey, as God is my witness.'

The other man looked at his watch, not really wanting to know the time, but using the deliberateness of the gesture to convey his impatience. 'I really do have to go.'

'No. Wait. Hear me out.'

'But, old chap, all you've done so far is confuse me with riddles and conundrums.'

Herbert rested his head on his hands and stared at Sir Geoffrey. 'Do you remember when we were at university that I was a bit of an antiquary?'

'I remember that while the rest of us quite sensibly spent the holidays with our families and on the Riviera, you were forever off round the countryside on a bicycle and with a box Brownie, taking pictures of dilapidated buildings that always looked as if they'd fall down around your ears if somebody sneezed. If that's what you mean by being an antiquary, then yes I do remember.' Sir Geoffrey smiled, as some recollection of those lost days flashed through his mind. 'We all thought you were slightly eccentric, or had a girl stashed away somewhere that you weren't letting on about. I always wondered why you gave it up.'

'Something happened,' said Herbert, the words almost a whisper. He reached in his jacket pocket and took out a photograph, which he passed to Sir Geoffrey. The photograph was brown with age, stained and crumpled. It was a picture of a gravestone, the words carved into the granite perfectly legible. *Ashley Mortimer 1970—2056.*

Sir Geoffrey frowned and made to pass the photograph back, but Herbert signalled for him to keep it.

'If this is a joke, Herbert, it's in deplorably bad taste.'

'No joke.'

'Then I think you'd better tell me the whole story, from beginning to end.'

'Yes. I can see that's the only way.'

But instead of beginning he got up and went to pour himself another drink, which he downed with the same alacrity as before. Keeping one eye on his friend, Sir Geoffrey looked at the picture again, his face expressionless, and then slipped it into his jacket pocket.

'It was the summer of 1951,' began Herbert as he sat back down, the whisky adding a warm glow to his cheeks and just the hint of a slur in his speech, 'and I had taken lodgings in the town of Penstanton on the North Norfolk coast, just across from Cromer. I had my trusty Raleigh two speed and looked forward to several blissful weeks exploring that part of the country, so rich in old churches and other delights to slake the antiquary's thirst for past glory.'

He paused and looked enquiringly at Sir Geoffrey, as if anticipating a question, but the other man only nodded for him to continue. There was something of a practised quality about the story, like a recitation that had been committed to memory and rehearsed many times before, alone in the darkest reaches of the night.

'In the second week I cycled down the coast to the village of Hambury, the site of a church that dated back to Anglo-Saxon times, quite an impressive edifice in its day by all accounts, but unfortunately the Luftwaffe had dropped a bomb on it during the war, though why Herr Stickelgruber's fly boys should have targeted a church is beyond me.'

'Cretinous vandals,' interjected Sir Geoffrey with real feeling. His parents had been killed during the Blitz and even now, more than fifty years later, some bitterness remained. It was ironic that his role at the FO under Thatcher had involved close contact with his German opposite number. Nowadays he acted in more of an advisory capacity, but was not without influence.

'I found the church easily enough,' continued Herbert. 'You could tell that it had once been a magnificent building, but the cretinous vandals, as you so rightly call them, had left hardly a brick standing. All that remained was a burnt out shell of its former glory. It was a big disappointment to me, having journeyed so far and anticipated so much.

'I was about to mount my bicycle and pedal away when some movement in the foliage off to the left attracted my attention. Going to investigate I discovered a concealed path leading off through the trees which, having come so far and not wanting to go away with no reward for my efforts, also being of an inordinately curious nature and with time on my hands, I decided to follow for a length or so. The path led me to a stone wall hung with ivy beyond which lay a graveyard.

'That graveyard was quite like nothing I had ever seen before, one of the most truly dismal places on the face of the earth I believe. It was chock-a-block with statues, all of them covered in a patina of dirt and hideous fungal growth, like the accumulated grime of many centuries. Nor were they the sort of sculpture appropriate to a Christian burial site, not angels and the like but terrible figures reminiscent of gargoyles and demons dropped from the walls of some Gothic monstrosity out of the Middle Ages. They had been artfully arranged to create a penumbra effect, so that wherever you stood you were always in shadow. The place gave off the most dreadful feeling of antiquity, of desuetude and decay, but the most unnerving thing of all was the gravestones themselves. There were literally hundreds of them, but to my consternation the dates on all of them were set in the future.'

Sir Geoffrey guffawed. 'I've never heard anything so preposterous.'

'I don't blame you for being sceptical,' said Herbert. 'I couldn't believe it myself. Nonetheless I swear to you that I am telling the truth.'

'Perhaps it was the burial place of some sect who follow a different dating system to the rest of us.'

Herbert laughed, the sound almost mocking. 'You're clutching at straws.'

'Well, what else is there?' demanded Sir Geoffrey, his own voice full of indignation. 'This whole thing sounds like something old Monty James would've dreamed up.'

'I only tell you what I saw,' said Herbert. 'But you've yet to hear the most important thing. I was unaware of its significance at the time. It was only years later that I heard once again some of the names I'd first read on those tombstones. Names such as Ian Brady, Myra Hindley, Peter Sutcliffe and Fred West.'

'God, man, this is insane. You're telling me that Ashley Mortimer is some kind of monster who'll harm my daughter, and your reason for spouting such nonsense is that you saw his name on a stone in a graveyard some twenty years before Ashley was even born. Caroline will have me committed if I tell her any such thing.'

'Believe me, I know how it sounds,' said Herbert. 'I've never told anyone about this before for fear of being dismissed as a crank. All my life I've tried to rationalise it away, pretend it never happened, but with Caroline's life at stake I can't do that any more.'

Sir Geoffrey sighed and looked out of the window, then turned back to his friend. 'Could you find this place again?'

Herbert shook his head. 'I spent over an hour in the graveyard, taking photographs so that I'd have proof my eyes hadn't deceived me. At the end of that time I looked round and saw someone moving towards me, a hooded figure in a black robe, like a monk of some kind. I opened my mouth to ask what place this was, but before I could speak the man looked at me and whatever words I'd been about to say were gone. What I could see of his face was covered in the same fungal growth as the statues, and I thank God that the hood he wore spared me the full sight of that frightful countenance. What completely unmanned me though were his eyes. I had never seen such implacable malice in anyone's gaze before. Pure evil is the only phrase to do it justice. I just knew he meant to do me harm. I was so filled with dread that I turned and ran from that place without looking back, as if the very hounds of hell itself were on my tail.

'The next day I was somewhat recovered from my ordeal, convinced that

I'd seen nothing of any significance, only delusions conjured up by the heat and my suggestible surroundings, something inconsequential that had brought on a panic attack of some kind. Feeling quite foolish and wanting to expose my fears for the harmless fancies they were, I cycled back to Hambury, but while I found the ruined church just as I remembered it, of the graveyard and its mysterious custodian there was no sign, although I spent the best part of the afternoon exploring in the area and questioning locals. I've visited Hambury many times over the years since, but always to no avail. It's as if that infernal graveyard never existed. All that remained to me by way of proof was the roll of film in my camera, but the photograph of Ashley Mortimer's stone was the only one that came out. The rest were just shapeless blurs.'

'How convenient,' observed Sir Geoffrey.

'But don't you see?' called Herbert, 'I was meant to take that photograph. It was a sign.' His voice, which had been steadily rising in volume, was now almost a shout.

'Steady, old chap. You're getting worked up over nothing.'

'Geoffrey, I believe that at certain times the barriers come down allowing us brief glimpses of all the future contains. I didn't just happen to be in the right place at the right time. There was a purpose to what occurred. I was meant to see that graveyard so that I could warn you and save Caroline.'

'You need a sedative, something to help you cope with these delusions. You've been under a lot of pressure lately. Let me call Andrew Carnie. Finest doctor in Harley Street. He'll soon get you sorted out.'

'Damn it, man, I'm not mad! I don't need a doctor!'

'Of course not.'

Herbert grabbed hold of Sir Geoffrey's wrist as he made to get up, holding him in a vicelike grip and glaring into his eyes with a wild intensity.

'Geoffrey, why won't you understand? It was a sign. A sign so that I could tell you to warn Caroline and save her from that heartless monster.'

'Yes, Herbert, of course I understand. A sign. I'll talk to Caroline as soon as I see her.'

'O thank God!' said Herbert, and shuddered all through his body. 'Thank God!'

'But first let me call Andrew.'

Caroline was staying with him, as she always did when a meeting of The Circle was imminent. When he got home that night Sir Geoffrey found her asleep in her room. Seen in repose she looked so like her mother, the same elusive beauty but with a streak of iron in her soul that had been missing from Madeline. Caroline's mother had taken an overdose soon after Caroline had been baptised into the faith, unable to cope with the demands of her station.

Sir Geoffrey touched his daughter once on the shoulder and she came awake instantly, rolling over onto her back, the sheets falling away from her naked breasts. Laughing she made to pick up a pillow and hit him over the head, but saw the warning look in his eyes and stopped herself in time.

'Why so sad, pater?'

'I've had to get Herbert Goodchild committed. He was growing paranoid, delusional.'

Caroline shrugged. 'It's only to be expected. You've been feeding off the old fart for half a century. Something was bound to give.'

'All the same.'

She sighed and placed her hand on top of his. 'Whatever you've done, I'm sure it was for the best.'

'Yes, I suppose so,' said Sir Geoffrey, certain that she was only humouring him. Caroline, like others of her generation in the faith, regarded any hint of fellow feeling or sympathy for those they used as hypocritical humbug, and he supposed that she was right, but it didn't make him any happier about how things had turned out. His friend was gone and he felt responsible. Later he would toast Herbert's memory in his favourite Glenfiddich, but for now there were other matters that needed his attention.

'I've been giving the matter of young Ashley Mortimer some consideration. I've decided that he's our kind of person. I want you to bring him to the meeting. I've already cleared it with the Priestess.'

'You've been unsure about him for months. Why the sudden change of heart?'

Sir Geoffrey smiled and kissed his daughter lightly on the forehead. 'Let's just say that I've been given a sign.'

DAGUERREOTYPE
Andrew Roberts

His first grey hair appeared on his thirty-sixth birthday.

There Michael Lyall was, merrily brushing his teeth, only slightly concerned at the way his gums had begun to tingle around the canines when he brushed a touch too vigorously, glancing up into the mirror between spits—not for vanity's sake, just curiosity—and he spotted it. Thick and coarse and right in the middle of his head. Surely someone had stuck that one in while he was asleep.

His wife spotted it at the breakfast table as he was reaching for the marmalade. She laughed.

He started to comb his hair a different way that morning. He was thirty-six years old and it was his prerogative. Three years later, the Devil spoke to him.

It was in a dream.

'How do I know it's you?' he asked.

'*Know anyone else with horns and a crimson hue?*' When the Devil spoke, he breathed in Mike's ear. It was a cold, insinuating breath and Mike could see the plume of condensation that rose with every sentence. The Devil spoke in his ear because he was riding on Mike's back. Mike couldn't see his arms or legs wrapped around in front the way he should have been able to, but the weight was back there, all right. That voice was in his ear.

Mike asked him why he hadn't sent a minion. The Devil laughed and told him he liked to deal with the important stuff himself.

'You have people under you—you understand that. They don't have our eye for detail.'

Mike nodded. The Devil was a wise man. First rule of business: the only person you can trust is the one who stares back at you from above the sink every morning.

The Devil shifted his weight on Mike's back. *I'm like Faust*, he thought suddenly, and wondered if the Devil had heard that. He realised he didn't even know how the Faust story ended—did Faust trick the dealer? Did the dealer trick the dealt to? Or was it a business arrangement, plain and simple? Bought—your heart's desires. Sold—one soul. *Non caveat emptor.* Just a shake and a signature—the American Way. Was the Devil American, then? Why not, everything else was?

What kind of tale would that be, he wondered. Man sells soul. Man lives happily ever after. That wasn't going to topple Messrs Archer and Grisham from the top of the bestseller lists, was it?

No, he thought he knew exactly how the relationship between Faust and Mr Splitfoot had transcended the purely business. He strongly suspected Faust had wound up contemplating the deal strapped to some horribly improbable instrument of torture in the warmest corner of hell for the rest of eternity.

The Devil coughed politely in his ear and began to discuss terms.

'Deal,' Mike said, and then forgot it all.

When he finally woke, he woke feeling like shit. It was 12:30 and the house was unnaturally quiet.

He stumbled downstairs, sat on the sofa and munched unenthusiastically on a bowl of Cheerios, hating the way they stuck in the crevices where the gums were pulled even further back around his lower canines.

He turned on the TV and flicked from the Open University to sport to a 1940s film and a Merrie Melodies cartoon. It was the one in which Yosemite Sam keeps finding himself back in hell. Even that didn't trigger the dream.

He rinsed his dish, went back upstairs and looked at himself in the mirror.

'You're old,' he said, and then wondered exactly what he meant by that.

When you were a kid, being old was being sixty. It was your grandfather with his pink scalp that peeled in the summer sun and his ridiculous car with its ridiculous metal dashboard and oversized steering wheel. A little later, when you became more discerning, it shifted to fifty. Half a century—that was up there, okay. When you reached mid-teens you looked at your father and his friends and realised some of them would never stay up dancing all night again. When you hit the big 2-0 yourself, you looked at the thirty-year-olds running around the same football pitch as you and wondered how they didn't keel over and die. Five years later you realised some of your contemporaries were going a little thin at the temples, had started carrying a rubber ring around their bellies in case they fell in any surprise canals. Teenagers began to look at you with an amused, sly pleasure. Bingo—you were fucked!

Twenty-five years old and your life was snowballing towards the world's biggest ravine. You could look back, but all you saw was the teenagers with their sly smiles and their arms around each other's waists, or your own friends clutching their hearts and heads as something came to a grinding halt deep inside their bodies. Or you could look ahead and stare at yourself in the dirty, black mirror as your own hollow-eyed, sallow-skinned reflection plucked out a knot of grey from your skull.

He looked down and there was a clump of hairs in his hand. He dropped them down the loo, urinated on them and flushed. Antiseptic blue water rushed around the bowl, and if that wasn't symbolic he didn't know what was. If being old was anything, it was antiseptic blue water gurgling its way into the sewage system.

When was it you started using things like antiseptic blue flush blocks, anyway? Was it the first time you saw that look on your kids' faces that said *Fuck, Dad—you're old*? Did it come with owning a £19,000 car that you changed every three or four years when false economy told you it was prudent?

Was it part of stopping doing things? Of having kids and responsibilities and domestic arguments instead of taking up hang-gliding like you had always dreamed of? When you found yourself thinking about your own name and what impact it had made on the world (Michael Lyall—it wasn't the kind of name you would ever find on the front of a magazine or at the top of a movie poster, but wasn't there somewhere it would sit comfortably?) did someone smile and slap a piece of blue sulphate in your hand? *There you go. You never learned to play the drums or tried to write a novel, but at least your toilet will always be clean.*

And what did you do? You took it willingly, dropped it in and watched it sink to the bottom of the cistern. And all the time, where it counted—behind the lines and the crow's feet and the roll of flesh someone had stuck under your chin one night while you were sleeping—deep down inside yourself, you hated what life had turned out to be.

You hated sitting in friends' living rooms, sipping coffee and listening politely to middle of the road vocalists—or, worse still, *jazz*, that most intellectual, self-congratulatory and soulless of all music. You hated sitting in a plastic seat with your paper cup as you watched a band you had loved turn into a sanitised arena tribute to nostalgia and middle age. You hated Neighbourhood Watch and TV quiz shows and mediocre sporting contests and what your kids were becoming and, secretly, you yearned for someone to whisk you back to the good old days. Only they wouldn't *be* the good old days, they would be vital and earthy and o-so-real.

You had a wife you still loved, even though *infrequent* and *stagnation* had not been the rallying cries of your sexual awakening. And you slept late and thought too much about names and faces you hadn't seen in ten or fifteen years. Names who had stuck together through your own particular summer of love, sworn they were never going to grow up, never going to leave for college.

But, of course, they had done both. It had taken three years before they were finally broken. He could console himself by remembering he had been one of the last, but they had all gone in the end. Just as they had all cut their hair and started to wash.

All except for one. Mr Sinatra, whose parents had deemed fit to nudge each other and nod at the registrar and say, 'yes, that's right—*Frank*'. *Frank* had insisted on being called Fran—despite it being a woman's name. Such stuff didn't matter. These were heady times, indeed, and everything—traditional gender signifiers included—was up for grabs.

Fran had died eleven years ago. Mike had heard various rumours, ranging from the sublime to the ridiculous, but one thing was certain—Fran had OD'd and they had found him lying on the floor. His hair, still long but now terminally dry and frizzy, had been soaking up his own vomit. Yep, Fran had lived the dream, all right. Fran was Peter fucking Pan and Cliff Richard all rolled into one. Fran had never used his daughter's tweezers to pluck the white hairs from his eyebrows and then placed them back in exactly the same spot so no one would ever know.

'You never found yourself staring into the bathroom mirror and worrying about getting dressed before your wife came home and realised you'd been in bed all morning either, did you—you son of a bitch?' Mike announced.

Railing at a dead man. Oh yeah, that made him feel much better.

It was six days before the Devil appeared on his back again. This time they were climbing up a series of small ramps that Mike couldn't see beneath his feet. There was a hot wind and a mist and it reminded him a little of the Hitchcock film Dali had designed.

'Listen,' the Devil said. 'Do you think I like doing this?'

Mike apologised.

'Sure, sure,' the Devil said. ' So—are you still old?'

Mike said he didn't know. He had been thinking about it and he didn't know.

'Sure you are,' the Devil whispered.

Mike wanted to ask him if he *was* American.

'Most definitely old. Don't you feel like dog shit when you finally fall out of bed in the mornings—dried and well-trodden dog shit? Wouldn't you rather sit up until three watching some bad movie or an episode of The Twilight Zone you saw less than six months ago when Deborah starts flashing you those signs around eleven o'clock on those infrequent occasions when she flashes anything at all?'

'I don't like The Twilight Zone,' Mike said.

'But you take my point.'

Mike nodded.

'So, what are you scared of?' the Devil asked. 'All I want is fifty people. They can be whoever you want—rapists, perverts, child molesters, sports commentators—and all you have to do is murder them.'

'Fifty—that's a lot of people,' Mike offered.

The Devil waved his hand. 'Nyah. One a week, it's over in twelve months. And you'll never get a day older. The sooner you start, the younger you'll be.'

Mike considered. 'I don't know—fifty people.' He knew he couldn't hide his interest.

'Damn right, you can't. Listen, tell me why you're worried.'

So Mike did. He told him about all the movies he had ever seen where someone was left screaming into oblivion. He told him about Ray Milland in The Premature Burial and Barbara Steele in Pit And The Pendulum and Prometheus chained to a rock to have his liver pecked out again and again and again. He told him about the parents who had wished their son back to life, about Dorian Gray and all the others who had found eternity in its myriad suspect forms.

He talked about fear and doubt and about how no-one wanted to be left holding a pig in a poke. But what he talked about most of all was being seven years old and thinking you were king of the world because, like all good seven-year-olds, you had dared to venture where you weren't supposed to go. You had scraped your knees and ruined the toes of your brand new sneakers, but you had done it. Twelve feet high and you had climbed it all. You were standing on top of the local substation, hearing the step-down transformers—whatever *they* were—hum beneath your feet, feeling that deadly power as it buzzed up through your legs and rattled its way along your entire body.

It was the most glorious and awe-inspiring feeling in the world. This had always been something to be feared and respected—the *Electric Shed*—and now you were standing astride it with the world's best friends. You had conquered it and you were invincible.

But, then, it had ended. The way all good dreams are ended. *Grown-ups*. There you were, with your arms around each other's shoulders as you congratulated and celebrated your own bravery, and some fool with a cap and a nasty-looking dog had come striding down the street and demanded to know what the hell you thought you were playing at.

That was it, you explained, you were just *playing*. But they didn't understand, because they had never been young themselves. They had come into the world with a hat and a vicious dog and a cheerless sneer across their face. *'What if it blows up?'* they asked. *'Do you want to go flying through space forever?'*

And that was enough. Because you knew there was a world of power underneath the place where your feet were planted. *A world*. And maybe a world was just enough to rocket you to the top of the sky and then out into space, where you would have only the stars and your own preciously clutched breath for company.

That was when a young Michael Lyall realised he didn't want to live forever. A long time would be enough. A hundred and fifty years, say. He remembered lying in bed and praying that night—*Dear God, please don't let me never die*. Of course, God didn't answer. God never did, but you said what you had to say—whether it was a promise, a plea, or all-out confession—and then fell asleep with the tears on your cheeks and fearful hope inside your heart.

When it was over and there were tears on his face, the Devil asked him a question:

'So, it's not the killing that bothers you?'

Mike shook his head. 'I really think I could get used to it.'

The Devil winked. Mike couldn't see it, but he knew he had. 'Maybe you won't want to stop.'

Mike said he didn't think that was likely. Once the deal was done, he didn't think he'd get the urge.

The Devil shrugged. 'You never know, Mikey. You just never know.'

'No,' Mike heard himself say unsurely.

'So . . . *fear.*'

'Fear,' Mike said.

The Devil considered. 'That old chestnut. Listen, take a while, do some research and I'll see you in a week. Jesus, those electric sheds—they'll get you every time.'

Then he was gone, and Mike felt his knees unhinge as he collapsed unconscious towards the hot, dusty floor.

Four nights later, he found himself staying up late and watching Logan's Run on his own. He cheered the part where everyone was put to death at thirty, and urged Francis to get Logan; he had always thought there was something very unctuous about Michael York, anyway. He booed at Peter Ustinov, who wanted to spend his wrinkled life with nothing but cats for company.

Research, the Devil had said, as though this were some academic pursuit he was considering. He supposed he should read up on the subject—see how immortality had been treated by the arts and science. He could watch films like Highlander, read the ethics of cryogenics (*forget murder*). But their arguments and warnings would fall prey to one undeniable fact: he didn't want to die. Years ago he had wanted to climb down from an electric shed and never go back up there again for fear of being left flying through space; now, he thought he might be able to hold his breath forever.

Because that was all it would amount to. A new existence every twenty years: fake i.d., a new city. It wasn't a big country, but if he kept a low profile he thought he could do it. *Twenty years.* Wasn't life over then, anyway? The family, the friendships, the enthusiasm for what you knew and did. Didn't they all turn to stone with the passage of time?

New wife. New family. He would have to cut all ties. Maybe even fake his own death. Certainly a mysterious disappearance.

Later, he lay in bed, hearing his wife breathe and thinking how, despite everything, he still loved her very much. But even that didn't ease his desperation. It couldn't, because now, at last, he knew there was a way out.

The Devil was blowing a party toot. It unrolled and tickled Mike's ear.

'It's your lucky day, Mike. Fifty per cent off. A gen-u-ine (*it rhymed with line*) sale. Today's very special offer—EVERLASTING LIFE. I'm not asking fifty. I'm not asking forty. I'm not even asking thirty. Twenty-five, Mike. *Twenty-five* lives. That's all it takes. One payment down. Sale guaranteed.'

Mike was shaking. 'Oh, God.' *But weren't God and Old Nick the same? Here is my body—eternal life. Who wouldn't?* 'It's a deal.'

The Devil gripped his shoulder. 'You said that once before and I had to come back. I don't want any more shit this time.'

Mike nodded.

'You can look at me now.'

Mike turned his neck, and the Devil was nowhere to be seen. Because the Devil was in front of him, grasping his hand and squeeze-shaking it in closure. It felt like the Devil had hawked and spat into his palm before they clasped hands; a real phlegmer.

'Done,' he heard before he could twist back, and then he woke.

The first was easy. He bought a kitchen knife from a shop twenty miles from his home and kept it in the glove compartment of his car for a week. Then, one evening, roaming a part of town that was nasty enough to have a reputation but not central enough to come under the auspices of security cameras and police patrols, he put the knife in the depths of his pocket and waited for someone to approach him.

It was just a kid with a white face and hollow eyes that were surely the product of a bad habit. The kid asked him if he could spare 50p like at least one of them didn't know the money would end up in his arm.

Mike reached into his pocket, drew out the knife and stabbed the kid in the chest. The kid looked at him in surprise. *What did you do that for?* His eyes screamed disbelievingly. *I only wanted fifty fucking pence.* Blood pumped from the kid's chest. He hinged backwards and sat on the pavement with a thump.

Mike watched the kid's eyes shut and, then, he ran. He dropped his keys trying to get back in the car, knocked his head on the handle as he bent to retrieve them. His heart was pounding like a bastard, adrenaline flooded every pore. It felt like the first time he had had sex. He looked down and the evidence was there—a hard-on the size of a housing estate.

Three days later, Deborah looked at him across the kitchen table. 'You're dyeing your hair,' she said, and he started guiltily.

He shook his head.

'Yes, you are—and I'm going to find the bottle!'

She dashed upstairs and started searching through cupboards and drawers, and for a while she looked young. She was trying a little hard, but she looked young. Finally, when there was nowhere left to search, she flopped down on the bed and stared at him.

'You're dyeing your hair at *work*. Or using one of those colour shampoos.'

'*At work*,' he said, and they laughed together while she clung to him.

She didn't ask again, and that was good. Because he couldn't tell her. Couldn't explain just what he was dyeing his hair *with*. It didn't come in a bottle and you couldn't buy twice as much as you wanted for one and a half times the price you wanted to pay, but it sure as hell got your hair clean. Washed that grey right out of there. *Satan's shampoo; just wash . . . and go.* Is that how he'd know? When his head was covered in lustrous, black hair? It seemed as good a sign as any.

Perhaps there wouldn't be a revelatory flash. But even without the hair, he would know. He was sure of that. Somewhere deep inside himself where his subconscious sat and reaffirmed its own existence over and over again, he would know. There would be a lurch and a murmur and then everything would settle back to normal as he and his newfound longevity went about the business of being immortal.

It was eight weeks before he could bring himself to do it again. Not because his mind and body were racked with guilt and confusion, but because the bargain he had made began to seem more and more like a dream or some half-remembered thought he had once had. He didn't want to kill twenty-five people for the sake of a mild case of *deja vu*.

Finally, sick of his own indecision, he took a knife from the kitchen drawer, walked the streets and stuck it in the back of the first person he passed. He had decided he couldn't make selective choices. That imposed some kind of morality or worthiness on what he was doing, and he didn't want to do that. No illusions, he just wanted to get the thing over with as quickly as possible. If he waited eight weeks between each killing, it would take almost four years. Four more years of lines and grey hairs and sagging, softening muscles.

The man he passed was unlucky enough to be out buying pizza. A day later, he was local news and Mike's hair was another shade darker. *There I am,* Mike thought. *I finally made the headlines.* Whether it was for the right reasons or the wrong reasons didn't matter. What did matter was that it was in motion now. Performing the deed twice had acted as some kind of Rubicon. He was marching on the Rome of his own mortality, and there were only twenty-three miles to go.

Number three was no difficulty at all.

By the sixth and seventh it was like shelling peas: a hit and run in a car he had passed in which the keys were clearly visible; a prostitute who had smiled suspiciously because he clearly wasn't the kind of client she was used to; a drunk; a courting couple; a blow on the head; a brick in his pocket; a push from a bridge; more knives. Twenty-five was beginning to seem like nothing at all.

It was eight and nine when the trouble really started.

This time, he had tried to stick the knife into someone and the blade had simply bounced off. Whatever the man had covering his stomach was metal. Mike had no idea what someone was doing walking the streets with a sheet of metal covering their abdomen, but that was the least of his worries for the moment.

His *victim* had recovered from the initial shock and was now twisting Mike's wrist and stamping down hard on his instep. The knife clattered to the floor and Mike followed, twisting as the pressure on his wrist increased. The man of steel aimed a kick at his ribs and grinned maliciously. He looked as if he had spent half his life waiting for this to happen.

Mike winced and rolled along the pavement until his back was pressed against the corner where two walls met. The man, who was surely going to beat him to within an inch of his life now, was walking forward and bending to pick up the fallen knife. He clutched it in his hand and stooped over, their new roles as victim and attacker now firmly established.

The man smiled.

Mike could hear his own breath.

The man smiled some more. He came on a step and feinted a jab at Mike's eyes.

Then Mike got lucky. Two streets away where people were spilling out of public houses and into taxis, a window exploded, amplified by the silence that followed in its wake.

The man with metal on his stomach and in his hand paused and looked up. Mike's hand reached out and grabbed the man's hair. He yanked forward for all he was worth and the man fell on top of him. There was a crack as the man continued over and struck his head against the wall. His body lost its tightness and slumped across Mike, the knife wedged flat between them. Mike kicked his way out and rolled over onto his stomach.

He lifted the man's head and let it fall to the floor with a sickening thud. There was no breath coming from the man's mouth. He waited and still didn't hear anything. He knew he should check for a pulse, but for some reason he couldn't do it.

Instead, he picked up the knife and ran for the darkness of the street where his car was parked.

It didn't stop there.

He was half a mile from where it had happened and everything was fine. He had stopped and let the knife fall into a grate. It could have been used again, he knew. But it was better down there in the sewers. It had been too close for comfort and he didn't need any souvenir to remind him of tonight; the memory of his own terror would be with him long enough.

He had wiped the dirt from his face, checked his clothes for rips and tears and set off again.

Thirty seconds later, he hit someone full on. Hit them hard enough to be able to watch them go flying over his head as they sailed through the night. He was doing forty and there was no way they were going to survive an impact like that.

His feet reached for the brakes, his eyes for the mirror, and then he was sitting with his head on the steering wheel, feeling himself beginning to shake because the police had appeared from nowhere and, Christ, it was all going pear-shaped now.

Someone yanked open the door and told him it was all right. They had seen everything and he hadn't had a chance. Mike looked at them and shook his head.

The guy nodded and switched off Mike's engine. He touched Mike on the shoulder, and Mike threw up all over him.

The police were gentlemen. They treated him as though he had been the victim of a particularly horrible crime—sat him down, explained things, sympathised, brought tea.

When it was over, they drove him home. They would need the car for a while, they said. But it was nothing to worry about—just routine. After all, he had had no chance.

He didn't kill anyone for three months. Now, there was fear. But, moreover, there was confusion.

Twenty-five, the Devil had said. *Twenty-five lives*. But hadn't he also said something about murder?

But even that wasn't the problem, because Mike knew he had sped up before he hit the pedestrian. He had seen them walk out into the street. Had had time to move his foot to the brake and apply all the pressure he could. But he hadn't. He had pressed down on the accelerator, knowing here was a cheap one. He had been deep inside himself while he did it, still shaken by the way things had gone horribly wrong, but the intent had been there. That was a definite.

It was the guy half a mile away that was the problem. Numbers. *Was it eight or nine?* Was the man dead and gone or was he lying in a hospital somewhere? He had been too scared to check for a pulse, and now there was no way of knowing.

There was nothing in the newspapers to inform him. He contemplated phoning the police or hospitals, claiming to be a concerned friend or relative—but there was no way he could work the story through. He had no name, no address, nothing at all that would fit.

Surely, it would have made the news if the man had been found dead. *Eight, then.*

Or nine.

Numbers. He knew that was what reality boiled down to. The numbers inside an atom, the maths that proved existence and space and time. Computer digits. Bar codes and bank accounts. Birthdays and ages and National Insurance identifiers. Chromosomes and DNA and rocket flights and two and two equals whatever the hell you want—

But numbers were far more important than that, now. He had made a deal with the Devil, and the Devil had said twenty-five. Not twenty-six. Not twenty-four. Not thirty-seven or a hundred and eight or three hundred million, just to be on the safe side. Twenty-five was the contract, and now he was well and truly in the mire.

Sometimes, he decided it didn't matter. When he had pulled the man with the steel stomach over his head, he hadn't meant to dash his skull against the wall. Even if the man was dead, it wasn't murder. *It was eight.*

Other times, he told himself he had approached the man with the express intention of ending his life by sticking a steel blade into his unsuspecting belly. If the man had died because he had been struck a blow on the head instead . . . well, that was still murder.

Nine.

If he was dead.

Finally, the dream came again without any prompting.

The Devil was sitting astride his back this time. Mike was lying on the floor and his face was pressed into the ground. One arm was bent up towards his shoulder and the Devil was tugging it hard.

The Devil's teeth bit down on Mike's ear and then, briefly, before all the pain disappeared, the Devil spoke.

It's eight, you stupid fucker, Mike heard as he felt spit dribble into his ear.

The day after that, he locked himself in his office at work and wrote down the details of each victim. He wrote them in sequence, in reverse order, and then at random. He shredded the paper he had used and dropped some of the illegible strips into eight different bins as he made his way home.

When his pockets were empty, he stabbed a woman outside her house and hurried away. He was one of the dangerous people now. The crazies you crossed the street to avoid.

But it was nine now, and for that he was thankful.

At twenty, he began to have dreams of failure. It was the same dream every time and he would wake from it in a sweat that was cold as the grave.

In the dreams, he is standing over his final victim. There has been a fight, but now the man lies on the floor before him, beaten.

Why? The man asks, and Mike tells him. *Because none of it is enough*, he says. He is uncertain what he means by this, but he thinks what he is trying to make clear is that no-one should be made to grow old when they feel fifteen inside themselves. *I'm fifteen*, he says. *Even when I'm slipping the knife in under the bottom rib, I'm fifteen.*

The cop arrives, then. Like the Devil, the cop is American. He wears mirrored shades and a gun on his hip.

Mike tries to look behind the shades into the man's eyes. The cop smiles. It is a smile of knowledge and amusement. Mike looks down and realises he is mistaken; the cop is not wearing a gun on his hip. The cop is *holding* a gun and pointing it straight at Mike's chest.

Something kicks him in the breastbone, then. It feels like a 10-ton truck. He sees the knife leave his hand and go cart wheeling upwards. Turning—red, silver, red, silver. That is strange, he thinks, because he has not yet drawn blood from his final victim. He realises his mistake. The blood on the knife is his own. It has come from the hole where his body used to be.

After that, he is staring at the sky. The sky and walls. The walls of the alley where he was supposed to become immortal.

The cop's boot comes down beside him and continues on. There is a sound, and Mike knows the man on the floor—the other man—has died. The cop has picked up Mike's knife and plunged it into his heart.

The cop is back, now. Mike cannot see him, because his eyes no longer work; there is only blackness. Nevertheless, he knows the cop is there. Knows he is close enough to see the white in the red in the hole of the body of this man whom he is leaning over.

The cop gives Mike's body a hefty kick with the side of his foot to make sure it is dead. It is not, but they both know it will not be long now. It would be nice to explain, Mike thinks. Tell this Angel of Destruction he is a decent man. All he wanted was to live forever.

The cop says something, then. His voice is cold and short, matter-of-fact, and Mike knows any explanation would be redundant. The cop understands everything; he has his own fears and dreams. Bargains are, indeed, cheap.

The cop straightens up and says it again: *'Twenty-five.'*

This is the point where Mike wakes. Always, it is before his dream-self dies, but he knows that is just his brain taking care not to kill his sleeping body with shock. The deal is over. He has not delivered according to the terms and now he must pay the penalty: death.

It is just a dream, he knows. But when it comes on four consecutive nights and he can no longer hold the drink he makes himself in a dead of night pitch-dark kitchen that has become ritual now, he knows he must act fast.

Act fast before he does something stupid. Like break into someone's home and kill all five in one fell swoop. His own family, even. Success is imminent, and like all successes the shakiness has set in. The finishing-line is in sight and God has tied his shoelaces prankishly together and planted one knee-buckling shove in the middle of his back.

As soon as possible, Mike whispers into the darkness of the kitchen and pours the liquid he has not spilled or drunk into the sink.

They caught him on the twenty-fifth. It was obvious, now he thought about it.

He has drawn the knife, shaking uncontrollably as he readies himself to use it one final time. It is a woman this time and as he stands behind her, he has already forgotten what she looks like. He cannot even see the colour of her hair. She has no person. He is standing behind her with a knife and she is nothing but sovereign remedy, his elixir of life.

He steps forward and someone tugs at his sleeve. Someone else is punching him in the face. They are a mob now, intent on justice and destruction, which is the same thing. He looks around as his head is flung from pillar to post. Between blows, he wonders where they have come from. The streets were empty and now they are full.

As he passes beyond consciousness, he smiles. The cop is nowhere to be seen.

He is in trouble now. All is not lost though, he knows that. Surely it is possible to kill someone in prison. Weapons can be bought. Failing that, he will use his bare hands. Then, all he has to do is escape. Escape and never kill anyone again.

The Devil comes the following night. *'You stupid fuck,'* he whispers in Mike's ear. *'It was twenty-five. That guy in the brace—dead as a fucking doornail. Pretty shitty trick, huh? Live long and prosper, Mikey.'*

Mike barely registers this (the police doctor has prescribed medication—eight pills a day. There is something in his food too, he is sure. Whatever, he has become slow and fogged in the thirty-some hours since his capture. It is not the indestructibility he had hoped for), but when he wakes five hours later, the visit is clear as a bell inside his head. The Devil has tricked him, he knows, but he might still get the last laugh. All he has to do now is escape. He wonders if that will be possible.

Before that, there is the law. Police and solicitors and cells and explanations; courts and guards and a trial with a judge in an ill-fitting wig who tells him he is the most evil man he has ever come across. *Life*, the judge says. *Because that is the maximum I can impose.* And he is led away from a shouting courtroom, full of people who want him dead. His family is there, too. They are small and speechless as he leaves them behind. His wife does not look well.

Later, she comes to visit him.

I love you, he says. *I'm sorry, and I love you.* And she looks away. Because despite spending more years with this man than she has without him, despite taking his cock in her mouth, despite letting him see her with her underwear around her ankles as she sits on the loo and her body rids itself of waste, despite rows and frustrations and disappointments that meant nothing, he has murdered God knows how many people. She doesn't know why and she cannot look him in the eye.

So he reaches for her fingers, wondering which will be worse—having her snatch them away from his grasp or taking hold of them and finding there is no longer any warmth there. He has stolen whatever is inside her that keeps her from freezing. Stolen and dashed it to a thousand pieces.

He will rise and leave because he cannot bear for her to be here and yet not here, and maybe he will never see her again. She will grow old and he will receive letters from his children that say too much about nothing and nothing about enough. He will read the letters once and throw them away.

Eventually, the letters will bring the news that his wife has died. Enough years will have finally passed for her to have almost forgiven him, and he will turn away because he is nothing now, less than he ever was.

And after that, the rest of existence stretching out before him like a road in the desert. Sitting in his cell while the mirror laughs at him and a succession of young warders' faces peer in at the door. '*How* long?' the warders will ask. Because even though they are green and these are their first days on the job, they are not stupid. Stories of the man who will live forever are just that—stories. The custodial equivalent of a left-handed hammer or long stand. Aren't they?

They will look surprised—because there is something about this man that tells them he is older than he looks. So he will say it again. *Fifty years. Sixty years.* All these years and more. They will repeat his words, respectfully but still with doubt, and he will nod. *A long time*, they will say, thinking they are hiding the fear and puzzlement that is taking them over by degrees. Fear and puzzlement that will, in later years when they are old and grey, cause them to veer away from his cell, request a transfer or retirement.

But he will shake his head when they say those words: *a long time*. Fifty years is not a long time. A hundred, that is a long time. Two hundred, that is even longer. Four. It does not bear thinking about.

These are the thoughts he turns to again and again in his solitude and confinement, and he gives them much thought and deliberation. Much more than he ever gave to the question of sticking a knife into someone's belly.

He has turned them over more than usual of late. Because he is alone now. He cannot remember when exactly it was that he last saw another human being, heard the slap of leather on concrete, the slam of metal on metal. There has been nothing now for some time.

It started weeks ago. There were reports in the press, stories on the radio. A new epidemic that made AIDS look like a summer cold. Then the rumours: the medical wing was full; half the prisoners were dead; the warders were falling like flies, the Army was being brought in; TV had stopped; the world was at an end.

Then silence.

The Devil had come before without being asked. Mike had done more than ask this time. He had begged and pleaded. Pleaded until his voice was a whisper, his throat raw and broken.

But the Devil hadn't come, because the Devil was dead. God was dead, too. It was the end of the world and there had been no judgement.

The world was over. *He* was God now. Only God had had at least seven good days. And all he had managed to create in this ten by six cell was a pile of feces in the corner (there were no flies and that was further proof, if proof were needed, that God was dead) and the smell of his own piss and sweat that was a constant assault on his nostrils.

He was getting skinny, too. He had begun to wonder if there were any nutrients in his own waste. And if there were, could he live forever in one endless perpetuity of recycling? You were truly what you ate. What went around came around, even though it would be difficult to get your teeth completely clean ever again.

There had been two packets of Polo's in his pocket when this started. He had eaten one mint a day. Except for two hours ago, when he had taken the last two and crunched them asunder with salivatory glee. Now, they were gone and he was beginning to wonder if—

He closed his eyes and he could see a small building built of white brick. Two metal doors made up one wall of the building. There was a small boy sitting on top cross-legged.

The boy was holding his breath and pressing down against the roof of the building with his palms, because the building was flying through space and that was the only thing that was stopping him from rushing off into oblivion.

He began to scream.

GAZELLES IN BABYLON
Cyril Simsa

Later, he could never remember what made him choose that particular store.

Chong's Curio Bazaar and Trade Emporium . . . Hardly an up-market name for the place where he was destined to make the find of a lifetime.

But there it was: just one of a whole row of little Victorian red-brick shop-fronts on a dusty sidestreet in a small market town, lined up in a sort of angular rat-run from the rise at the back of the church to the County Museum on the large town square. Maiden Harborough. Yet another of those genteel and faded English towns whose moment of glory had come and gone in the sleepy centuries between King William's Domesday survey and Sir Walter Raleigh's first voyage of discovery to the Virginia plantations. Somehow, Rigo rather doubted it had ever managed to do more than to roll over with a faint roar and grumble in the whole half-millenium since.

MAIDEN HARBOROUGH. Wulfweard and Drogo hold it of the Bishop. There is land for 20 ploughs; there are 10 slaves, 25 villains and 22 bordars; and woodland for 50 pigs; and a mill rendering 22s. 6d., and 80 acres of meadow . . . Plus, of course, parking space for 300 tourists and Chong's curio bazaar.

The thing was, the shop was not even especially impressive. Its window was cramped and dingy, with flaking brown paint on its woodwork, and glass so long unwashed it was beginning to look more like a particularly nasty Jungian archetype, than a pioneering sales pitch of early post-historical capitalism. The inevitable trays of bric-a-brac by the door were old and faded—genuinely old and genuinely faded, to be sure, but no more attractive for all that—and the tiles around the entrance itself were so chipped and rotten that a dentist might have been tempted to give them bridge work.

Perhaps it was the Chinese coin that did it—three thousand years old, if it was a day, and swollen green with verdigris—discarded so casually in an open box on the sun-flecked pavement. Or perhaps it was just some kind of collector's instinct. Either way, Rigo suddenly found himself reaching out for the elaborate brass doorknob—an incongruously Byzantine affair of bald-headed monkeys and unchastely prolific lilies, polished to an obscenely smooth finish by the hands of a million customers—and pushed . . .

A bell rang dimly in the back as the door swung open, but otherwise there seemed to be nothing inside but clutter. Ancient, dusty furniture . . . faded family portraits and neoclassical landscapes gravid with the pimpled pink backsides of maenads and satyrs . . . unclassifiable *objets d'art* in what was surely not real gold and lapis . . . something that could perhaps have been a Roman oil lamp . . . About par for the course, in short. So what was it that had compelled him so strongly, out on the street, to reach for the handle?

It was at that moment that, picking her way carefully through the lumber like a bower bird, a girl emerged from behind an ornate Anatolian tapestry which had evidently been used to separate off the sales area from a more private inner sanctum to the left of the shop.

From such small acorns . . .

She was dressed in silk—sea green, and subtly patterned with a repeating pattern of birds' wings and deep-sea breakers—breaking silently over the timeless swell of the waves that rose and fell with the curves of her body. Her face was painted a rare, speckled white above her Mandarin collar, like the delicate eggshell of an almost extinct species of tropical hummingbird in a green satin egg-cup. Her hair was short and black, her eyelids hooded, as if in memory of a long-lost Oriental past, though somehow she didn't quite look Chinese—more like one of those post-Colonial grandchildren that came out of Macau or the old silk road out of Xinjiang.

She regarded Rigo impersonally—evidently not yet sure whether she should be pleased to see him—with impossible eyes the colour of peaches.

Must be contact lenses, he thought.

And then she spoke:

'Can I help you?'

The words hung like bubbles in the grey air between them, refracting colours, the images of objects, the smudgy spring light from the window . . . all his uncertain impressions of this first encounter with this most peculiar lady. And was it his imagination, or did her voice carry the faintest hint of an accent? A strange one—something mid-way between Chinese and the cidery burr of the West Country. Not one he had heard before.

He shrugged.

'Just looking,' he said weakly.

There, so now they had their first ritual exchange behind them, he reflected, turning away quickly to busy his eyes in a nearby display case.

But he was not getting away so easily. His gaze settled with a sense almost of inevitability on a bowl of Japanese porcelain, boldly decorated with a pattern of fruit bats and peaches.

'It represents long life and happiness.' The girl had come to stand next to him, enveloping him with a pervasive scent of myrrh, aloes and cinnamon. 'A fine combination . . .'

And which combination was that?—he wondered. The three herbs and spices? Or the glazed clutch of full, ripe peaches exactly the colour of her eyes, with three little bats squiggling away unobtrusively in the background?

But aloud all he said was: 'Really? It seems pretty bizarre to me . . .'

At least he had found his voice.

'So you're Ms Chong?' he asked carefully.

She shook her head and smiled.

'No, Chong is my uncle. I'm Morvenna Lee. Call me Morvenna.'

'Amerigo Wippler.'

He held out his hand, and she shook it vigorously.

'Come to discover?' She laughed, showing for a moment her small, pointed teeth.

Insectivore teeth . . . Fruit bat teeth . . .

'I'm more of an Old World person myself . . . ' She indicated a small sandstone statuette of what at first looked like an Ancient Greek hero, but on closer inspection turned out to be a Buddha. 'Old World-Older World hybrid . . .'

She smiled again at his evident puzzlement.

'Early Buddhist sculpture from the Greek kingdom of Ghandara in Northern India,' she explained. 'Part of the legacy of the great Alexander...It's very old, twenty-odd centuries give or take. One of those many forgotten meetings between East and West . . . '

But what was she trying to tell him?—Rigo mused. Was this in some sense a symbolic autobiography? Surely she could not seriously be suggesting she was descended from the Alexandrian diaspora of Central Asia?

'So what else have you got to show me?' Rigo tried to get into the swing of things.

'Well, we have this rather fine papier-mache mollusc.' She pointed at a dusty over-size model of a snail standing close-by on a rosewood sideboard. 'It was made in Paris about 1880 for an unknown zoologist, and if you split open the shell, it comes apart to display the full internal anatomy. Look . . . ' She plucked gingerly at a crack in the snail's papery carapace and swung open a flap to expose a chaos of bizarre geometrical forms which would not have seemed out of place in even the most nameless of crumbling palaces at the Mountains of Madness. 'This yellow thing here is its digestive gland,' she demonstrated. 'And over here in purple is its gonad . . . '

She closed the lid delicately.

'When we first got it in, we spent a very jolly afternoon taking it apart, but it took us ten days to put it all back together, and we had to call in the local biology teacher to help us. So now we never do more than peer.

'And over here is our xylotech . . . '

She led Rigo to what at first appeared to be a glass-fronted bookcase, except that the books seemed to be bound, not in leather, but in bark. Morvenna pried open the doors of the cabinet, and pulled out a book at random, passing it over wordlessly to Rigo. To his surprise, he found it was made of a single, solid block of wood.

'This one is cherry, I think.' She peered at the label on the spine. 'Yes, look at the bark and the colouring . . .You see? Every one of these books is made from a different tree, with cross-sections in three different directions, and samples of the bark, and sometimes even the characteristic lichens . . . As far as we can tell it was originally produced for the private collection of an 18th Century Czech-German bishop naturalist, but his foundation had to sell it off after the 1918 armistice to cover its debts. It was in Wiltshire for a while after that . . .

'And then over here,'—she reached into a ancient brass bowl of trinkets, and handed Rigo a miniscule cylinder of steatite—'is a Babylonian seal with a representation of an elephant. No, turn it the other way up . . . ' She flipped the seal around on the palm of his hand. 'Look for the ears and the trunk . . . ' And Rigo discovered, to his embarrassment, that he had been squinting short-sightedly at the elephant's rump.

'The question is,' Morvenna continued, 'is it an Indian or an African elephant? We know the Romans and the Carthaginians tended mostly to use elephants from Africa, but that was probably no more than an accident of geography. Who knows what they preferred by the Euphrates? And how the elephants got there? Unless, of course, there was once an indigenous population, left over at the end of the Ice Age. Goodness knows, conditions were still rather confused in those days, what with all those lions in Assyria, hippo swamps in the Sudan, and gazelles in Babylon . . . '

But Rigo was scarcely listening, for he could still feel the electrifying after-shock of her body, where her fingers had fleetingly brushed his hand. It was as if he had been stung.

'I sometimes wonder whether we will ever have a true idea of how many lost cultures and lost civilisations rose and died in the Near East, even after the Egyptians . . . ' Morvenna continued blithely, apparently unaware of his distraction. 'The area seems to have grown them like chickpeas . . . Look at those mysterious pre-Dynastic megalith-builders of the Sahara, with their astronomically aligned rows of menhirs, and their stone circles, and their round barrows full of ceremonially dismembered cows . . . Or all those sacred stones in the Bible, from Jacob's pillow to the twelve great stone pillars of the Canaanite temple at Gilgal . . . No wonder the Egyptians ended up having such an obsession with putting up morbid stone monuments in the desert, full of the mummified remains of their illustrious dead and ascetic animal-headed deities carved out of huge blocks of basalt . . .

'And those mummies . . . '

She paused, and Rigo realised, self-consciously, that she was watching him. Like Anubis weighing the souls of the dead before the court of Osiris against an obsidian bowl of chaff. Evidently, whatever it was she was testing him for, he passed.

'You know, the Egyptians were capable of mummifying almost anything.' She said, choosing her words slowly and meticulously. 'Dogs, cats, antelopes . . . hippos, deer, crocodiles, ibis, elephant . . . even scarabs and molluscs . . . They always sent the pharaoh on his way to the afterlife with an animal accompaniment. What most people don't realise, though, is why . . . '

Ah, and here it comes, thought Rigo. *The real reason she brought me here.* As if she really *had* brought him there. When had he started believing in predestination?

'Have you ever considered the structure and function of mummies?' she asked.

Rhetorical, my boy, rhetorical, Rigo said to himself. *But shake your head just in case.*

'The masks and the bandages . . . the spices and rituals . . . the weird little lotus pictograms painted on at the knee? The essential organs lined up in jars of coagulated oil on either side of the dead pharaoh's resting place like macabre clay bowls of *pate de foie gras*, and the solid gold tresses on either side of his head that glowed like an aura . . .It all served as a kind of distillation of life, a highly effective concentration of the essence of the animal—or the human—that was being preserved . . . a store of the living creature's psychic presence, to be drawn on later.

'Perhaps you've noticed just how similar the dried-up flesh of a mummy is to the hard tack of the Victorian explorer? No self-respecting Victorian traveller would ever have set off into the hinterlands of the Dark Continent without a full train of porters and a goodly supply of essentials. It works much the same way when you want to visit the Underworld. You have to have your own ritual food supply with you.

'You could say that Mummies are a kind of astral pemmican, and each different species has its own particular uses, with the pharaohs themselves as the real beluga . . . You eat them to keep you alive in the afterlife. And in this one, when you've overstayed your time.'

She leaned closer and put her hand on his shoulder, and suddenly her scent became quite overwhelming.

Rigo sniffed involuntarily.

'Yes, I know,' she laughed. 'Every good boy learns from his Bible that he should beware women who perfume their beds with myrrh, aloes and cinnamon . . . or their decolletage . . . especially when they find that the Book of Proverbs has inadvertently discovered the secret anointing oil of the Witches . . . But what does your heart tell you? Never mind regrets, never mind opinion . . . What do your viscera have to say? What does your gut want you to do about your innermost desires and longings?'

But Rigo was tongue-tied again, and with all the best will in the world, he couldn't manage any more than a confused and undiginified silence.

Morvenna smiled. 'What's the matter, viscera got your tongue?' she asked laughingly. But she said it kindly. And it was true, his viscera filled him with an inchoate, anxious roaring.

'Come on . . . ' Morvenna passed over his continuing silence. 'There's something you need to see before this goes any further.'

She moved off to the back of the shop, and pulled aside the Anatolian tapestry from behind which she had emerged earlier, to reveal another, deeper, and altogether less cosy chamber, which sloped away into what seemed at first to be an infinite darkness . . . The inner room was dim and austere, filled with the vague outlines of mummies and sarcophagi, and larger-than-life statues of baboon-headed deities and magicians carrying wands made of the living bodies of petrified asps . . .

Moses and Hermes . . . Thoth and Osiris . . .

A wave of cold air swept up into Rigo's face from the chamber's massive stone walls, and he saw that they were slithery with a peculiar species of microscopic grey dust and speckled silvery-white with mica, which sparkled now even in the faint light of the torches that flamed to one side in a long line of black metal sconces . . .

Speckled and sparkling like the cold night sky, he thought, viscera finally snapping into in gear.

Morvenna turned, and the torches cast highlights off what he now realised were multiple rows of bobbing ibis patterned into the weave of the shiny green silk of her bodice. Her peachy eyes shone like twin planets, casting back their ruddy glow over the twilit sands of Asia's forgotten history.

'So are you coming?' she asked in that East-West lilt of hers. 'We've all done it, right on down from the Taoist sages of Ancient China to the to the toothless and scarified medicine men of your own Pictish ancestors . . . You could live forever.'

Yes, perhaps. Or maybe he could end up embalmed with camphor and myrrh in a second-hand sarcophagus.

He hesitated.

Morvenna, watching him struggle with his fears, smiled slyly to herself. Her face filled his field of vision like the pale disc of the moon-goddess Isis.

'Will I not live to regret this?' Rigo asked aloud.

'Yes, perhaps,' she echoed his thoughts ambiguously. 'People are capable of regretting almost anything in the morning. But tell me you still regret it as you board the Boat of the Dawn at midnight. Tell me you still regret it at the court of Osiris. Tell me you still regret it when your viscera come to life.'

She opened her arms, so the light of the torches shone like an aureole around her body.

'Welcome to eternity,' she whispered regally.

And helpless to resist her, Rigo stepped forward into the warm embrace of the Goddess and the coolly impressive enormity of the age-old mystery of night.

HIDE AND SEEK
John Paul Catton

It was nearly sunset, and dusk was oozing through soft, absorbent clouds like blood from burst capillaries. A mournful skyscape was reflected in the unreadable glass-windowed face of Okamura Heavy Industries Head Office, West Shinjuku, Tokyo. It was also reflected in the dusty spectacles of Mr. Yukawa, the company's executive director; a thorn of the day's last moment of sunlight stabbing him in the eye as he squinted across the conference table.

'As I see it,' Yukawa began, 'we'll need at least two hundred thousand square feet. That will more than double our present capacity, at least as long as we continue operating in the Toyama area.'

'Right, and by increasing capacity we can lower unit costs, which should improve our profit picture.' This was from Kuroda, the office's chief of planning. He stood before his assembled fellow employees, outlined against the window, behind him the ubiquitous skeletal cranes standing silently amongst anonymous concrete giants. Kuroda continually dipped his head table ward, not just as a show of respect to the assembled businessman but also to prompt himself from his notes. A slender, bespectacled man, Kuroda's hair was only just beginning to acquire its distinguished shade of executive gray. 'Besides, new equipment will be more efficient and easier to maintain.'

As he sat by the right of the chairman, as befitting his rank, Yukawa wallowed in the luxury of being passive throughout most of the meeting. As the only director present, he could speak the least, and he would speak the last;

and his word would have the weight of experience, of seniority, of authority.

The fifty-eight-year-old Yukawa folded his arms, sucking his teeth thoughtfully as he surveyed the staff around the horseshoe-shaped table. The middle managers, on each side, looked preoccupied as they took notes and nodded their heads. In Onoda's case, his faraway look was probably due to him pondering his marital problems rather than the day's business, Yukawa thought ruefully. Perhaps a tactful word, concerning Onoda's suitability for promotion, was in order.

At both ends of the table were the flushed and expectant faces of the junior *salarymen*. The next generation, looking very serious about things that didn't concern them yet. Young Yoshino, holding his pencil like a Kabuki actor about to thrust with his dagger.

Kuroda had already spoken with several estate brokers. 'So considering possible locations, and whether we should build something of our own or lease a facility that already exists, we have a number of options. I propose setting up a sub-committee to study the available properties, and their descriptions and financial data.'

'Hmm.' The meeting's chairman, Mr. Nasu, deliberated for a silent moment, and then inclined his head towards Yukawa. 'Would that be acceptable, Mr. Director?'

Yukawa began his summing-up. 'I think—'

As he looked up, at that precise moment the dying sun slipped behind Kuroda's head and shoulders. The younger man was thrown into eclipse, a fiery corona of light playing about his hair. He had turned into a shadow. Yukawa instantly forgot what he was about to say.

'I think—'

Yukawa stared at the enigma that the standing man had become, and it was like looking into a well. The shadow had lost all outline, all perspective; Kuroda had become a man-shaped hole cut in the air, showing the darkness behind the scenes.

His face. I can't remember his face. Which one was Kuroda? What does he look like? Gods of Mercy, he thought with panic beginning to clog the back of his throat and fill his mouth, I can't remember what he looks like, I can't—

'Mr. Yukawa?' The chairman had bent his head closer to Yukawa's. 'Is everything all right?'

Yukawa jumped, and stared at Nasu's jowly face as if meeting him for the first time. He turned back to Kuroda, who was bending forward in concern, his face returned, his head no longer obscuring the setting sun.

As he stared at Kuroda in relief, Yukawa noted each feature of the younger man's face. The eyes, the high nose, the mole, the quizzical expression. With a sudden, unwanted clarity, Yukawa saw that there was no distinguishing mark he could think of that would separate Kuroda from the image of Yukawa's own son. Whose face was he looking at? The younger man's features blurred momentarily, refocusing themselves, adjusting to fit the correct template. In the distorting mirror of age, Yukawa next saw his own face, younger, dedicated, hopeful, looking with envy and sly mockery at the cold, unapproachable director; himself. The only thing that separated Yukawa and Kuroda from swapping chairs was a walk of twenty years.

Still trying to separate his gaze from Kuroda's, the director said quietly, 'Yes, I'm all right.'

And then he heard it. Reedish, piping, almost musical, like the call of a country bird. The voice, arcing across the rooftops. The voice, splitting through the conference's warmth to spear him in his chair.

The voice, clear and cold in his ear. *'Are you ready yet?'*

'No,' he breathed.

'I beg your pardon?' the chairman asked.

'No.' Yukawa stared wildly about him. 'No, I'm not ready.'

All eyes in the conference room were upon him. 'Gentlemen, will you excuse me? I'm not feeling very well. The chairman will conclude the meeting.'

Outside, in the executive washroom, Yukawa stared at the droplets of water running down his stricken, open-mouthed face. It felt as if his eyes had retreated into their sockets, and it was an effort to pump air into and out of his throbbing chest.

Before him, the emptiness in the mirror warped and fluttered, and the voice repeated—with a touch of petulance—*'Are you ready yet?'*

'No!' he whimpered. 'Give me more time.'

Out of the building. Nobody must be allowed to see him hiding, he thought. He would make an excuse for his sudden 'illness'. A minor annoyance, to be explained later.

In the foyer, the staff were surprised to see Yukawa leaving alone, and unannounced. Head down, his hunched form scurried with unseemly haste through the automatic doors, a chorus of polite, formulaic farewells dripping from his polyester-suited back.

Shinjuku, early evening, the smog of the day slowly becoming the shroud of the night. The windows of camera-shops blinked and beckoned. The ever-changing neon of the discount hardware stores cast ephemeral shadows against the dull gray concrete. The tangled smells of stewed curry and grilled chicken from a nest of tiny restaurants tickled his throat, making him cough.

As he stumbled towards the station, feeling the late summer heat close in upon the places where his clothes snagged against his skin, Yukawa looked warily around for young mothers and their children. Surely, most mothers would have finished their shopping by now. The primary schools and middle schools had closed, but the evening prep schools would now be open. He had no time to lose.

As Yukawa hogged the middle of the sidewalk, shapes moved unexpectedly at the edges of his vision, slow and shadowy, in the tiny gaps between certain buildings. Arms and legs wrapped in unidentifiable cloth stirred feebly. Slumped bodies lay with filthy hoods and caps pulled over their heads, hiding their faces from the light. Down the entrances to tiny alleyways hunched these figures of the homeless, silent and shapeless in their ancient grimy clothes.

Yukawa shuddered violently, despite the heat.

As he entered the gates of Shinjuku station, he was swamped by the crowds from both the offices to the east and the shoppers from the neighboring Keio and Lumine superstores. Carried along by the flow, Yukawa soon realized he had made a tactical error. There was no safety for him in a crowd.

Not any more.

His fingers fumbling and clumsy, he bought a ticket from the vending machine. Pushing and thrusting through the people crowding the platform, Yukawa leapt onto the Sobu train, his shoulders buffeted by the sliding doors, the station guard scowling silently, eyes obscured by his cap. The sweating businessman steadied himself, mumbling an apology to anyone within earshot, and leaned back against the doors to get his breath back.

Every seat was taken, naturally, but there were not too many people standing. Good. Yukawa could still command his own personal space. He could prevent, if necessary, anyone from getting too close to him, without drawing attention to himself.

It was not crowded, not like that terrible evening, one week ago . . .

On that evening, the flow of commuters onto the train had seemed it would never end. Grey-polyester skins of *salaryman* meat, stuffed into the carriage by an invisible machine for squeezing and pumping. At length, the doors had mercifully closed. Yukawa had found himself lodged near the far door, with someone constantly snorting mucus to his left, and to his right, someone else breathing mist onto a windowpane uncomfortably close to his face.

Shuffling his feet, easing his shoulders into a less cramped position, Yukawa eased his right hand upwards to wipe the sweat from his brow, his left hand holding the briefcase pinned to his side, assuming the expression of distracted calm that it was advisable to wear on trains.

It was in this position that Yukawa had first felt the tug on his left sleeve.

At first he had ignored it, thinking someone's bag had caught the jacket material; but shortly after wards it came again, harder, as if someone was trying to pull the button off his sleeve. Odd. Yukawa glared around him, turning his head with difficulty, looking for a likely suspect. Was it that demure-looking secretary with her eyes respectfully downcast, her breasts warming the back of his jacket? Was she a reverse groper, a female masher? Such things were not unknown.

Several times, during the journey home that day, Yukawa had felt the annoying pluck on his sleeve.

At length, the train had reached the station named Mitaka, and with a sigh of relief, Yukawa slipped and slid through the crush to get off. As he did so, he noticed the tug on his sleeve increasing, as if he was unwittingly dragging something with him. Stepping into the smoke-tinged atmosphere of Mitaka's large, open-air platform, Yukawa heard the doors close with a pneumatic wheeze, and turned around to find out who—or what—had got off the train with him . . .

'Uh!'

The grunt of surprise and fear turned several heads on the train, and led Yukawa, who had just shocked himself out of his reverie, to swing his face quickly to the window. He must have been dozing. Daydreaming, thinking too much. Gods of Mercy, these days, he could hardly think of anything else except—*that.*

The number of passengers on the train had lessened; there were only a few people standing now. As this was the local train, the next stop would be Asagaya. The clatter of wheels accompanied the low hum of isolated conversations.

The carriage seemed to fall into a hush, like dipping into a shallow cleft of silence, and there it came again;

'Are you ready yet?'

'No!' The involuntary gasp was louder this time. Heads turned in the opposite direction to Yukawa, and gazes were tactfully averted. His eyes bulging, Yukawa turned around and stared through the double coating of glass framed in the doors leading to the next carriage.

A shape was moving there. Difficult to make out, because of the people standing in the way, and the swaying of the train, but someone there was moving. A short, hunched-over someone, thin, sickly legs exposed by short trousers, head down showing the crown of a school-uniform type cap, a satchel strapped to its back . . .

The platform of Asagaya station slid into view and the doors hissed open at the halting of the train. In utter panic, Yukawa bolted from the train and fled through the platform gates.

He wouldn't make it home in time, he thought, he had to do something unexpected, he had to do *something*.

A short time later, seated on an undersized bar stool in a tiny red-lantern saloon, Yukawa was pressed tight between total strangers like a layer of fish pressed in Osaka sushi. The smoke rose from the quickly filling ashtrays and the ceaselessly active patron's grill. The customers—all of them male—huddled around the tiny square bar that more or less filled the drinking area, middle-aged, rumpled, wrinkled, in almost identical suits, easing themselves past each other's backs and shoulders to slip in and out through the sliding door.

As the warm *o-sake* blossomed in Yukawa's face, he shouted louder and the jokes he told to his unexpected companions became cruder. He told himself that nobody he knew was here. He was safe.

He was lying to himself.

How old was Yukawa when it had happened? How far back did it go, this memory, this thing that he thought had been deleted like an unneeded computer file? Yukawa thought about his grandchild in elementary school now. Yukawa had also been in elementary school, perhaps seven or eight, when it had happened.

On that day. The day when, after school, in the echoing shadows of the local playground at dusk, ten children had joined hands, but the figures of eleven children had been counted in the circle.

The day when Yukawa, standing as part of that circle, puzzled but expecting someone to explain the trick, felt the hand to his left loosen its grip and tug at the sleeve of his school jacket.

The day when Yukawa had turned and stared into the face of a boy, a face that was not a face. It was blank, featureless, a mask between the turned-up collar and the peaked school cap. A smooth expanse of flesh, no eyes, no nose, no mouth.

The boy had no face.

Yet on that day, Yukawa had heard the boy's mouthless voice, a voice as clear as a temple bell.

'Let's play a game. You hide, and I'll come looking for you. Are you ready?'

Fifty-one years later, Yukawa was still not ready.

That day, the playground had cleared itself in mass panic. Panic the children had learned to deny afterwards, as they grew older and adopted the roles of early adulthood like a heavy, formally tied kimono. But Yukawa had stared into the creature's empty face. He had succeeding in forgetting for so long, but now it seemed the game was approaching its end.

According to society's rules, Yukawa had achieved what had been required of him. He had worked unstintingly for his wife and children, genuinely regretting the time at home he had not shared with them. Unlike other colleagues, he had not sought shallow pleasure in mistresses, pornography or the excessive use of *o-sake*.

But there had been another game being played. A more subtle game, and Yukawa now realized that in this, he had not performed very well. Although he had disguised himself in the featureless gray of the *salaryman*, for some unknown reason, he had still been observed. Watched from an impossible distance. Watched by a face without eyes.

Now he would once again look upon *Nopperaboh*, the ghost-boy. The wandering spirit, looking for a playmate, a friend, a parent, someone to take care of him. Throughout all eternity. Or until at least, the childhood stories went, Nopperaboh became bored, and looked about for a new companion.

In the small smoke-filled bar, the *o-sake* suddenly tasted very bitter, and the jokes lost all meaning. It was time for Yukawa to go home. Back to his house and family.

Hailing a taxi from the closet main road to the bar, Yukawa half-drunkenly ordered the uniformed driver to go to a temple near to the businessman's home. He would resist, thought Yukawa. His home was still his home; he would use the love of his family as his armour. He had real children, and grandchildren, not this ageless shadow of a shadow that was trying to adopt him.

The taxi stopped, the door springing open automatically, Yukawa clumsily counting money into anonymous white-gloved hands. Shambling to the temple gates, litter danced around his feet in the fetid breeze, and childish laughter seemed to echo from the rooftops. On the houses around him, the ugly entrails of air-conditioning filters, electrical wiring, meters and pipes bulged outwards, like living creatures turned inside-out.

The paper lanterns cast a soft, rust-colored light as they hung from iron hooks around the temple premises. Yukawa washed his hands carefully in the fountain of purification, stood before the collection box, quietly dropped coins into its slot. He stood with his head bowed for a long time, but the words of the Buddhist *sutras* would not come into his head. The plot of land beside the temple housed a car park and a small playground for children. In the shadows, at the edge of Yukawa's vision, a swing was rocking to and fro, as if pushed by invisible hands.

In Mitaka, the faint sounds of the TV and the smell of cooked rice were drifting from the modest Yukawa house. The householder, arriving late, unlocked the outer door and slid aside the wood and paper screen that led to the parlor. 'I'm home,' he called gently.

Fumbling as he took off his shoes, Yukawa felt a film of sweat ooze over his pinched skin. He almost overbalanced, drunk with relief, apprehension, confused by the night's liquor. He was home. Had he reached the end of the game?

There was a shuffling in the hallway, and his wife emerged, in kimono and house-slippers. She held their grandson's hand in hers, as they entered the parlor side by side. Yukawa felt the blood pounding in his head, and heard the terrible unreal sound that ground out from deep in his throat.

Beneath her immaculately gathered hair, the woman had no eyes, no ears, no nose, no mouth.

The boy too, as he advanced upon Yukawa with his arms outstretched, had a face smooth and blank as paper.

CEREBRAL DEMONS & THE SPLIT
Rachel Kendall

Through the fissure of an open window the scent of carbon monoxide seeped in over frosted glass and dirty London sky. Robyn reached up to shut out the night but the smell and sound of the street had already infiltrated the dayglo bathroom. Exhaust fumes and children's empty voices weaved around her head as she sat on the edge of the bath to wait for peace.

'What are you doing in there, honey?' Nick's deep voice radiated through the wall from the bedroom next door. Robyn curled her lip into a plastic smile.

'I'm going to run a bath,' she called back, and quickly locked the door so she was secure inside her enamelled coffin.

Turning to the mirror, she was faced with the enemy, a voodoo doll ready to be crucified. And then she laughed because she looked ridiculous and in a way she knew that what she was about to do was ridiculous, but it could also save her life. Above her forehead a patch of shiny grey skin was encircled with light crimson hair. Beside her on a table surgical instruments shone like silver—hair clippers, syringe, drill, sunglasses, and beside these, cotton wool, surgical tape, bandages and plasters. As she hunched over her tools, Robyn's grey shadow engulfed her like a death shroud and the speed of the world was set on slow.

Taking the syringe in her right hand Robyn carefully drew back the plunger and sought out the centre of the smooth skin. As she inserted the needle to release the clear liquid, the sting and snag of flesh was a sensation she could live with. But thoughts of the operation were swimming around her head now and she was feeling a little nervous. Shaking hands were slick with sweat and ghost fingers were tapping a melody on her spine, causing the hairs on her neck to rise and her throbbing veins to run unsatiated.

It would take a moment for the anaesthetic to take effect. Next door, Nick was probably watching Sky TV, unaware, uninterested. He had brought Robyn here for the weekend in an attempt to kick-start their relationship, to seal in a little magic where it had started to leak. Robyn admitted she was the problem—the depression, the mood swings, the freak-outs, black outs and various tempestuous evils in her head. Eventually Nick had told her she had to find a way to exorcise her demons or he was gone. So she had seen therapists, analysts and psychic healers, had swallowed various noxious medicines and mind-altering substances that worried her head further and made her limbs ache with a heavy grief. But it seemed Robyn transcended professional aid. It was not just the depression, that was bad enough; it was her bisected mind. It was her ego, superego and id all mushed up where everything else was a perfect dichotomy so all she knew was confusion, and a lot of noise. But now she had the perfect solution, a beautiful release of pressure through a hole in her skull. Of course Nick, her boyfriend knew nothing of her plans. He would tell her she was crazy. Two years ago they had literally fallen into each other's arms at a party and a relationship had been inevitable. Robyn had been whetted by Nick's charm and childlike energy, and she, to Nick, was a tempest. He said she was beautiful in her turbulence, crazy in her vulnerability and savage like an animal untamed. They had been happy in their eclectic lives, their opposites seeming to attract. But a year and a few months down the line, Nick had taken it upon himself to administer punishment to Robyn when he felt it necessary and fair. But it never was necessary and it never was fair; it was cruel. Robyn had accepted it because it was her fault. He told her she was ugly; her self-hatred was vile. Mascara lines down her face, black shadows under her eyes, bruised legs and self-inflicted wounds, were not beautiful anymore. She knew that. She also knew that anyone of sane mind would tell her she was mad. What these people did not realise was that to perform the operation was a risk, but to not perform it was a risk also. It was the pressure you see. There was too much pressure in her brain, so she had to create a puncture. It was that simple. After today she would be surfing a higher plane and would reign over everything she had once succumbed to. It was a momentous day, both exciting and terrifying. She had dressed in her best, even decided to wear her pink micro mini skirt to reveal her shapely legs, which Nick had slapped and tickled earlier, before plunging his hands between to check everything was still intact. She thought that today she was not ugly. And in a few hours not only would she not be ugly, she would be fantastic. Life would be better after today. She would see colour and light reflecting from everything in a rainbow of creative energy. And she would be happy and her mind would be still.

It was time. As Robyn's exhausted heart crashed to the floor a million ruby shards migrated in every direction. A voice told her she might go too far, drill right through, but the preachers of trepanation had informed her that she would know when to stop. That to feel no more resistance would mean she had broken through the skull. With a tiny hole in her cranium her future was set for success.

Robyn slipped on her sunglasses, then picked up the small dentist drill and hooked it over the rail of the shower curtain where it hung down in front of her face like a metallic corpse. Taking clumps of cotton wool and tape she formed a padded barrier around her forehead, above her shades, to prevent the blood from seeping into her eyes and blinding her with redness. Trembling fingers unbuttoned her blouse and she let it fall to the floor silently, as an angel descending onto the ridges of her spine, wings outstretched like silver slivers, black nails digging into the flesh of her shoulders. Robyn turned on the tap in the bath to release a steady gush of water and then taking the drill in both hands she inhaled deeply and switched it on. It whined with feral undertones. Holding her breath in swollen lungs, the taste of saliva diluted with fear lingered in her throat before she exhaled, leaving a dying transparent mist on her reflection. As it melted away she brought the point of the drill to her naked head and pressed it to the numb flesh. Demons danced around her, naked and filthy, as the tearing of skin brought forth fresh blood for the devil cherubs. Robyn was void of pain, but felt the crack as the drill pierced the skull and tiny fragments of bone shot out like gunfire. She had been told the whole operation would take about half an hour. All she had to do now was keep on drilling.

There was a little spurting of blood. Mostly it trickled. But it trickled rapidly. It poured down her forehead, soaking into the cotton wool until it was dyed red and putrid. She continued to drill as her hands became slippier from sweat and spilled blood. It escaped down the side of her face, matting the hair near her ears, leaving ruby tracks down her cheeks, dripping off the end of her chin. An odour of burning bone like hot rancid breath traced its way to

Robyn's nostrils, making her feel nauseous. The angel on her back was weighing her down and she felt her legs would soon crumple from standing in this nervous, tense position. All muscles were twisted little knots tied around the wooden sinews of her body. Her face, underneath the red, was cold white and her lips, zipped together tightly, had the texture of a scar. The blood was soaking through the cotton wool and the tape was beginning to peel off. Now the blood was hurrying towards Robyn's eyes. When it reached those small green wells, it stung. It was thick and sticky and blinking would not remove it. Damn, she would have to switch off the drill and get this sticky shit out of her eyes. Her long fingers played with the handle of the drill, searching out the switch. It seemed noisier now, as though it were playing a harmony to her senses.

Suddenly the sky turned to pink as a blast of light exploded from the centre of Robyn's head where all thoughts were created. The whole world was bathed in red and yellow viscous fluids that rained down from the Temple of Robyn and there was a magnesium white pain so agonising it could only turn to paralysis if it were to be called pain at all. The drill carried on buzzing, wheeling, twisting and turning beyond Robyn's skull, through the dura mater and further into the sticky whorls of her brain. And her fingers, frozen around the handle, began to twitch and tickle the metal machine. From the widening orifice in her head, voices, thoughts, emotions and hordes of riotous parasites drifted out one by one, set free from their caged existence. And Robyn fell. In a twisted searing of flesh the drill was forced out of her head and danced suspended in the air, the tip holding onto globules of white and red. Robyn hit the floor in a swirling mass of angels and demons and her own brand of conscience that swooped down to feast. As she punched the air they took flight, freeing her to roll over heavily onto her front, feeling no pain now, just a slight grey restraint circling her like an aura and the loss of a life in her skull. Snatching off her sunglasses Robyn was able to rub the red from her eyes and see the blood on her hands. Hitching herself onto unsteady limbs, fluid red palms and knees left an imprint on the tiled floor. She grabbed hold of the sink and levered herself up, coming face to face again with her reflection. How beautiful did she look now? The hole in her head was as wide as a five pence piece and blood was still gushing in a river. Swiping a demon with the back of her hand, she picked up her bandages and began to dress the wound.

Twenty minutes later with only minuscule copper brown traces left on the floor and sink, Robyn opened the bathroom door and stepped out. She waited for a torrent of remonstrations from Nick but received only a silent smile and a look of something like awe. She looked fantastic, radiant, in a wide pink smile and glowing complexion. She looked better than she had for months. Nick opened his arms wide in an invitation of touch. Robyn smiled. With a beret pulled low to her finely plucked brows she sidled over to Nick with an army of demons behind her and the drill feeling wicked in her hands.

INVISIBLE DUST
Mary Williams

The African walked slowly along the sea front of the small English town, window-shopping. What strange things these people ate—walking sticks made of sugar, and potatoes, always potatoes, everywhere, and hot dogs. What were these things? The street was full of the stink of hot fat and fried onions. It turned his stomach. Back home there was street food, but not like this. At home it was good and spicy, making your mouth water. He crossed the road and admired himself in the reflection of the shop window. Six foot three and lean as a wand, long straight nose, dark skin with a hint of copper, he looked like the Doh tribesman he was. At twenty-six he was fit and strong and handsome, and he knew it. He straightened his tie and walked on and peered through the window of the curio shop, where the owner, having nothing better to do on a midweek morning in early June, was reading the racing pages of the Telegraph.

The owner looked up see a neatly dressed tall young black man come into the shop and look around. He put his paper down. M'Bye had learned that impeccable manners quickly disarmed people.

'Good morning,' he said in his slightly accented English. 'You don't mind if I have a look around?'

'Not at all,' said the owner. 'Are you looking for anything in particular?'

'I am interested in the things that have been brought back here from my homeland—Africa—do you have any such things?'

The man behind the counter became quite animated. His old tweed jacket looked shabby in comparison to the young man's suit as he felt in the pocket for his key.

'Which part of Africa are you from?' he asked, trying to establish a connection. The African did not reply. The shopkeeper went on, 'I have spent time in Sierra Leone and the Gambia—before it was overrun with tourists—as well as Ivory Coast, and I've brought a few pieces back with me from my travels. You might be interested in these —'

He fished behind the counter and unlocked the glass case in front of it. He reached in and pulled out several small objects. One caught the eye of M'Bye immediately. It was four inches long, rounded, like a skipping rope handle, with grooves in it and a leather thong knotted around one end. It was rounded at each end.

M'Bye looked at the price tag. It was high.

'Do you know what this is?' he asked the man, holding it in the palm of his elegant hand. The shopkeeper looked uneasy.

'I was told some fanciful story when I bought it,' he replied, 'but the fellow who sold it to me made such a song and dance about parting with it that in the end it made me want it even more. It undoes in the middle, so something must have been kept in there, but what I couldn't tell you.'

'The fanciful story,' said M'Bye, pronouncing the words with an exaggerated emphasis, 'was it true?' M'Bye leaned forward and looked closely at the face of the shopkeeper, who took a backward step. 'You have paid for magic, my friend,' said M'Bye, 'strong magic. The story was a true one. I too have used such a thing, when I was a boy and went hunting in the forest. So it's magic in some way. What does it do in this fanciful story?' He snorted the last two words. The shopkeeper kept calm.

'You take the top off carefully and inside there is magic dust, a powder that makes the hunter invisible to his prey. The deer does not see or hear or smell the hunter approaching. Then it is too late and the hunter has killed the deer.'

'You have learned well, my friend,' answered M'Bye. 'And does it work, this invisible dust?'

The shopkeeper was perplexed and a little frightened. Africa had come to his door and was asking to be heard. He wished he'd never started this conversation.

'I keep an open mind,' he said, 'You hear some queer things. Maybe it does work, at that. To be honest, I haven't opened it since I bought it.'

M'Bye looked at him thoughtfully.

'You could test it,' he said.

M'Bye left the container of invisible dust behind in the shop. He bought only some old books, showing natural history specimens. The shopkeeper thought it was an odd choice, but said nothing. As five o'clock approached his thoughts turned to home, where his wife, Lindy would be waiting for him. He had not long been married to her and she was a good few years his junior. He felt himself to be a lucky man.

I know, he thought, *I'll sprinkle some dust on me as I go up the path, just for a laugh. She'll think I'm mad but she'll like the story.*

He took the small rounded object, feeling as he did so the smoothness of the many hands that had held it in the past. *This should be back where it came from* he thought. It didn't belong in a rainy seaside town curiosity shop, thousands of miles away from Africa.. It felt warm and light in his pocket. He imagined plains and hunters tracking game, shadows and spears and heat.

He noticed a strange car in the driveway as he came close to his home. *Must be one of her friends paying a visit*, he thought. He crept up to the house and took out the container of invisible dust from his pocket and stopped to open it. It unscrewed in the centre. In one half when he peered in, was darkness, nothing else. He could not see any dust; he couldn't even see the bottom of the small container. He looked in the other half. Nothing. Of course, it was invisible! Somehow he had expected something. He held one half over his head and shook it, just in case. Creeping round the corner, he could see his wife looking in his direction through the window. Someone was next to her on the settee, a man. The man patted her bottom as she stood up, still looking towards the shopkeeper. She put her hand out behind her to quieten him and the man took it and pulled her back into an embrace. Furious, the shopkeeper banged on the door, quite forgetting his plan. There was swift activity inside the house, and then the door opened. He stood there, in front of his wife, and she looked right through him.

The young woman looked around her and called over her shoulder to the man on the settee.

'Must be those damn kids again. Nobody here, anyway. Stop worrying, he's always late.' And she closed the door and went into the house.

Next day the shopkeeper returned the container to its rightful place behind his counter.

He spent a boring morning stocktaking, then decided to close for lunch. He chose a small cafe down by the sea front. The African was there, eating fried fish delicately with his fingers. He glanced up when he saw the shop-keeper enter.

'Did it work?' he asked, one eyebrow raised, as he broke off another piece of fish with his tapered fingers.

'You lot and your superstitions,' answered the shopkeeper, sitting at the next table. 'Of course it didn't work.' His grey face sagged slightly. He hadn't shaved.

'Of course not,' affirmed M'Bye with heavy sarcasm and an enigmatic smile that the shopkeeper found infuriating. He popped another piece of fish into his mouth. 'I may come and buy the thing to take home. You will not mind.' It was a rhetorical question.

'Of course not. I'll even give it to you. I have to get back, if you'll excuse me.'

The African watched him leave with his dark, steady gaze, and a small twist of amusement around his lips. He had already seen the bloodstain on the shopkeeper's tweed jacket and drawn his own conclusions.

BRIGHTNESS
Sean McFadden

What was it about the moon that night? He never could decide, not even years later, still undergoing treatment, when the question of blame arose . . .

Back then the sheer sky had hung endlessly on the bruised hills below, tepid and blue. And nothing mattered but the moon in it. It was utter and realised amongst the oppression of so much space. It was immaculate, new born; it signalled another creation, echoing aeons before. It penetrated the sky, was certain, undeniable. And it held him transfixed for long spells as he drove dustily along the barren roads, alone and unregarded. Through the half-shut nothing towns, on, towards the border.

Outside, little streams he crossed pulsed like ores of metal the moon dug from the soil. Tonight nothing could withstand it and not be altered as it wished; it had ownership tonight. Its long hands got held out, bleached by the vacuums of fathomless space, hammered as thin as bones: a touch stirring and imminent.

. . . On the passenger seat, that hadn't been cleaned before he hired the car, folders were fanned out. They shuddered from the journey and slid accidentally, getting creased; his work, his plans; his name printed on the tags: Stedinger, A; like on half a dozen gravestones that were all laying claim to an element of the corpse. Like a saint's relics, say.

He smiled at the thought. Who doesn't have a weakness for sainthood some nights, when all there is between you and it is loneliness? When that's all the choice there is?

'If no one ever missed you would you cease to exist?' It rattled through his sleepy mind to the rhythm of the car. 'Would you fade then, bit by bit?' No one answered but the moon, peering through the windscreen, through God's emptiness outside, where the insects got pulled to it, sinking in its tide, murmuring and struggling, madly awake, and crawling . . .

Arthur Stedinger felt the steering wheel wrench beneath his hand as the car tipped into a pothole and lurched. 'Back roads,' he hissed. But the back roads were essential he knew that; they were where other traffic rarely went, and authorities hardly bothered about or mended. Where illicit trades could go on, and potholes seethed like so many secrets that got run down, that still blindly tug at the speeding passers-by; that complain.

Secrets, and their profession; their reasons and resolve; the views that they engender that blot out any others like shadows across the landscape; their pitfalls and codes; it was in scenarios like this that Stedinger liked to feel he operates. It was here he got his work done, work he said he fits. It was through the chilly routines it demanded that he sought to contain himself, draw an outline that he could cling to and call by that name of his: Stedinger, A.

It was defined. It'd come to terms.

And so he kept on towards the border, where payment's all that counts; and time, and the appointment. But not nerves or the need to rest, or how the moonlight was . . . only the arrangements and what it means when they fall due, noon, tomorrow, there.

'And, Christ, I'm going to be there . . . ' As he glanced at the weary folders that were the only passenger, his only companion out here that he needed. A smile grazed his eyes, his gaunt dark face. 'And after that we'll see . . . ' The smile got contained as he nodded at the blank road. 'Perhaps settle down, at that. Marry, like I said. A nice and lonely girl she is, not a hair out of place. Sucks like a pro. Could easily do worse . . . '

Or better? He tapped the dashboard and wished the radio were working. Hmm, the dial did nothing. And the silence was like a headache: silence, car, and creatures. All vaguely living, dying, so distantly from him. And if talk won't close the distance at least it keeps it quiet. Hmm, the smile sank on his lips.

'Or could easily do better? If all this gets handled properly . . . if this wreck doesn't fail entirely.' And he knew it wouldn't. Fail. An instinct, like you get when it's a question of what matters.

Like the moon has its instinct, like it's all it ever has. All that keeps it flooding there, accurately, its way. On its pinpoint decisive wandering in the absence, the steerless grey.

And he was watching her again, slack-eyed, a fascination. Wondering if his eyes might fail from simply gazing in that pool, so unreservedly; if his mind might altogether . . . if they won't sink and ripple, go . . . into that all-meaning eye, its streams and silver welcome. Like a cat's eye that prowls the world, opening in the silk-sore night, in the depths and utter space.

That faceless stare hung in the night sky, unyielding, annihilating, going blankly on forever. It sways lamp-like above the hills and trees, above the desert tracks and houses, as if it's guiding him, his path. And gazing up through the grime, through the tickets on the windscreen, he felt faintly like the Magi: called and knowing why. Unswerving through that silver wave, through the dust, the dark, the throng that midnight here consists of, filling out the air, filling out the isolation.

He saw past them to the heart now, to its glistening mad skin. And was numb now with the swell of it. Forsaken, feeling clean. Forsaking, like the Magi had, all that went before. And safe, with only hours now, only hours till it's done.

'What?' The moon asked, deeply. Deeper than he thought. Its slight grey in his dark hair: thirty-seven years old, not having got what he deserved.

—Doesn't a spy act like a shadow acts, because he's unable truly to act? And was this the link he felt to the moon? This allegiance she seems to have to hurt and discriminate, the dispossessed that he felt close to by virtue of denial, of blame? A liar needs resentment; frustration is his tool. And remorse is, and panic, and aberrations of the will . . .

'No matter,' the moon breathed back.

No, it pulled him simply, desertedly along. It steered the creaking wheel he steerlessly tried to follow. And all he needed was to look, crawl wisely along the thread of it that it let loose along the road. That it wept with sly hard looks and didn't dare to stop.

'Only minutes now, and miles,' he thought. If you crawl and don't stop, if you look and never stop. Why would you, after all? Having dropped inside those placid arms, those sheets of sheer existence. An unknown, and unpronounceable. An utter silver presence wringing out his mind, frozen in his skeleton.

The car heaves. He didn't notice.

And what he thought is 'only seconds.' Only seconds, unencompassed . . . a second is all it takes, if the heart pulsates inside of it. And that's all that hearts can do. The pulsation steep and dark enough for eternity to fit within, for it to open like a gate, call death out, other dreams . . .

'SCHEEOWLLH!' Like demented children, when that shriek attacked the night. And the wheels thumped over ruined limbs, car sliding off the road at once, and jolting.

It brought him back, swerving on the trackless soil, shivering and sick. He screeched the brakes; it made him sicker. And the car slumped to a halt; the shrilly anxious engine cutting out. And that was that. Only loneliness was left. His heart like a tantrum in his panting throat; his knuckles locked and white against the wheel, its cold rebellion.

And disaster sat outside, in the wind, the desolation . . . outside, what mutilation?

Slowly he let go of the wheel, his indecision, and peered back through the smeared glass along the road he'd driven. Scanning there, reluctantly. But nothing; he got out, tangling arms and face amongst the thin cowl of the trees that overhung where the car stopped. And feeling numbly round the headlights that were blindly streaming out, he walked off the desert onto the road, and peered again where he thought the car had swerved, still dreading what he'd find: a tramp who got pissed, or a girl who'd run away.

But no . . . 'It wasn't anything,' he frowned, and felt relief. His dry mouth able to swallow, and his heartbeat sliding hollowly, through bewilderment, unbelief, to its echoing proper place. Then, habit coming back, he rubbed the buttons on his jacket and felt the night air bristling coldly round his neck. He frowned again and pulled his collar. 'Still, better check the car . . . '

And with that he bent and shuffled around it, left hand along the chassis, toe tapping at a tyre. Fine; he's no mechanic but as far he could tell it all looks . . . fairly . . .

'Ah,' he stopped and winced. Bending closer now to check at the rear wheel, along the axle. 'So it's you that put me off. Almost scared me to death. Well, you paid for it. Christ . . . What a freak show.'

And he murmured to that half a victim that still clogged his rented car: the bald skull and shoulders, the fore claws and ceaseless blood of a twitching, hissing cat. Still hissing with half its energies, poised across the brink between the world and non-world. As Stedinger crouched to drag it loose.

'They'll charge extra for corpses, see. And you wouldn't want that, would you? Wouldn't want much of anything now . . .

'Not that it's like you to bear a grudge, eh? Slaughter's the rule. I don't have to explain that here, not to you.

'No . . . One turns a switch on; one signs a note; one uses a suitcase; one sinks her teeth. And one swerves a car, trying to keep awake.'

And he carefully wrapped his hand inside amongst the metal, his left hand that wore the ring. Inside, where the rust was bad, amongst the guts and grime and sopping fur. All the bones in little shards like jewels for a bride say, for an ancient house of royalty, glinting; yellow; red.

And how sad he was to get his shirt wet, trying to hold his breath. As he knelt, prepared to wrench, fingers slipping in the gore. 'After three . . . '

One, two . . .

'AAEYSHI!' An echoing and responsive shriek, wordless, numberless, to that earlier inhuman cry broke between his teeth as the half-thrashed, half-clinging, existence which was all that ghoul had left caught him as he tugged at it. Out of instinct, out of nakedness. Out of desperation, faith. As its wild nails sought the world still, ripped and sank across his hand as he shook and tried to pull.

They ripped and froze, and held on dearly. As he felt sick, then had to stop. Knuckles curling in a spasm, as the other's deadly energy flowed into him. Trying slowly not to panic because to rush'll make it worse. And trying out of screwed eyes breathlessly to wait, to ease and extricate as delicately as he can; once the chance comes; if it does . . . from the seething, icy claws tearing in his hand.

Meat is what they'd call it. Predators like her.

And the shadows of the cat and him were twisted, bent together, as he reeled loose from the car. Hissing, bleeding, cursing, they splattered on the dust. Like soul mates in the solitude, twinned against the black. As if closeness depends on blood alone, no matter how or why it's mingled in the emptiness and quiet. As if blood alone contains responsibility, as if longing, fear, or spirit, were all housed and fed in that.

And they were, at least for seconds there. As what's done, what's still existing, what's rational, what's cursed, bestial, or bit, sprawled and moaned together in the moonlight's quivering arms; its smile; for only seconds.

And then the cat stopped dead, uncoiling from his wrist, fallen in his lap in puddles of fur and formlessness, shamelessness, and eyes. Stedinger retched and wiped the mess off, staggering as he stood; kicked the corpse away for the cars to grind, shoe sinking in its chest. And only slowly did he stroke his hand then, checked it in the glow of the headlights that grew dim. Gnawed and gaping open, blackly pulsing blood; he was surprised it doesn't hurt more, as though anaesthetised with shock. But no point dwelling on it or watch the tendons sadly flex.

'Have to get on, get it clean. And make sure I arrive in time . . . ' Although the car failed when he tried it, half a dozen times. So that, winding an old rag that smelled of petrol on his cuts, that he took from the seedy glove compartment, he ditched it there, took the folders, the door slamming like applause, so brief and hollow.

Heading for the motel that glimmered faintly down the tracks, where he knew it from the old days; his dusty steps too rushed and awkward, leaning in the dark. As the silver cold and isolation, the bleeding starts to worry him. But in truth it wasn't far.

And having got there he could catch his breath, calm down after that horror; smile about it almost: scars of honour from the war. That constant, seeping war that made up his career . . .

All that had faded though as he rang at the cheerless and dingy reception, flashed the money that he carried at the old man whose shift it was, who noticed. It matters, because you get what you pay for. And Stedinger wanted agreement, no doubts or recollections, no delays at this stage. That alone he can't afford.

After that, he'll settle in; use the phone to book another car; his voice tired and business-like. 'When's the earliest it can be here? The extra cost doesn't matter . . . Okay, fine. That's fine . . . ' Then ask for antiseptic, a bandage; show the wound.

'Have trouble out there, eh?' The sleepy and bald sub-hotelier murmured through his beard, its greyness like a web.

'Could say that,' Arthur Stedinger smiled, aiming at complicity as a guard against the anxious night, the hurt and wincing that he felt. 'There're devils in that waste of yours.'

'It's haunted there alright,' the old man growled back, coughed twice, then passed the key. 'Number eight, to the left . . . ' And that was all he had to offer; the lamplight tearful in his grey eyes, on his thin red lonely nightshirt; 'but I'll bring along that medicine,' he nodded as an afterthought, furrowing his brow.

. . . In the cheap room like a thousand others the visitor settled down. Those folders where he could see them, neatly on the bed; his shoes kicked off like a dead man's shoes that no one came to steal.

He dabbed the cat's blood in his lap with a towel that's on the back of a chair, then carefully unwound that rag he'd had to use where it stank around his cuts, where it already starts to glue.

Then, apprehensive still, he flicked the curtains shut and went to check the mirror. What for: this reassurance, the ghost of company out here? 'But don't look,' he heard a voice warn grimly through his head. But he did, and he looked drawn.

'Loss of blood,' he muttered. 'Nerves . . . ' As he breathed between his teeth, and slowly took it in: a dismal, blank succession of silver parts of him; of what's allowed, of what's been led to, all held up to his face. Where he waits like a witness before this slim and sorry mirror that hangs a pale gash from the ceiling; where it bled its emptiness and doubt slyly in the room, across his clothes, the stains . . .

After that he'd like to rest, but can't. Although he stretched out on the bed, legs dangling off the edge, arms out as though to welcome sleep. 'Sleep . . . ' Except he can't. Not yet, because the heat, the dust; because the chill he caught out there; the medicine he's expecting, soon . . . because the glowing that's taken root in his claw-like hand, a glow he felt but couldn't see; claw-like with a withering spasm he watched but couldn't feel . . .

Because of that and then this tapping at the window where he'd shut the world out . . . the ugly curtains breathed the draught in. And he answered 'Is anyone there?'

The door creaked and she came in, the girl that he'd ordered it seems. Like you order drinks usually, or medicine or the bill quietly on the phone.

Young, too young for him: a girl like a highness from an old dark fairytale; silver; sure, well balanced, and now reduced to this.

In the doorway before the door closed her hair was tangled in the night, like smoke that's bent, ascending. Like frosty branches . . . it's all he felt: the magnetic pang of yellow hair, offering itself. As the door clicked at her back and she gazed across her shoulder to where he sat up, wants to hide; then gazed across the thin strap of the sleek dress she wore, where it left her shoulder bare.

'Have you got it . . . the medicine?' he faltered, rubbed his thighs. As she moved, her limbs orchestral, weaving closer to the bed.

'All you want,' she smiled, and let the first aid drop on the mattress. Stedinger looked inside the little case then back at his nurse, pushing the folders out of sight underneath the dirty jacket he took off, although he's cold. 'What else?' she asked.

'. . . Surrender' was the word that came into his mind, though he couldn't tell why. It had been welling there, thirty years perhaps, and now it seeped out. Like a theme from an instrument.Nent.

Her hands were held out, awkwardly, like a greeting, so he took them in his hand that wasn't hurt and let her sit. The old springs in that nobody's bed wincing beneath them both.

'What d'you mean?' He tried to rouse himself. As she reached across his lap to stroke the other, grey, caked hand he'd prefer to keep hid; uncurling the locked fingers on the shredded palm; then pulling him where she was.

'I mean . . . what are you offering?' And he could feel her baking breath as her eyes gleamed into his, his own already answering.

'Anything you want.' A kiss . . .

'But wait . . . what girl?' the stray thoughts in his head insisted faintly.

A candle to a goddess is what she looked like, nothing less; like silver days, intoxicants, all held up to his face.

And love. He'd never made love. Sex, but never love . . . where it's tender in her eyes and skin, tongue and breath and teeth; where it streams inside his shirt, underneath the flickering light. Where the darkness takes over, smoothly; and there is coldness, nudging him. Darkness that got cut with white lances of foam; it plays across the skin. And he felt how her kissing grows, rises and strokes, and the iciness of her breathing. It glistens in the air and on the walls. It weeps.

'It's yours now,' it echoed through the gaps where his thoughts had been. 'This scene . . . alone . . . against her golden head, turned upwards . . . ' And he saw how the droplets mist slowly on her eyes; in the depths; in reflections; and got lost in the flood.

As he goes under, once, twice. Where the droplets mist on him and splatter in the moonlight. Where outlines distort and sweat.

And his breathing goes into hers, achingly, scared, on thin hollow lips he parts then, to speak? Through rushing dark kisses that closed tight on his neck; like water, so quick; with fingers like night made her for an instant; their surface so pure.

As he obliterates, sinks. Not a ripple, not a sigh . . .

. . . Until, tired out from sobbing, he woke out of sleep that hadn't happened, he was sure, and opened bloody eyes. Bloody where his hand was laid across them like a shield against the daylight through the open curtains. An unavailing shield that he tried to use to wipe the blood off, not realising what it was . . . Till blinking through it at last he saw the ceiling; no hand, but simply ceiling; blood, and simply bones from knuckles to wrist that he's staring through, all gnawed . . .

His sobbing turned to shrieks, arms flailing on the empty bed; his ring dropped on the floor.

THE MASTER'S CALL
Philip Robinson

This is Hell. We twisted, revolting creatures, wallowing in the eternal slime at the very bottom of the pit, are the demons it spews from its ranking womb with uncaring alacrity. Every moment another rancid batch of us is birthed to further clog the works. We eat our brethren to create space; devour each other to survive.

The Master Himself forgets we are here . . . until he needs us.

It is said that when The Master Calls, only one hears the summons. But no one knows because The Master never calls.

Until now.

For I have heard The Master's Call.

A presence finds me, and only me. It encircles me, lifts me, pulling me upwards through my infinite brethren, through the thick, black and scalding slime. Do I believe I am the one? The multitude around me would rip me to shreds in their jealousy. I do not blame them, for I would be no different. So I come, slipping through cracks between their bodies, chewing my way through their cold meat when their unbudging forms block the way. And I ascend.

It is a long journey through the black oceans, but then something so strange . . . something so impossibly beautiful it burns me to behold it.

Light.

It is the complete antithesis of what my prior existence has been.

The slime has thinned around me; I can breathe. The din which has wracked my brain for so long has now waned, but this is not the end, for still I carry on at the urging of The Master. I do not fear. I am the chosen one. I do not hesitate.

Everything is now tepid, supple and yellow. The light from above grows stronger.

Upwards; I feel naked without the gelatinous wrapping. I have left everything behind. This is existence beyond the slime. This is not Hell.

I hurtle forward and slam into a creature, horrible and revolting to my very being, and it sucks me inside, swallows me deep into itself.

*

This being is called George Shock and in an instant I know everything about him and his world: this long, pale shape is his natural form; he, and the rest of these creature, are human beings. People. They are the dominant ones in these strange, painless surroundings. The Masters. This world is nothing like the slime, George Shock is nothing like me. On Hell's filthy floor we must conform, bend to its will, but George Shock is the master of his own.

Though I am deep inside him, in his brain, my presence goes unnoticed. His senses won't detect me. I pass myself back and forth in here . . . does he tense slightly? He does not scream at my touch.

From here I can look through a window into another strange world, a world of experience he calls Memory. Through this window I see my task, the reason I've been chosen to come here . . . George Shock has met The Master.

Arrangements have been made, and I have arrived.

*

George is sitting on a hard floor in the middle of a barren room; an electric guitar lies heavily across his lap with a lead running into a small amplifier by the wall. There are three others here—the rest of his rock band: *Shock*. They know nothing of George's meeting with The Master. In front of him is a recording device, a DAT machine, and he leans forward, activates it. He settles the guitar comfortably on his legs, then places his fingers on the neck of the instrument, holding what he calls a D-minor chord. He drags a plastic plectrum across four of the steel strings, then opens his mouth, making a noise to match the pitch of the guitar—

And I come flooding through him in a violent torrent, pulsing down through his body and out of his mouth, out of his hands. His inner workings leap into chaos; adreneline surges through him, his heart positively slams, his stomach is knotted and his muscles are spasming. His fingers are clutching at the neck of the instrument, leaping up and down on the notes and chords while his other hand pounds and hammers on the steel strings. From his mouth soars a powerful voice:

Tears of blood, flowing free, through gutters running down to Hell,
To save yourself, to take, to taste, it's your own soul you sell . . .
When you hear The Master's call . . .

The hands working the instrument are his; the voice ripping up from deep in his chest—utilizing no more than the same twelve notes he's been using all his life, but pulsing and throbbing with more passion and fire than he can comprehend—is his, but what he is producing now is far, far greater than the sum of the parts. His voice will never again portray such intensity and emotion, nor will his hands ever find such a natural combination of rhythm, speed, and precision. The plectrum is hot between his fingers. There's magic ripping through the room, bouncing off the walls and floor and ceiling and pouring into the DAT recording device. The song is bewitching . . . the song is mermerising. The song is me.

He finishes, gripping a final D-minor chord, a melodious, longing moan emanating from his throat; he holds these final sounds, squeezing every last, dripping nuance from them as they fade.

Even before the guitar sound has died, Davey Walsh says, 'When the fuck you write that?'

But for a tiny, insignificant echo, I am no longer in George Shock. I live in the remaining note ringing from the amplifier, the dying breath of that final chord hanging almost inaudibly on the air around them. Then I am disappearing as George prises his fingers from the strings. 'Just now . . . ' I hear him say. 'Just this min . . . '

*

I live on here.

In those dying moments I feared a return to the slime. But no, I remain. I fill this room again, soaring all around George and the others, above them, through them. I rush full and vigourous from the tape machine. All four faces are quite pale in the presence of the song.

'Look at my arms . . .' Davey whines in an unsteady voice, ' . . . I'm covered in goosebumps.' He looks to George. 'This is . . . fucking *Stairway To Heaven*, man. This is *Imagine. Voodoo Chile. Sergeant-Fucking-Pepper*, man!' He pauses to catch his breath. 'This is fucking—'

Brad leans over and vomits on the floor. George only stares at the tape-player; Davey continues vociferating and the fourth presence, Alex, is lying on his back staring at the ceiling.

The song ends . . . fades from the air and I lose them once again, but now I know it is not the end for me.

*

Once again I flood the room at tremendous volume. Nothing has changed in my physical surroundings, though some time has passed; I know this even though I remember nothing of the period in between. From then to now is instantaneous for me, and for the duration of the silence I didn't exist.

There's a tension on the air between the four. Harsh words have been exchanged. Argument. The four stare at the tape machine as though capable of seeing traces of actual music pour from it . . . as though looking for a sign of me.

George's guitar has been flung aside, his hands are clasped to the sides of his head, his fingers spread over his ears as though trying to block the song out of his head.

'Try it one more time,' Alex says. 'Your voice can't change that much . . .'

Ah, so George has tried a repeat performance. His glare is cold and hard. 'I don't even know the fucking words.'

Davey is shaking his head slowly. 'You must have been fucking possessed, man. I mean . . . your voice has never . . . and fucking Steve Vai wouldn't be able to play what you were playing. Thank Christ you got it on tape . . . that's all I can say.'

They replay it again and again until there is barely a break between my jaunts into the room.

*

Everything has changed now. A new room. New listeners surrounding the tape machine, rapt expressions hang heavily on faces. I can sense that hours have elapsed since the other room.

And more. And more. Different locations. Different people.

An office. A man behind a desk, unable to conceal the ecstatic grin on his face. The song ends and as I fade I hear him say, 'Gentlemen, I think we can do business . . . '

*

I am flooding through a room filled with technological equipment, filling the heads of all present. None of the original band is here; others are playing, session musicians—a drummer banging out a rhythm, a bassist filling in with runs between the chords. A guitarist lightly strums an acoustic.

A producer mixes this additional material with George's original record-ing. The quality of the vocal on the tape is very high, usable for the stu-dio-version of the song. Very fortunate, since George's performance could never be repeated.

When the work is done, the additional material has been kept to a mini-mum, and it is George's guitar and vocals which are kept at the forefront of the mix.

*

The playings have become constant, perpetual.
I am being recorded.

*

I am everywhere.

Suddenly, through a wide variety of different media, I am flooding through record megastores, simultaneously appearing in the domestic hous-ing of millions of listeners, the workplaces of millions more; out in the streets I'm thrown to the winds, pouring from hand-held machines, pummeling di-rectly into brains through small ear-pieces, filling moving vehicles. I now ex-ist in not only one world, as I had with George, but in a multitude which over-lap in a continuous blur of images, infinite tidbits of existence with no com-mon connection other than myself. Some cry over me, some jump around in their bedrooms screaming while others simply lie still, playing me repeatedly as though trying to absorb my very essence. Listeners can't seem to help but give me their attention and I enter them. Not in the very intimate way I first entered George, but for moments they are loving me. When the song fades and I leave them, I know they hang onto a small remnant, tossing it around and around inside their heads.

'That's George Shock with 'The Master's Call' screeches an ecstatic radio voice. 'Song of the decade? Gets *my* vote! And rumours abound about the elusive man himself. A report in this morning's 'Times' claims he's been committed to a psychiatric institution ... fact or publicity hype? ... who can tell in this crazy rock'n'roll world . . . .'

It is true.

George was left the worse for wear after our brief intimate acquaintance, his mental health deteriorated with my departure; whatever trace I left with him has been too much. He assaulted someone with a knife, then tried to slit his own wrists. Alex, Davey, and Les have all been arrested in separate, rather violent incidents. They have known me from the beginning, since the birth, I've been with them longer than anyone else . . . .

*

'There you have it, George Shock,' sighs that same DJ over my final notes. 'Just keeps getting better. A contender for Greatest Rock Song Ever Written? Gets *my* vote! No word as yet on an album ... let's hope we see one on the horizon soon . . . .'

My popularity continues to grow as people suck me into themselves. They have no sense that they are ingesting anything other than a song for pleasure.

But I am the song, and I was born of the slime.

In snowy Edmonton, Canada, a man who plays the song over and over in his car suddenly stamps down on the gas pedal and ploughs through the crowd of pedestrians crossing in front of him. At an all-night rave in Bristol, England, an extended jungle-mix of the song pumps from the giant sound-system, and the DJ throws himself off his podium and into the crowd, slashing with his knives; his berserk actions spread through the crowd like wildfire and the mayhem pours out into the street.

Similar events occur around the globe, all to the soundtrack of The Master's Call.

I am everywhere.

People are gathering in huge crowds in late night car lots and I rush at them from giant speakers. They suck me into their brains.

In prison, Davey Walsh has killed two guards with a makeshift knife.

A connection is made between the song and a number of violent acts. The floodgates open for a plethora of claims, and blame is slung at me.

*

George is dead.
The Master has called him.

*

Does 'The Master's Call' contain subliminal messaging?

The question is bannered across the world, in one variation or another.

George's remains have been buried anonymously to prevent massive crowds taking up residence around his gravesite. Instead, they gather around the hospital where he'd been taken, around the house where he'd lived, around the school he'd attended . . . anywhere remotely connected to the person who had been George Shock. His death only heightens the notion of something malicious in the song. The other members of the band have also deteriorated, physically and mentally; no one knows who the session musicians are; when the producer is tracked down he is found naked, perched up on his kitchen table with all available evidence suggesting he hasn't moved in four days.

The scaremongers surge into overdrive.

The recording is recalled from all stores; radio stations delete it from their playlists; even the so-called rebellious television shows bow to the pressure.

I am feeling a significant decline in the power of my presence, a weakening lurch as though a great chunk of my self has been severed away from me.

Still I am being played continuously. I haven't experienced that 'death' between playings in a long time . . . someone somewhere is always listening to me.

But those who have been listening the longest . . . those who discovered the song soon after its release . . . have come into what has been termed, 'Final Phase'—hiding in their homes, slinking out only when they have portable means to bring me with them. In towns and cities around the world they slouch in darkness. They still commit beautiful acts of violence on their fellow humans while I pound in their heads.

On and on and on, and I preside over every moment.

*

Much time has passed now, and I am dying. My listeners are gone . . . locked away in some dark place. Copies of me are still being destroyed, and new converts have dwindled to a trickle. New songs are capturing the world. I am yesterday's fad. Hailed a classic, but it seems even classics can die.

I fade.

This one girl now is my final link to the world. I want to cling to her but these are my final seconds. She plunges towards the rushing water below; the phones slip from her ears and, engulfed by water, her small machine swallows the rank liquid and . . .

*

That drowning girl feels like only moments ago, though I know many years have passed for the people.

Harold Steinke has discovered one of those cumbersome, obsolete compact discs in a basement. He has transferred me into the vast banks of his music-library chip. From this he has uploaded me into something called the Microsoft-AllTech, from where I immediately feel millions and millions of virtual fingers reaching for me, pulling me in infinite directions at once. They suck me into their lives and suddenly I am filling the world once again. While before everything was frustratingly manual, this new world is fully automatic. It moves very quickly, trying to keep pace with its own advancement.

The Master speaks to me now, and it is good news. It was my honour to be the first of my kind; now we are legion.

THE SPECTRE
Rick Hudson

Alice didn't recognise herself in the mirror anymore. Her reflection never seemed quite right. She always felt as if she was looking at an alternative, other Alice.

Age was part of it; the reflection was always five years or so older than the internal Alice, but that wasn't what troubled her most. Alice was now thirty-six and she had always assumed that she would have become what she was due to become by now. Whatever that was. The face in the mirror didn't suit her. She imagined herself to be free spirited, creative, a little wild even—but the face in the mirror was mundane, prosaic and conservative.

There was something oafish about the face in the mirror, it appeared wilfully stupid and drably mocking. When the face in the mirror smiled it did so with a contemptuous, prudish sneer—it was a collaborator with monotony.

Alice was becoming preoccupied with the image and what it signified. Her mind wasn't on her mundane job and every conversation, every TV programme and every magazine resonated with the same chord of restless dissatisfaction: you are not what you hoped you would be.

At night she lay awake, staring at the ceiling, calculating. What could she do? Nothing was actually wrong with her life; nothing really bad had ever happened to her—it was just all so disappointing. So mediocre.

Alice dreamed about grand projects that would rescue her from boredom. She went back over the years, imagining what would have happened if she had this, if she had done that.

It had gone midnight when the tapping began. Was someone knocking on the window? Surly not. It must be a twig snagging on the glass. The tapping continued, it maddened her. She filled her head with trivia to bar the noise from her head, but still the insistent, staccato drumming went on, nagging like an itch.

She leapt from her bed and dashed to the window. A tiny childhood fear of bogeymen and murderers made her hesitate before reaching for the curtains. Chastising herself, she pulled them back to reveal . . . nothing. There was no twig or branch to rap against the window.

And yet the tapping continued to taunt her. Alice swallowed a lump of chill fear. She knew what was making the noise. It was a finger tapping on glass, but not the window. Alice turned around; she turned to face the grinning Alice in the mirror.

THE SCAVENGER
Alison L R Davies

The Rattler greases those snakeskin boots of his, oils them up real good, feeling the wet kiss of deceit against rough skin. Toothy grin, and a smack of lips way too thin to be human but that's another story. One of many that he spins. Some say the Rattler tells so many stories he doesn't know the truth anymore, wouldn't know it if it smacked him in his narrow wolfish jaw. But I say he's just become part of the dance, like so many of us, just a character in a never-ending story. The Rattler picks at a ragged nail, scrapes at lodged grit like a lump of decaying gristle. Wouldn't do for him to look dirty, nobody likes a stinkfist. He's sitting in Jed's, pruning himself, counting time with bloodshot eyes, and drinking. Oh the Rattler's forever drinking, the sweet rot of whisky, the musky scent dripping from his pores.

'Line me up another.' And he's back at his boots again, always the perfectionist.

Jed eyes the clock. Sluggish time has a lot to answer for. The door creaks, click clack as heels carve their inevitable path.

'Hey babe, you been waitin' long?'

The scuffle of whiskers as the Rattler grins.

'I'd wait till the end of time for you, Darla.'

Jed sighs, at last a reprieve.

'Get another shot for the lady.' And Rattler's pulling out a wad of notes like you've never seen before.

'In fact, just give us the bottle and two fresh glasses, and when I say fresh I mean clean, none of your usual grubby fingered receptacles.'

'Oh honey, you don't have to do that for me.'

'You're my lady, I'd do anything for you.'

Darla shrugs, pretty hunch of her rounded shoulders and a flick of hair. Strawberry blonde today.

'How you been?' He kisses her cheek.

'Fine. Been fine. Just the usual going to work at the diner, trying to sort my life out. Get Jerry off my back.'

'He still bothering you?' The Rattler's sniffing the glass now, leaning his poker snout right inside.

'I wish he'd leave me alone. I've told him, it's over. I don't want him anymore, haven't for months. God, he's repulsive!'

Rattler moves silent, moth-like fingers caressing her fluffy curls. He leans in, snorts her hair, gets a good strong mouthful.

'Beautiful,' he smiles.

'You listening to me?'

'Always darlin', I always listen to every word you say.'

It was in the early 80's when Jed first met the Rattler. He remembered the day, smoky heat, searing blood red through the August sky. Sand a river of pain against bare flesh and way too many juicy flies dizzy from sunstroke. All the fans were going, the jukebox pumping out 'She Sells Sanctuary' like it was going out of fashion and amongst it all the clink and tap of leather that signified custom. Jed had smiled but inside something tightened. The lank haired stranger with the courteous manner and pearl cast teeth threatened him in a way that nobody ever had before. Sure, Jed had had his fair share of drunken trouble, but this was different, this was clinical. They shared a beer, in fact they shared two. The Rattler cracking jokes, his lazy grin becoming addictive and Jed found himself wanting him to stay, not because he felt comfortable with the stranger, more because he was enamored. It became a regular thing.

The Rattler would stop by whenever he was in town. Sometimes it would be a week, sometimes two, even a matter of months, but always he'd be back with that same doe-eyed smile, that same charming manner. And at first Jed kidded himself that maybe the Rattler was o.k. that his first impression no matter how acute had been wrong. Surely a guy could make a mistake? But that was until Stacy. That's when he glimpsed the truth, as sure as eggs is eggs, his intuition had been spot on.

'She's a real doll isn't she? Don't you think?'

Jed busied himself cleaning glasses; dull clink clink as he stacked shelves pretending not to hear.

'Hey Jed buddy, I said what do you think?'

'If you say so, when she comes back will you be staying long?'

'As long as it takes . . . you can't rush these things. She's been awful long in that powder room. But hey, that's women for you!'

Jed shivered. How many times had he heard that expression? It was the Rattler's favourite. He usually said it right before the final kill. They'd lie there twitching, jittering bones and blood and he's take a swig from the bottle and spit out those words like it was nothing.

'I'm back, did you miss me?'

She swung her legs round, the stool wobbling for a second on the polished floor.

'Cause I did. Now then, honey, where were we? Oh yes, about this little problem of yours . . . '

'You mean Jerry? I'd say he's one great big fat problem. Stupid Asshole!'

'No, Darla, I was talking about your other problem.'

Jed took a breath. Here it comes . . .

'I don't have no other problems. I'm happy.'

'Ah honey, you don't know how good that is to hear.'

They kissed, a long, noisy confusion of tongues and jaws, and mulching of skin.

'So, Darla, if you have no other problems and you think he's a stupid asshole then why the hell you been screwing him?'

'What? What you on about?'

'You heard or are you deaf as well as dumb?'

Darla froze, poetic almost fragile look invading her features. And Jed's reminded of Stacy, cool, petite little butterfly Stacy, and how he broke her there and then, a crushed petal taken to task by those claw like fingers.

He hadn't been there from the start, only walked in half way through; when it was still evident whose body it was decorating the tables and chairs. The smell had been awful, meat, and dirt and souring blood. Yarn the colour of Ravens wing scattered on the floor, a dark gauze, which he later discovered, was matted hair. Carcass cut, no, torn into pieces, and bone polished, glistening with spittle, the Rattler's spittle. And the forager himself chin raw, eyes of coal for one second looking so much like a wolf, elongated snout and hungry flash of jaw, before returning to human skin. Jed had been scared then, so petrified he wet himself, a pool of urine slapping the hard floor. And the Rattler had laughed. Had laughed so hard it made his head ache. He'd forced him to dispose of the body, forced him with just a look that said it all, and Jed had done exactly that. Forever the coward, he took his instructions. The Rattler said there could only be one leader of the pack and Jed had backed down, cowered into complacency. From that moment on he was an accomplice, as much to blame for the killing as if he'd done it himself. And the Rattler all shiny with southern pride, wearing his arrogance like a polished medal. 'I smell it on them.' He'd once boasted. 'Can always tell, and sometimes I can even smell their seed as it wallows inside. They can't hide it. I'm too good for them. And its nothing they don't ask for. I tell them right from the start, nobody cheats on the Rattler. I mate for life. All good Wolfies do.'

Jed knew the score, but each time it got harder.

This one didn't put up much of a fight and he was glad. It was always worse when they did. The Rattler would rip them so much more savagely, slobbering and chewing and pulling at skin like it was dough. But Darla went down just fine; honeyed profusion of bubbly hair and moon flecked skin, and a sharp inhalation of air and pain. And that was it. The Rattler sighed.

'No spirit. Don't you just hate girls with no bite?'

Jed averted his eyes from the mess.

'But you know what galls me more? She didn't stop lying even at the end. I mean you'd think she could have told me the truth then, but I figure she was covering up for someone. Funny that.'

Jed wiped his forehead with a frayed bar towel, vinegary sweet stink of ale turning his stomach.

'You o.k., Jed? You looking a little peaky there, bud. Wouldn't be feeling a tad guilty would we?'

Jed frowned. 'No more than usual.'

'Ah and here's me thinking you'd be feeling bad. Still you humans can be awful gutless about things. No soul, just no soul at all . . . .'

Jed was about to protest when he saw something in the Rattlers eye, something he recognised and feared.

'What's up, Jed? Scared that I might find out your little secret?'

The Rattler sprang on to the bar, legs flexing and falling feather soft against the smooth surface. Snakeskin boots, rattle tap, and he's intently leering.

'I don't like betrayal; I can't be having that in my pack. And I can smell betrayal Jed, reeeeaalll bad.'

He sniffed at the air, at the barrels of ale, at the floor and then ever so quietly, angels wing in flight, he sniffed at Jed and he smiled.

'You thought I'd never know. You thought I could only smell it on them, but you under-estimated me buddy and I really hate that. You've been playing with my little Darla, making me think it was Jerry when all the time it was you having your fun with my girl.'

Jed lifted his hands, all jingle jangle nerves and shock sending him off-balance but the Rattler was too quick, too animal ferocious with those needle thin nails of his. He caught him above the eye, sent him shimmying along the floor, a cacophony of limbs and muscles twisting.

'You know the score. You got to pay.'

And the Rattler laughed, a hell bound monster roar that sent the dust-mites spinning. He laughed as he pounced, as he tore and devoured, until feeding consumed all his energies and the silence was silted only by a constant snuffling and smacking of lips.

I don't know if Jed really was fooling around with the Rattler's girl, or if it was another one of his stories. Maybe he just felt like another kill, maybe he simply tired of the glassy eyed barman whimpering, or maybe he just snapped, red-hot crack of bones and temper to addle his brain. It's irrelevant. When he left the bar, face clean and glistening like a freshwater spring he glanced over, his expression speaking a language only another of his kind could understand.

'They're all yours, Jackal, I've had my fill,' it said. And I didn't thank him; if it hadn't been his kill I would have found another. And anyway it doesn't pay to get too close to the Rattler, he's a storyteller, he makes it up as he goes along. And so I followed the trail of prints to the bar, jagged paws carved in dirt and sand and I had me some fair pickings that evening—like the true scavenger that I am.

THE STORM CHILDREN
Cullen Bunn

In the dim lamplight, Grandpa Grant's face looked almost skeletal, all bone and shadow. As he spoke, though, with the children huddled close, his eyes gleamed, as if the light had decided to swim within them. His voice calmed the children, and little Stevey, only three, crawled into the rocking chair and onto the old man's lap.

Rain pelted the windows, pouring down the glass in thick, rippling sheets, and lightning ripped bright gashes in the pitch-black sky.

Frightened, Stevey buried his face in the crook of his grandfather's arm and shivered. Thunder boomed, closer now, ever closer, and window glass rattled in the pane. Jenny and Samantha, sitting with their legs crossed on the floor, jumped, scattering the pieces of the puzzle they were working on. The puzzle had been intended to distract them from the storm, but the storm would have none of it.

The oldest of the four children, Kenny, stood in a corner and rocked back and forth, back and forth, quietly.

'Don't you worry about that old storm,' Grandpa Grant said. He turned his attention away from the children and stared out the window as he spoke. 'It's just pitching a little fit, wailing like a baby. That's all.'

Outside, wind thrashed through the trees, and the branches clawed and scraped at the sides and top of the house like bony fingernails. The children—except for Kenny—shuddered at the sound.

From across the room, Beth watched her father entertain the children. She held a cup of coffee in her shaking hands and listened to the stories—stories she had heard before, she supposed, when she herself was a child. It struck her how quickly the years slip by, how easily the stories were forgotten. It didn't seem that long ago that she had sat on his lap and listened to his tall tales. Now she had four children of her own, and her father would never be simply 'daddy' again. Now he was Grandpa Grant.

'The storm will pass soon enough,' the old man continued, 'taking its thunderboomers and lightning with it. You'll see. Everything will be just fine. And if you sit real quiet, you might even be able to hear the storm children out there playing in the rain.'

'Who are the storm children?' Samantha asked, chewing nervously on a strand of her dark hair, a bad habit she might never outgrow.

'You see,' Grandpa Grant, answered, 'folks around these parts say that when we lose a child in a storm, he or she might come back on nights just like tonight. That's why the storm's pitching such a fit, because its children got away and are out playing.'

Beth looked down, urging her hands to stop trembling.

Her mother—Grandma to the children—hissed. 'Grant!'

'What?' The old man looked up. 'I just—' His eyes strayed to Beth, and his mouth fell slack. 'Oh. Oh, Beth. I'm sorry. I didn't mean to . . .'

'It's all right, dad.' She placed her coffee cup aside. 'No harm done.'

'It's the storm,' he said. 'I guess it's got us all worked up a little. I wasn't thinking.'

'It's all right,' Beth said, but even she could hear the icy edge in her voice.

Sitting on the floor, Jen looked back at her mother. 'What's wrong?' She was eight and almost too smart for her own good. 'Did Grandpa do something wrong?'

'No, honey, he didn't.'

Beth knew that the little girl didn't believe her. Jen wasn't old enough to remember her brother, Kenny, before the accident, before the change. The change—that's what the family called it, and wasn't that just a nice and clean way of explaining something they didn't understand and didn't like talking about? No one could explain how Kenny survived the accident with only a few scrapes and bruises when all of the other children had died.

Nor could anyone—not any one of a dozen specialists—explain why he could no longer function on his own, why he couldn't speak, why he couldn't eat or go to the bathroom without assistance, why he seemed so empty.

The school bus driver had been going too fast, especially for the weather—that much Beth understood—and it was a miracle that any of the passengers survived. She should have been thankful, or so her friends and family members said, but sometimes she just didn't have the energy for thankfulness.

She suddenly felt as if she might vomit, and if she did, she wondered if she'd see the color of her shame. Even after five years, she still held onto so much anger and guilt. She had blamed her husband for not sending Kenny to a private school, like they had wanted, but those were leaner times, before his business had taken off. She had blamed herself for not picking him up after school, but she had her hands full with the girls at the time, and riding the bus wasn't so bad, after all. She had blamed the bus driver, of course, but he was dead and she found no relief in the act. She even, at times when her nerves were shot, blamed Kenny for his condition.

But she knew where the real blame lay.

The storm.

The storm had glazed the road and obscured the driver's vision. The storm had prevented the brakes from taking hold on the wet pavement. The storm had sent the bus careening into the wrong lane, right into the path of oncoming traffic.

The storm had brought on the change.

Even now, years later, a storm struck Beth not as an act of nature, but as something more, something dark and hungry that had taken her son away—

'When will daddy get here?' Samantha asked.

'Not for awhile, sweetie.' Beth forced a smile. 'He has a lot of work to finish before he can leave the city.'

'I doubt he'd be able to get to the house anyway.' Grandpa shook his head, set Stevey on the floor beside his sisters, and walked to the window. 'Way it's coming down out there, the creek's bound to have flooded the road by now.'

'I hope he's not out driving in this,' Grandma said. She busied herself, checking flashlight batteries, pulling dusty candles from drawers, just in case power failed. 'Weather like this, he'd be wise to wait it out.'

'Don't worry about him.' In fourteen years, Beth had never known her husband to leave anything to chance, and it wouldn't be that unusual for him to miss another weekend visit to her parent's anyway. 'He'll be fine.'

The lights flickered as thunder grumbled in the distance.

Kenny rocked back and forth in the corner, his expressionless features coming into the light for but a moment before vanishing again into shadow.

'What do the storm children want?' Jen asked, challenging her grandfather's story.

'Oh, they just want to play, but when they come, the storm follows, seeking to grab them back up.'

Grandma gave the old man another dirty look and clapped her hands together to get the attention of the children. 'I think it's about bedtime.'

'But I'm not tired,' Jen answered, looking over her shoulder at her mom for some sign of sympathy.

'Sorry, kiddo.' Beth nodded towards the stairs. 'Up you go.'

Jen muttered under her breath as she and her sister followed their grandmother upstairs.

'Don't pout so,' Beth called after them. 'Look on the bright side. By the time you wake up, the storm will have passed.'

Grandpa Grant hoisted Stevey into his arms. 'Let's go, boy. Time to get some shut-eye.' The child giggled. The old man had a way of making even sleep sound adventurous. He looked over at Kenny, then to Beth.

'I'll get him,' she said.

She approached her son, who continued to rock where he stood, completely unaware of the world around him.

'Let's get you to bed,' she said, but gave up on speaking to him further. What was the point? Her words might as well be drowned out by the thunderstorm.

*

Jen sat up in bed as thunder rolled across the top of the house, threatening to peel the roof away, reach in, and snatch her and her brothers and sister away. The chandelier hanging in the center of the room rattled. She always had trouble sleeping while visiting Grandma and Grandpa's. She wanted to sleep, too, because she hoped that, like her mother suggested, the storm would be over when she awoke and, if she were lucky, her father would have arrived, too. She crawled out of bed—the hardwood floor felt dusty under her bare feet—and looked out the window.

A low blanket of slow-moving clouds blotted out the stars and the moon, and lightning jumped back and forth through the darkness.

Jen wondered if her father was caught in the storm, if there were other kids, back home maybe, who were awake in bed right now, waiting for the storm to pass. Black clouds stretched across the sky as far as she could see, and it wasn't hard to imagine that this storm was as big as the world.

'Rain, rain, go away,' she whispered, finding little comfort in the words, 'come again some other day.'

But she didn't want it to come again. She wanted it to go away and never come back.

In the bed next to hers, Samantha lay, wide-eyed. 'Maybe the storm's coming for us,' she said. She held the covers up over her mouth, and her voice was muffled. 'It might be coming for the storm children, like Grandpa said, and if it doesn't catch them, it might come for us.'

Lightning flashed, frightening shadows into corners. Jen peered out the window, and her mouth fell open in surprise. In the distance, she saw movement. Several child-like figures took flight across a hilltop, running, running, running as lightning streaked after them, and the lightning, forking and splintering, took on the shape of a grasping hand.

She hopped away from the window as if she had been slapped across the face.

Samantha sat up in bed, clutching the covers to her chest. 'What? What is it?'

But Jen couldn't answer. Her mouth worked, opening and closing, but only a startled gasp found purchase. A queasiness roiled in her stomach, and she wondered if this is what Kenny felt like, wanting to speak but unable to do so, and she thought for a dreadful second that the lightning and thunder and rain had somehow stolen her voice.

'Mama!' Samantha cried. 'Mama!'

Jen stepped cautiously towards the window again. In the darkness, the trees dotting the hillside swallowed up the figures, but when lightning flashed, tearing the darkness open, she saw them, dancing and running, playing in the storm.

The door flew open, spilling light into the room.

'What's wrong?' Her mother came through the door, panic in her eyes.

'Jen saw something,' Samantha blurted.

'Jen? What is it? What's wrong, honey?'

'Out there,' she said, finding her voice again. She pointed a shaky finger towards the hillside.

Beth eased her daughter aside, holding her shoulders, and leaned down to peer out the window. A flash of lightning colored her face blue. She touched the glass, leaned closer.

'Who are they?' the little girl asked. 'Do you think they're—'

Beth turned away from the window, fear crawling across her face.

'I-It's nothing.' Beth's features calmed. She brushed the hair from Jen's face. 'There's nothing out there.'

'But—'

A blast of thunder warned the girl not to argue.

'Go back to bed, baby,' Beth said. 'You . . . just had a nightmare. That's all.'

Jen crawled back into bed, pulling the thick covers up, and glanced over at her sister. Samantha lay quietly, and Jen hated her for not coming to her defense, hated her for being too afraid to look out the window. Beth, smiling sadly, watched them for only a few seconds before stepping into the hall and pulling the door closed.

Darkness.

Jen listened, and the storm growled, angry with her for revealing its secrets.

The rain came down harder now. Wind howled. Thunder chased lightning. Lightning sizzled in the darkness. In the distance, masked by the sounds of the storm, Jen imagined that she heard what might have been children laughing and singing.

She looked over at Samantha, who was already asleep.

Still, she could not sleep. She rolled on her side so she did not have to look out the window. She closed her eyes, squeezed them tightly shut, but still she imagined the storm watching her, flowing up to the window and staring at her, rattling the latch, trying to force its way in—

Outside her room, she heard movement, the shuffling of feet across the hardwood floor, the hiss of clothing. The stairs creaked. The front door opened. Wind swept into the house.

'Mama?' she said, but there was no answer.

The little girl sat up, but didn't dare get out of bed again. Who, she wondered, was going out in this weather?

*

Beth led her son into a torrent of wind and rain. His grasp was weak, and she checked herself, afraid she might break his fingers if she gripped his hand too tightly. He wouldn't complain, she knew, even if she was hurting him. Rain stung her face, slicked her hair and skin. Her clothes were soaked and heavy. Kenny, too, was drenched, even though he wore a red rain slicker over his pajamas, and his hair dangled before his expressionless eyes.

Mud tugged at Beth's feet as she pulled her son through the darkness, leading him up the hill and towards the forest where she had seen the storm children dancing.

That was what she saw, wasn't it? What else could it have been?

Lightning snaked through the clouds, carving a zigzagging grin in the night.

A gust of wind whipped past her, so strong it almost knocked her off her feet, and she saw the tops of trees, bending almost to the point of snapping.

She felt like she was living in one of her father's stories as she approached the hill. A hint of fright jumped through her body as she saw perhaps a dozen figures, all hazy outlines in the rain, dancing, moving in slow motion, their high-pitched, singsong voices chanting in an eerie rhythm.

Beth stumbled towards them, dragging Kenny along behind her, thinking how insane she must be. But as she drew close, a curtain of rain fell before her, and the force of the wind pushed her back. A spray of water blinded her, and she held her free hand before her face.

Her vision cleared.

And she saw that the storm children surrounded her.

*

Jen hated the basement, and when her grandmother had pulled her out of bed, suggesting that the family might be safer downstairs, dread filled her. There were scorpions in the basement—nasty, pale scorpions skittering out from between cracks in the wall and from under boxes. She knew that she needed to wear shoes in the basement, but Grandma did not give her time to put them on. Once she had stepped on and been stung by a scorpion, and she remembered how it burned. What she remembered more, though, was the way the tiny creature, broken and oozing from its shell, twitched and spasmed as it tried to get at her, wanting to sting her again and again.

She thought of the storm, raging outside, and how it only grew stronger, more furious, as the storm children eluded it.

Patches of mildew crawled along the basement walls. Cobwebs covered dozens of stacked boxes. Along the wall, an old lawnmower leaked oil, forming a glistening stain upon the floor, and in the corner a tattered broom was propped next to the washing machine and drier.

Water dribbled down the walls, pooled on the concrete floor. Jen saw a snaking stream of water oozing towards her, reaching for her, and she stepped away, afraid to touch it.

Upstairs, Grandpa Grant stood at the front door, calling for Beth and Kenny. The sound of the wind consumed his voice.

Grandma held Stevey in her arms, rocking him, as she paced back and forth.

Thunder boomed. The single, bare bulb fluttered, dimmed, dangerously close to dying out, and Jen held her breath, because she knew that if the light went out, the scorpions, waiting in the shadows, would come scurrying out of hiding for them. Another crash of thunder, and the bulb sprang back to life, washing the walls in a dull glow.

The storm, Jen thought, was playing games with them.

A door opened at the top of the staircase, and Grandpa Grant rushed down to join them. His clothes were wet.

'Where's mama?' Samantha asked. 'Where's Kenny?'

Grandma and Grandpa looked at each other in silence. Grandma started weeping softly.

'Nothing to worry about,' Grandpa Grant said, unconvinced. 'We're safe down here.'

But even as he said it, the light faded, and darkness devoured them.

*

The storm children circled Beth and Kenny, staring with blank, expressionless eyes, but also smiling gleefully, and the effect reminded Beth of a doll, grins and giggles, but no soul. Wet strands of hair hung down in their faces. Their clothing clung to their bodies like wet tissue. Wisps of spectral fog rose from their bodies, writhing slowly, dissipating into thin air. They regarded Beth, their heads titling curiously, and then they looked at Kenny.

Beth grabbed his hand more tightly.

'This is my son,' she said, drawing in a deep breath, tasting salty water on her lips. She was unsure if these children understood or not. 'I . . . I believe he might be with you.'

The children, moving in unison, turned their attention back to her. Their skin was pale and slightly bloated, and Beth imagined that they had perhaps been underwater for a long time.

'He's with you,' she continued, 'but you can see he's not like you. He's not—'

Dead, she almost said, but the word caught in her throat.

Wind shrieked. Lightning jumped down to the earth. The hair on her arms stood on end.

'Please.' She raised her voice to be heard over the storm. 'I want him back.'

Pellets of ice struck her face, leaving stinging red welts upon her flesh. Thunder rumbled, loud and constant, as if something large—something behind the storm—had awakened.

The children turned from her. They giggled and squealed and sang their song as they danced away, mud spattering their pale legs, moving like ghosts.

'Give him back!' Beth cried, chasing after them.

Her foot twisted in the mud, and a knife of pain stabbed at her. Kenny's fingers slipped from her grasp, and she tumbled down the hill into a rippling pool of cold, gray water. She struggled to her hands and knees, and saw Kenny standing at the top of the hill, and behind him, clouds pooled, gathered, and contorted; roaring and whirling; reaching down with a twisting funnel to touch the earth.

'Oh God,' she cried, struggling to climb the hill, slipping and sliding in the wet earth. 'Kenny! Get down, baby! Get down!' But the sound of the rushing air drowned out her voice, and Kenny wouldn't have responded, even if he heard her.

The wind and rain writhed in a chaotic cyclone, tearing trees from the ground and tossing them aside, churning the earth and spitting debris into the air.

As Beth reached the top of the hill, she saw the tornado ripping over the ground towards her. She stood, dumbstruck, as the storm children, dancing nearby, reached up as a toddler might reach for a parent and were sucked into the torrent.

She grabbed Kenny, swept him into her arms, and threw herself back down the hill just as the screaming tornado might have torn them both apart. She covered his face with her arms as the winds buffeted her and debris scratched her skin. She risked glancing up and saw the tornado pass over her, spinning sluggishly, and the currents flowing around the inner wall of the funnel looked like the writhing bodies of children.

She forced her eyes down. Sobbing, she clung tightly to Kenny.

The wind passed and took some of the rain with it. She lay very still, shivering, weeping. With the sudden passing of the storm, the night seemed too quiet. The storm was gone, racing off and vanishing into the night.

Beth didn't stir for several seconds, afraid that even the slightest movement might upset the delicate peace around her.

What had she been thinking?

She had almost gotten Kenny—and herself—killed.

Kenny shifted against her. She looked up in stunned silence and saw her son looking back at her.

'Mama?' he said softly.

*

Downstairs, in the darkness, Grandpa Grant whispered, 'I think the worst of it has passed.' He turned his flashlight towards the ceiling. Tiny dust motes whirled in the beam of light.

'Maybe we should stay down here a while longer,' Grandma said.

'What about Beth?'

'What could have possessed her? Why would she go out there?'

'I don't know.' His voice was drawn tight.

'Is mama all right?' Jen asked.

'I'm sure she is,' Grandma said, but she did not sound sure.

Little Stevey mewled softly.

'I'm going to take a look around,' Grandpa said. When Grandma grabbed his shoulder, he patted her hand and moved it aside. He walked up the creaking wooden stairs, pulling the upstairs door open. As he ascended, taking the flashlight with him, shadow poured back into the basement.

'I don't want to wait down here anymore,' Jen said.

'Me either,' Samantha said. 'We don't have to stay down here anymore, do we? The tornado's gone.'

Grandma looked upstairs, then at the children. 'I suppose it's all right,' she said, and they followed her up the stairs.

A branch had pierced the kitchen window, carving a jagged scar stretched across the front of the refrigerator, showering glass and water over the kitchen floor. Shattered dishes covered the counter.

Grandpa walked through the mess, heading for the front door.

'Be careful,' he warned. 'There's broken glass all over the place.'

Grandma shook her head at the ruin and drew the children close.

Grandpa opened the front door.

'Lord almighty!'

Snapped limbs covered the yard. The barn had been torn asunder and lay split open like the ribcage of a massive skeleton. An old rusted swing-set lay on its side, twisted, and a cement birdbath was smashed into chalky pieces. As they looked over the yard, they saw two figures approaching.

Beth and Kenny, dripping wet and covered in scratches, bruises, and cuts, stumbled towards the house. Beth was crying, crying and smiling at the same time.

'What were you thinking?' Grandpa asked as they reached the front porch. 'You could've gotten yourself killed.'

But Kenny looked at him and spoke.

'Grandpa?'

The old man looked at Beth, a dozen or more questions forming on his lips, but she was crying and shaking her head, unable to answer, unsure herself of what had happened, except that she had managed to bring her son back.

Carrying little Stevey, Grandma led Jen and Samantha towards their mother. When Beth saw them, she started crying anew.

'Girls,' Beth said between joyful sobs. 'Come say hello to your brother.'

Samantha took a step towards her brother, looked down shyly and giggled, but Jen could not even look at the boy.

'Don't act like that, Jennifer,' Beth said. 'This is your brother.'

But the girl turned and ran away, going upstairs to the bedroom and curling into a ball upon the bed, shivering. She could not explain how she felt. She could not find the words.

She listened to them, downstairs, talking for hours, asking question after question, listening to Kenny's answers, and then laughing and crying and sometimes a mixture of the two.

Much later, as they all went back to bed, her mother stopped in her room as she tucked Samantha in. 'Jen,' she said. 'I know this is strange for you. I know. But you have to try. Your brother has been through something very traumatic. Do you know what that word means?'

Jen nodded.

'Well, if you do, you know that he needs our help and understanding. Samantha did her best to get along with him. I need you to do the same. Can you do that?'

Jen nodded again.

'Good.' Her mother kissed her on the forehead. 'Get some sleep. We can start over in the morning.'

Jen lay awake for some time, considering what her mother had said. She wasn't exactly sure why she had reacted the way she had, treating her brother like a stranger. But in a way, that's what he was, she supposed, a stranger. She had never known him in any other way. Still, she resigned herself to be nicer to him.

With the storm gone, she realized exactly how tired she was, and her eyelids grew heavy.

Later, she was roused from sleep by a flickering light filtering into the room. She did not rise, but saw the door creaking open, a narrow sliver of light growing across the floor, climbing the bed, and touching her face. Her sister remained asleep, breathing deeply, steadily. As the door swung open, she saw Kenny standing in the hallway, watching her.

His eyes were narrow and gleamed like silver. His hair and skin looked wet, damp footprints trailed off behind him, and water dripped off his body and pooled at his feet.

And Jen might have cried out for her mother if fear hadn't clutched her throat, choking her silent. She didn't know what her mother had brought in from the storm, but it wasn't her brother. A light rain speckled the window, sending undulating shapes crawling across the floor, walls, and ceiling.

The boy smiled.

In the distance, new thunder bellowed.

And in the water pooling at the imposter's feet, the reflection of a little boy, lost and alone in the storm, screamed.

MEANS OF DELIVERANCE
Simon Bestwick

I look in the mirror, and what I see there I can destroy. And I will; the means lie close at hand.

In just a minute, I'm going to reach out and take hold of it. And then I'm going to do what I have to do.

But first:

*

I wasn't always like that. Or was I? Sorry. How can I expect you to understand that? I barely understand it myself.

My name's Gavin Warne. Occupation? Bank clerk. Not exactly exalted, no, and not exactly what I wanted to be. I never quite understood what happened to my life, but I don't really mind. My wife Deborah makes more money than me in any case. We have two children, a five-year-old boy called Christopher and a four-year-old girl called Lynn.

I remain jealous only of Alan Henders, my best and oldest friend. After he graduated from college, he roamed all around the world. Thailand, Egypt, China, Outer Mongolia, probably parts of the world I've never heard of. Or you, for that matter.

No family ties for him, a loss in a way but a source of freedom too, letting him loose to globetrot whenever his feet started itching. Good old Alan.

Bastard.

But I managed to beat Alan out in one respect. I was the first of us to see a ghost.

About seventy-two hours ago, to be precise.

*

It happened around lunchtime. I work in Salford, the rougher sister city to Greater Manchester, so there aren't many places to go.

Since I have a car, I've one way of passing the time pleasurably.

I take a packed lunch, buy a cold can from the off licence next door to the bank, and drive out to the Landslide. It takes about five or ten minutes. As the name suggests, it's the site of a landslide, and you can find the remains of god knows how many houses there. Plus the river Irwell running through it and some thick woodland that's sprung up over the years. Depending on the weather, I'll either wander down there, breathing in the smell of grass and leaf mould and looking for somewhere to sit and eat, or I'll stay in my car and eat there, overlooking it all.

This day was a nice one. Summer, warm, making my shirt cling and stick to my back. I left my jacket in the car and went down the flight of steps to the woods.

I ate sitting by the river, legs hanging over the steep bank. The river was shallow and shrunk in at the edges, exposing pebbles and dried waterweed and the usual flotsam and jetsam- a child's doll left abandoned, beer cans, part of a discarded bicycle rusting in the water.

I'd finished and I got up, dusting down the seat of my pants, when I saw something move behind the trees. Something dark but with a flash of pale and white.

I don't know what it was. Something about it I still can't put my finger on, but it made me sure there was something wrong. I moved towards the trees, slowly and cautiously. 'Hello?' I called. 'Are you all right?'

The figure was small and slight and dressed in something black, a sort of cloak or cape. That didn't surprise me too much; you see people dressed like that round my neck of the woods. Goths and rockers mostly. A second intuition followed on the heels of the first; as well as being in distress, it was female. I advanced into the trees, towards her. 'Excuse me? Miss, are you—?'

She half turned, then bolted wildly. I ran after her. Why? I can't tell you. I knew she was in pain, distress, something— OK, that you could put down to body language. But I was sure, without the slightest evidence to support the theory, that there was something I could do to help.

I called out to her a couple of times as I ran, but I lost her among the trees. Well, dressed in black, among all those shadows, wouldn't you? I ran out of breath and came to a halt, gripping my thighs and gulping air. When I got my breath back I found myself calling out to her again, twice.

She didn't answer me. Not directly, anyway.

But after a minute or two, when my breathing wasn't quite so hoarse and my heart wasn't thudding so much in my ears, I was able to hear her over the chuckle of the river and the distant noise of traffic on the main road nearby.

She was crying. It sounded like small bells tinkling, but off-key, wrong somehow.

I followed the noise through the trees. I made a few wrong turnings, but she kept up the weeping throughout and in the end I found her.

I came into a clearing in the woods. The remains of a fallen tree lay across it, almost covered with ivy so that it looked like a lump of leaves with the odd piece of mottled black thrown in. She was perched on it, her back to me. Bent forward, face in her white-gloved hands. And she was crying. I saw her shoulders shake.

I padded through the thick, shin-high grass towards her and finally reached out a hand. 'Miss?' I said cautiously.

And touched her shoulder.

She turned around and screamed at me. Rage, terror, agony—they were all there somewhere and something more that I couldn't readily identity and had no desire to. And I ran from that sound, blundering through the woods back my car.

No. That's not right. Not quite right, anyway.

It wasn't just the sound. There was something else. Something I saw when she turned.

The cloak or robe she was wearing was all black. It had a hood, a cowl that covered her head but left her face bare. Or should have.

But her face was covered with something else. It was a veil of white cloth, with two holes cut in it for eyes. The scream came out from under there, sucking it into a mouth that even then, now I remember it, seemed to gape impossibly wide.

I had no idea what lay under the veil. I didn't want to know. Just the sight of it terrified me. But there was more. Something that made it worse, the veil was stained. A rusty brownish red in some places, ochre yellow in others. I'd seen stains like that before, on white gauze bandages in hospitals. They were the stains of blood and pus.

I drove back to work shaking, almost bumping the car twice on the way. How I managed not to I'll never know. I was five minutes late back and got a rollicking from the manager, but it didn't seem so bad. I'd survive. But I couldn't stop thinking about the woman in the woods.

*

Deborah was sympathetic. That evening she massaged my back after we'd put the kids to bed.

'Look, she was probably some kid dressing up.'

'I don't think so,' I said. 'You didn't hear her.'

Deborah kissed the top of my head. 'She was dressing up and she had a fall out with some mates or something. It happens, you know. She was crying about being called names or splitting up with her boyfriend or a barney with her folks, something like that.'

'You didn't hear her screaming.'

Deborah rolled her eyes and cuffed me gently across the top of the head. 'Honestly. A strange man chases her through the woods and grabs her and you wonder why she screams her head off? You're lucky you didn't come home in a police car.'

I sighed. 'I suppose. Just seemed . . . weird, somehow.'

'Weird,' She hugged me from behind, and kissed my ear and neck. 'That's the story of your life, Gavin.'

'I know.' I turned round in her grip and kissed her. 'Don't know how you put up with me.'

She kissed me back and stroked my face. I stroked hers in response. 'You've got your uses.'

We kissed again and I stroked her through her blouse, cupping a warm breast in its bra cup. She pulled out of the kiss. 'Weren't you going to Alan's tonight?'

'Bugger Alan,' I muttered.

'Only if I can watch,' she said primly.

'He'll understand,' I murmured, kissing her again.

'Yes, well,' she removed my hand before it could go anywhere else, 'there was a reason you were going there, wasn't there? Something about this huge report I've got to finish tonight?'

I groaned. Sod's law.

'Sorry,' she said. 'I did tell you.'

'I know, I know you did.' I sighed. 'Oh, well, another time?'

'Let's see how much energy we have when you get back,' she said, smiling wickedly.

'Your wish is my command, ma'am.'

*

Alan lived in a tenth-floor flat out in Old Trafford, with pretty extensive views of Moss Side and Hulme. A spectacular tie-dyed sheet of fabric hung on one wall of his living room, looking like a sunburst in orange, blue, green and vermilion among other colours. On another, there were concert posters for Hawkwind, the Prodigy, the Sisters of Mercy, Gong, New Model Army and more, a huge collage the few gaps in which were filled with ticket stubs.

Of the remaining two walls, one was mostly filled with a window offering the aforementioned view, with his video collection stacked up under it. The other was mostly bare, except for a big poster of some sword and sorcery type hero standing over the body of a slain dragon. Alan was into that kind of thing; his favourite video was *Conan the Barbarian*.

The occasional but regular visits I made to Alan let me drift back to my student days; Alan played loud psychedelic music, we said uncomplimentary things about the government, authority in general and pretty much set the world to rights. We watched *Conan* every other visit and crappy old Italian horror films or pirated video nasties. And of course we smoked pot. Lots of it.

Somewhere in the druggy haze, I remembered the weird incident at lunchtime and told Alan about. I figured, he'd travelled the world and the seven seas (as the song goes) and maybe he might have seen something like it. He snorted at the suggestion.

'Come off it, mate,' he said, brewing a couple of late night coffees in his small kitchen to give us our second wind for the marijuana marathon to come. We'd watched *Conan* yet again, followed by the uncut *Zombie Flesh-Eaters* or some similar classic of twentieth-century cinema, but he had a couple more up his sleeve—*Three On A Meat Hook* and *The Driller Killer*, if memory serves. Ah, youth.

'You see one bird dressed up like the flying nun and you reckon you've seen a ghost or something? Give us a break!'

Put that way, it did sound pretty stupid. But all the same . . .

'Look,' Alan said seriously. 'I've been to Egypt, Thailand, Borneo, Israel, and more places than I can name off hand. I've been there drunk, caned, tripping— even straight. And I've never seen a thing. No ghosts, no monsters, no demons, gods, devils, angels, *nothing*. I don't believe any of it.' He waved at a particularly ugly mask he'd brought back from Bali. 'See that? That's Rangda, the Witch Widow. Great mask, yeah? And some great legends. But they're stories, man. Nothing else. She isn't real or anything.'

He passed me my coffee and started rolling his latest joint. 'Same goes for ghosts and stuff. All I can say is if there are any, they're bloody hiding, which they aren't supposed to do.'

'Probably more scared of you than you are of them,' I grinned. 'Anything trying to take a bite out of you'd start seeing pink elephants or something.'

He beamed, blinked and fluttered his eyelashes in a way that was supposed to say, 'What, me, guv? Pure as the driven snow, I am!' I didn't believe it for a minute.

'Don't give me that look,' I grinned. 'Remember that bender we went on when we graduated from Uni?'

Alan bent forward to concentrate on his joint-rolling, his long hair dropping down in a screen round his face. 'Remember it? I'll never bloody forget it.'

After the official 'graduation party' (read 'massive piss-up') Alan and I had recovered our bearings and sobriety and had taken off on a week-long spree. We both had things lined up— a job for me to pay off the huge overdraft I'd incurred, and in his case a holiday in the Tropics (no money worries for him—his dad was loaded). I was never sure exactly where he went to begin. Or if he planned on it becoming a six-month trek around the planet before returning home to catch his breath and exercising the old wanderlust again.

So that week had involved touring several cities, getting wasted in every way known to man, woman or sheep, and, of course, girls. Alan was a ladies' man and a half. He went to pubs, we went to clubs, and unless he wanted to, he never left alone. And thanks to him, I had my first experiences with the opposite sex. To begin with, it was usually on the lines of 'have you got a friend for my mate?' on his part, but with time I watched and learnt, copied his technique and profited by it.

Big chunks of that week are still a blur for me. So, I always assumed, it must have been good.

'So,' I said after enjoying (or should that have been enduring?) *Three On A*

Meat Hook, 'what do you reckon it was I saw?'

Alan, caught in the act of changing tape for the player, reefer dangling from his bottom lip, looked up and shrugged. 'Beats me, man. Probably what Deborah said—some bird in fancy dress.'

'Halloween in't till October,' I pointed out. (It was the beginning of August).

Alan shrugged again, took another drag of his joint and passed it to me. 'Maybe she's got a skin disease or something, has to keep it covered up.'

I puffed on it. 'You reckon?'

'I reckon. Now stop harping on about it. You want to see something scary? Try this.'

And on we went with *The Driller Killer.*

*

And that should have been that. You'd think so, wouldn't you?

Not a chance.

I arrived home around two or three o'clock, stopping en route twice—once to buy a doner kebab from an all-night pizza parlour, along with a packet of chips and a can of Diet Coke, to combat the dreaded midnight munchies and again to bin the can and wrappers. If Deborah found any evidence of eating that kind of crap my life wouldn't be worth living. She had enough trouble turning a blind eye to my sessions with Alan at the best of times.

I let myself in and tiptoed upstairs. I was just about to go in the bathroom and brush my teeth when I noticed it.

The door to the children's bedroom was ajar.

I stopped and frowned. The door was always closed. Always. The window might be open, but the door never.

I took a step forward to close it, and got my second shock of the evening.

The light in the kids' room was dim; the only light there was filtered through the drawn curtains above their beds, a greyish square. Something was silhouetted against it. A shape.

'Debbie?' I whispered, but even as I said it I knew it wasn't her; too short, too slender. Then who? I thought about burglars, paedophiles and serial killers and tried to look for a weapon.

For all of half a second.

Because then the figure turned, and although it was a dark blur in the gloom, I could see the shape of the dark hood round its head, and the pale blur of the white veil, the two black holes for the eyes. It took a step towards me. I took a step back. It took two steps, to the threshold of the children's' room.

I remembered Christopher and Lynn and made myself step forward again. The figure cocked its head to one side quizzically, studying me.

I looked at it. It was the same face of white cloth I'd seen before. The same stains of blood and pus.

It whispered something to me, but I couldn't hear a word. Then it lunged. Its hand took me in the chest. It was like half a dozen knives made of ice had plunged through me. I couldn't even scream.

In the moment it struck, its black-clad body seemed to crumple in on itself and fall against me like rags. Tumbling backwards, I caught a glimpse of what looked like a twist of smoke, dark with a whiff of something pale, like a face without any features but huge, dark eyes. And then it was gone.

I hit the floor of the landing hard and cursed in a whisper. Mercifully the children didn't wake, but Deborah did, pulling open the door. 'Gavin, for Christ's sake.'

Before I could protest she grabbed me and pulled me into the bedroom. 'You'd better not have woken them up, it took me ages getting them to sleep tonight—what the hell have you been eating—sh—' and she was out on the landing. 'God's sake, can't you even close the bedroom door?' She drew it gently shut.

There was no point telling her I hadn't opened it, or what I'd seen. She'd have just assumed I was taking something stronger than usual round at Alan's, and then it really would have hit the fan.

*

I was looking over my shoulder for the rest of the next day. I didn't want to see the thing again, but I was frightened now that if I didn't see it during my working day, when I was away from home, I'd see it at home again. Standing over my children's bed.

I was at a loss. In the end, I took a deep breath and drove out to the Landslide as per usual. Even though the sky was heavily clouded with grey and it was spitting rain, I walked down the steps and down to the river, watching the trees.

'Well?' I called. I hoped there was no-one else around to hear. No answer came.

A fine drizzle of rain was falling, like a thin mist. Visibility dwindled and a pale haze shrouded everything.

'Gavin.'

It was a whisper; thin but sharp like a razorblade. I spun round, looking into the woods.

The figure stepped out from behind a tree. 'Gavin,' she said again.

She, yes—there was no doubt from the voice—she just stood there, gazing at me through those empty eyeholes. Her arms rose, spreading out. 'Come to me, Gavin,' she whispered.

I'd never felt less like doing anything, but I managed to. I kept thinking of her standing over the children's beds.

I began blustering as I came near her. 'You listen to me,' I snapped, 'you stay away from my family, do you hear me? You—'

'Ssshh.' She raised a white-gloved finger and put it to her lips. 'Gavin.'

'What?'

'Gavin.'

'What?'

She took the white veil in her hands. 'Look.'

And she lifted it.

I screamed blue murder and staggered back, but she came after me, thrusting her face into mine so I couldn't look away, wouldn't, *couldn't*, ever forget it, making sure I'd keep on seeing it till it was burned into my memory like a brand into a child's flesh. Forever. That face.

Except that it wasn't a face. You couldn't call it a face. Skinned, I think. There were cuts and what looked like burns there. And no eyes. But she was still looking at me. She still saw me. Somehow. I don't know how.

She was trying to speak to me again, but something was different, as though only the presence of the veil gave her the ability of coherent speech. Her jawbones were practically exposed and I don't think she had a tongue any longer. I collapsed to the ground and she bent over me, thrusting a horrible mess of red and black into my face, bloody foam frothing from that ruin of a mouth. I moaned and clapped my hands over my ears, trying to shut out the sounds she was trying to make. But they wouldn't go away.

Blackness.

Rain falling on my face.

I woke up. The drizzle was fast becoming a downpour. I scrambled up and ran like hell for my car.

*

I was half an hour late back for work this time. I made up some excuse about a stomach upset and being stapled to a pub toilet as a result, but even to my ears it sounded pretty lame. I could tell my manager didn't believe me. I think she suspected I was having an affair, especially with the damp and grass stains on my clothes.

Luckily I was home before Deborah and I had my clothes in the wash ahead of time. I picked the children up from school and put dinner in the oven. And wondered what the hell I was going to do next.

*

I spent the rest of the afternoon and the whole of the evening in a state of absolute panic.

The more I thought about it, the more I thought that she, whoever she was, had a reason for what she was doing. Of course, it could be something as simple as scaring me to death or into a psychiatric ward, but I didn't believe it somehow. Why? I couldn't tell you. Just instinct, intuition. Well, it had been doing all right by me so far, hadn't it?

I remembered reading somewhere that ghosts—if that was what she was—came back to right the wrongs done to them in life. What the wrong was in her case was pretty clear. But why me? What could I do? Presumably she hadn't just picked me out of a hat. Had anyone been murdered around the Landslide? Even if they had, why should the victim pick on me and expect me to—what? Find her murderer? Find her missing face? Had she mistaken me for a copper or something?

No solutions.

And no clues.

At least, not until that night, when I was lying in bed with Deborah. She was fast asleep, a short distance from me. The distance had grown between us over the evening. She had known that something was wrong, but of course I couldn't tell her what it was. In the end, my refusal to admit that anything was up had been too much and she'd given up, cold-shouldering me for the rest of the night.

I felt drowsy. My eyelids flickered and fluttered. I was drifting off . . .

And then a piece of ice landed across my lips.

I was shocked awake but the cold-gloved hand changed position, clapping over my mouth. I stared up into that stained white veil, the eyes black holes, a blank, pitiless face.

'Ssshh,' came the cold sibilant whisper again from beneath the veil.

It took its hand away.

'What do you want with me?' I whispered fiercely.

It cocked its head in that quizzical, maddening way. A ghost had no business acting like that, I thought crazily.

'Why?' I whispered. 'Why do you keep coming after me? Into my house, standing over my children?'

It cocked its head to the other side, almost teasingly. 'You know.'

'No, I don't. For God's sake, I don't know——!'

My voice rose; Deborah stirred in her sleep. The cold hand was shoved down on my mouth again. 'Ssshh,' she repeated. 'You don't know?'

'No. I swear to you.'

She stared at me for a long, long time. 'Can it be?' Her hand fell away. 'So, you don't know?' There was anger in her voice, disbelief. 'You don't *know?*'

My eyes flicked sideways to Debbie as the voice rose; terrified she'd wake and see it. The ice cold hand grabbed my face, twisted it to face the stained, descending veil. 'You don't know?'

'No,' I managed, though it probably sounded more like 'Nuhh,' being strained out through that grip on my mouth. Her breath blew in my face through the cloth of the veil. It was cold too, and smelt foul. I kept thinking about what was under the cloth.

'Then ask your friend,' she whispered. 'While you can. You haven't much time. I'm impatient. I'm angry. I'm ready to take revenge. And I've the right to be all three. I'm tired of this. Ask your friend, ask Alan Henders about little Maria.'

Deborah stirred and woke. 'What . . . '

'Nothing,' I whispered, cradling her. The room was empty again. All that remained of the veiled woman was a faint smell of corruption, one that was fading even as I smelt it.

'You're cold,' she mumbled. 'Come here. I'll warm you up.'

I let her. But I was thinking about Alan.

*

Deborah's work started first, so she usually took the children to school. The house was empty. I lay in bed and thought. Then I picked up the phone and rang the bank, and told them I was ill. Recurrence of the food poisoning.

I'd be back in on Monday (it was a Friday that day). I didn't know if my manager believed me or not. Or care much either.

I showered and dressed, then got in my car and drove out into town. I ate bacon, eggs and fried bread at a greasy spoon. I was treating myself. I was also putting things off. Did I really want to know that my best friend was a murderer? That he could have cut a girl's face off, or whatever it was that he'd done? But I couldn't put it off forever. I kept seeing *her*, standing over my children's bed, standing over Deborah and me. They had to come first. Finally, I kicked myself up the backside, got in the car and drove out to Old Trafford.

*

Alan looked surprised to see me, especially when I got him out of bed at the uncivilised hour of half past eleven. He was never what you'd call an early bird.

'Morning, man,' he said, rubbing his eyes blearily. 'What the hell's up?'

'Can I come in?'

'Yeah, sure.' He padded down the hall, the flip-flops he wore in the flat flapping on the tiled floor.

I closed the door behind me.

*

'I need a spliff,' he said. And, of course, he set about rolling one with his usual skill.

I'd told him some of what I'd seen, but by no means all. I was saving the best till last.

'Who's little Maria?' I asked finally.

His fingers slipped and skidded, tobacco and grass scattering everywhere. 'Fuck! Bollocks! Shit!'

I jumped up. He was my friend. He was my best friend. I knew that. But this was my family. I pounded both my fists on the table. 'Who is she?' I shouted. 'Or who *was* she? What did you do to her, Alan? What did you do?'

'Nothing!' He yelled back. 'I didn't do anything!'

'Don't give me that! I've had that—thing in my house! Standing over my kids! And then it tells me to ask you, to talk to you! Give me some answers!'

Alan jumped up and paced, fists clenching, mouth working soundlessly. I paced alongside him, pushing my face in his. 'Come on, Alan, talk to me!'

'No!' he shouted. 'No, no!'

He ran past me. Ran out. He was in the lift before I could stop him, and going down.

I went back into the flat. What now? His flat was on the tenth floor. By the time I could make it to ground level he'd be out of the car park and on the road. And OK, perhaps that other side of me was in action; perhaps I was trying to put off the crunch point where I didn't give him a way out, when he had no choice but to tell me what he'd done to her. I flopped down on the sofa. What now?

There was a click and sound filled the flat. The radio had been switched on. But not by me, and there wasn't anyone else there.

It was the midday news bulletin.

I felt my stomach collapse, my throat constrict, the blood drain from my limbs and my face. The kids hadn't arrived at school. The school had rung home and no-one had answered. Deborah hadn't reported for work. And I'd rung in sick.

Deborah's car had been found abandoned in a country lane just off her route to work. In a ditch. Doors open.

Empty.

Police were anxious to trace them. And they were also anxious to contact me. I wasn't slow to spot the distinction. After all, I was the only one who'd rung in to explain their absence. But I wasn't where everybody thought I should be. My car was missing.

Paranoia. How long before they traced the car? How long before the police came here? There wasn't any time to waste.

The phone rang. And rang. And rang.

I snatched it up. 'Alan?'

Whatever I'd hoped to hear, this wasn't it. Not the sound of children. Crying.

Sobbing.

Screaming.

My children. I was almost sobbing myself. Especially when I heard Christopher's voice sob 'Daddy, it's cold here, it's dark, make her stop it, make her let us out . . . '

Then Deborah. 'Gavin! Gavin for Christ's sake! GET US OUT OF HERE!'

And then they were cut off. As simple as that. For a moment I thought the call was over, but then another voice came on the line. No screaming, no panic. But then, I guessed her to have done all of that she was going to many years before.

'I've got them, Gavin Warne.'

I gripped the phone till I felt the plastic squeak. 'Where are they?'

'Safe.'

'Where—'

'Shut up.' Contemptuous. Cold as ice. 'You'll never find them.'

'If you hurt them I'll—'

'What? Tell me, Gavin. What will you do?'

There was silence. We both knew that I could do nothing.

'Good,' said her cold, cold voice. 'Now, you're in Alan Henders' flat. I suggest you make a thorough search.'

'What for?'

She gave a cold laugh. 'You'll know it when you find it. Start looking now, if you care for your children.'

'You—'

Click. And I was talking to a dial tone.

*

I set to work.

Methodically, I ripped Alan's flat apart. The videos tumbled across the carpet, every box opened every tape played through on fast forward; books flew from shelves, held up and shaken for loose papers to fall out. The cutlery out of the drawers, the crockery out the cupboards . . . no luck.

Alan's room. The logical choice. I stormed in, heaved the bed over, ripped out the drawers from the chest of them. Porn mags, baggies of marijuana.

Nothing.

A floorboard creaked underfoot. I looked down. It gave slightly, and the screws, the screws looked . . .

I rummaged through the devastation of his flat till I found what I was looking for. I used the screwdriver to twist the screws free, pry the board up.

Underneath was a battered tin box, its paint flaking off.

I tugged it free and sat back against the wall. My legs and arms were trembling; I could barely pry off the lid. I pushed it free with my thumbs.

Inside, something was covered by a piece of black satin.

I took it out. Was this it? Was this what she'd sent me out after?

I unfolded the cloth. Something pinkish-yellow lay there; I reached in, picked it up—and dropped it with a cry of revulsion.

Twisted and stiffened by shrinkage, with holes for eyes, a human face looked up at me from the floor. And from the cloth fell a switchblade. It was closed now, but its handle was crusted with dried blood.

*

I barely heard the flat door open, or Alan's muffled cursing as he saw what I'd done. Then his shadow fell across me and I turned to see him standing framed in the door of the bedroom.

Strangely enough, he didn't look angry, murderous, even afraid. Just sad. Resigned.

I was still sure even then that he was going to kill me.

I wish he had.

I made myself pick it up, that thing on the floor. I held it so that it was unfurled, so that he could see it, every details of the thing he'd done. 'Who was she, Alan?'

He was pale as smoke and didn't answer me.

'Why did you do it, Alan?' I felt a stab of pain, not physical, but at a level so profound it was far, far worse. 'I thought I knew you. And you're carrying this.' I almost threw the horrible bloody thing at him; I stopped myself and almost screamed 'Why?' at him instead.

He took a deep breath, tall, still, straight, the colour of milk. 'I didn't do it.'

'Oh no?' I was swaying, dizzy, weak. I took deep breaths to keep myself straight. 'Then what? Buy this off a market stall at Bangkok or Singapore, did you?'

'No. I was there when it happened.'

'And you didn't do it?' I wanted to believe him, but I didn't see how I could.

Not until he spoke again, and when he did I didn't want to believe him anymore.

'No, Gavin, I didn't. You did.'

*

The whole block of flats seemed to spin round under me like a merry-go-round. 'What?' I whispered. 'Pull the other one, Alan. It's got bleeding bells on.'

'It's true,' he said. There was no fire in what he said, and his voice was so quiet I could barely hear it. Thin, pale, drained, etiolated.

'I think I might just remember something like that,' I said. I tried to sound sarcastic but it came out like a plea. Alan shook his head and his eyes met mine. They were alive with pain.

'No, mate. You were too drunk. And stoned. And off your head on other stuff. My fault.'

'No,' I said. 'No.' But it was hard not to believe him; Alan was never this subdued, never this sad, never this . . . this . . .

He came slowly into the bedroom. A chair lay on its side where it had fallen. He set it up straight and sat on it.

'That last week,' he said, 'that week after we left college. Remember? That bender we went on?'

Of course I did. But how much did I remember? I *had* been drunk. I *had* been drugged up. There were holes in my memory of that week, big long hazy blurs in the film.

'Do you remember Brighton?' I had to strain to catch his whisper.

'Vaguely.'

Very vague; Brighton Pier in the rain, seen through a haze of booze and acid . . .

'There was a place. I knew about it cos my dad had one of their cards in his wallet. He gave it to me as a graduation present. It's called Deeray's. They . . . they can lay on anything you fancy. Whatever you want. If you've the money. *Anything.*'

'No,' I whispered. But something was rising, coming back, awakening down in the pit of the brain like a snake stirring in a bed of slime. A flash of memory came up like a bubble of swamp gas bursting in the dark water of a foul marsh. Only a second but it was enough—a bar, all dim lit, a live band playing an old swing number, a lot of little round tables—Alan sitting next to me at one of them, a bottle of brandy between us.

In the middle of the bar, a dais. And on the dais, bathed in an overhead light, performing to the music, there was a girl.

A

A girl

A girl and

A girl and a

'A girl,' I croaked, squeezing my eyes shut to try and blot out the memory, the image, and failing. 'A girl and a donkey.'

Alan nodded. Lines were graven in his face I couldn't remember seeing before. 'That's right, mate. That was the floorshow. The appetiser. Then we went upstairs for the main course. Remember?'

'No,' I said. 'No!'

But I could.

The stairs weaving in front of me at the far end of a tunnel made of alcohol, cannabis resin, LSD and Lord Jesus Christ alone knew what else.

A room with the biggest bed I'd ever seen and half a dozen girls besides. All on the tab—did I mention that Alan's dad was loaded?

I didn't catch the names of half of them, I remembered that. One of them, though. One of them did tell me her name. Why couldn't I remember? My mind kept shying away from the name like a horse from fire. She told me her name. But why?

Why?

Because I asked her.

She told me that her name was—

'Maria,' This time I was the one speaking barely loud enough to hear.

'Little Maria,' nodded Alan. 'There was the big room, with the big bed, but you took a shine to little Maria. She was a beauty, she was. About eighteen, nineteen, dead small, but—' he held his hands out from his chest. 'Gorgeous. Dead dark, too. Big dark eyes, long black hair. Not surprised you fancied her. I should have seen it. You were really mooning over her. There was another room, a little one next to it if you wanted to get a bit more private. You took her through there.'

Alan shook his head. 'You'd come up for air and then go back in. They gave you stuff at that place, kept you going all night.' He pushed all his fingers through his long hair. They were shaking. 'Shit, I should've seen it. You were going on with yourself, saying you loved her, saying . . . I don't know what. I was out of it too, but nothing like as bad as you were.'

I couldn't answer him. My mouth was dry and my throat had closed up. I was seeing horrible things happening behind my eyes.

'Then you started turning nasty. I'd never seen you like it. You scared me. You started slapping her about, ranting. I mean, I guess she was up for it, they're up for anything there, but I think she was getting scared. But you'd tied her up and there wasn't much she could do long as you were paying for it. You were blabbering, but it sounded like you were saying you were in love with her and you were angry because she didn't, or couldn't love you, cos she was just a body, just a face—'

I was remembering too much, seeing too much, now, and I put my hands over my ears, but I couldn't shut it out, what he was saying, what I was seeing.

'—because tomorrow it'd be someone else, you were just another punter to her, nothing to her, and you couldn't bear that, couldn't bear that you wouldn't leave a mark on her—'

A mark on her. Oh God. I remembered the slim body, the tawny skin. Marked with blood, straining against ropes. I clutched and clawed my head, dug at my scalp till it was bleeding, but I couldn't get the sight out of my skull.

'You ran to the—whatever he was—the floor manager or whatever you called him—you talked to him—you ran back in.' He jabbed a trembling finger at the knife on the floor. 'You had that, I don't know if he gave it you or you'd already had it. But you were in there before I could stop you, and you slammed the door and locked it, and I couldn't get in and he wouldn't let me stop you because you were paying for it—'

I couldn't tell him to shut up, I had no breath for it. All I could see was that face looking up at me, that lovely face, those big dark eyes and her mouth, lovely, soft, full, beautiful mouth saying *please* . . .

'And then all we could hear was the screaming. And in the end you came out again.'

Blood. Screams. A wet red mess that had been a woman's face.

'When you came out you were covered in blood. You had the knife in one hand and you had . . . that . . . in the other.' He gestured towards the terrible thing on the floor. 'You told them you wanted it, the face, preserved or something for you to keep. So that you'd always have her.'

'But you've got it,' I managed to say at last.

'Course I do. I made you wash the blood off, and I got the knife off you and made damn sure they gave the face to me. You were so out of it I just hoped you never remembered what it was you did. And you didn't.'

I tried to stand, collapsed against the wall instead. 'Not till now,' I said in a croak. 'Why did you—?'

'Keep them? Maybe I felt responsible for what you'd done, taking you there, getting you in that state. My dad knew. It was on his tab. He never said anything about it. I don't know what he might have done in that place. I don't like to think. If I'd thrown 'em away, it'd have been like it had never happened. I'd be doing my bit with all the others to cover it up. And . . . ' he stopped and fumbled out a cigarette.

'And what, Alan?'

He lit his smoke. 'I wondered if you'd ever do something like that again.

And if you did, and you didn't cover your tracks as well . . . '

'You'd have gone to the police and shown them the evidence.'

He nodded. I shrugged weakly and sank down the wall.

'Why'd she wait so long?' I whispered. 'Why didn't she come for me before?'

Alan looked at me. 'Oh, shit. You didn't know, did you?'

'Know what?'

'She didn't die at once, man. She survived what you did to her. Just. But she was stark staring. They locked her up somewhere; I don't know where, not the details. But I kept track through my dad. She died. A few days ago.'

And I could bet which day as well.

'She's got Deborah, man,' I heard myself say. 'She's got Debbie and the kids.'

Alan didn't answer.

The phone rang, and rang. I pushed myself up and blundered past him, picked it up. I knew who it would be. 'Hello, Maria.'

'Gavin.' Her voice was pitiless and cold. 'You found what you were looking for.'

'Yes,' I said.

'So now you know. Come home, Gavin. And Gavin?'

'Yes, Maria?'

'Bring my face.'

*

Alan offered to come with me, but I turned him down. God knew he'd been through enough on my account. I just accepted the loan of his car; I didn't want to get pulled over on my way home.

The police, if they'd been there, had gone. Maybe they'd had a tip-off. Or maybe not. It didn't matter. Nothing mattered anymore.

I got out of the car and walked up the drive. The front door swung wide at a touch. When I stepped into the hall, it swung softly closed behind me.

The curtains were all closed and lights off and it was almost evening. All I could see in the hall at first was blackness. Then a blur, advancing towards me. And then, finally, out came little Maria in her black robe and the white veil stained with her blood and pus. And the two black eyeholes.

'You're here,' she said coldly.

'Yes,' I said, as coldly as her. 'Now what do you want?'

'What you took.'

I held out the package, the bundle of cloth. Her face inside, and the knife.

Her gloved hand took it from mine. 'Thanks,' she said, but there were no thanks in her voice. Why should there be?

She unwrapped the package and unfurled her face from it. It hung limp as a rag from one hand while the other lifted the veil. The second time around, the red and black mess underneath didn't look so bad.

Little Maria, whose second name I had never learnt, moulded her face back on the rotting meat and bones. The skin fused to the face, a thin red line, ugly and ragged, marking where I'd sliced it. Then that was gone. For a moment, she stared at me with gaping eyeless sockets, but then her lids lowered for a moment, and when they opened again those deep, dark eyes I'd drowned in that night at Deeray's stared back at me.

'I liked you, Gavin,' she said, and for an instant her voice lost its coldness. 'You seemed like a nice guy. But you hurt me. You really hurt me.'

Her dark eyes trembled with tears.

She sounded so like a child that my loathing of what I'd done rose up all over again in my throat like bile and threatened to choke me.

'I'm sorry, Maria,' I whispered. 'I'm sorry.'

Her eyes hardened, her mouth became an unforgiving line, and that, I suppose, was no more than I deserved. 'Too late now,' she said, icily, and then every light in the dimmed house blinked on and I was alone in the hall.

But a moment later, from upstairs, I heard the children crying, and I ran up to find them.

*

They were in our bedroom, the three of them.

When I kicked open the bedroom door, the kids screamed and Deborah flinched violently, burying their faces in her breasts and giving me a blank, dead glassy look.

I feared for their sanity, for their health, for everything. They were huddled in a corner of the room, sat there, and Deborah's cheeks were stained with dried tears.

Then I ran to them, but Deborah twisted her body, twisting the children away from me. 'Get away from us,' she spat. Her voice was rough and hoarse. As though she'd been watching something that had made her scream for a long, long time.

I stood mute and numb and staring down at her. She raised her head and met my gaze, eyes flinty. And when she spoke, her voice was no less cold and unforgiving than little Maria's had been.

'I mean it, Gavin. Get away from us.'

I stumbled away back onto the landing. Tears were flooding down my own cheeks once more.

'You bitch,' at last, I whispered to the air. 'You showed them, didn't you? You showed them what I did.'

I received no answer but for a faint, tinkling laugh, receding, like a little bell of silver steel. Fading slowly away, into sweet oblivion and something close to peace.

As cold as cold as cold could be.

*

And where does that leave me?

Well, as the song says, this is where I came in. Sitting in front of the mirror, repelled by what I see. But with the means of deliverance at hand.

Deborah left that night, with the children. I don't know where she's staying. Maybe with her parents. Maybe with friends. Maybe anywhere she can think of where it might just take me forever to find them.

She needn't bother; she might as well have saved her energy and kept the house. Why should she think I expect her forgiveness when I can't find any in myself?

And besides, I don't think matters are even in my hands anymore.

You see, when I came back into our bedroom a few minutes ago—I don't know why, maybe to try and remember the good times just once more—I noticed something, lying on the dressing table, in front of the big wide mirror where Deborah had put her make up on every morning. The chair Deborah had always used was there too. I went and sat in it, looking down at what was left on the table for a long, long time, and then at the mirror, to study the face I saw there. And draw the conclusions I've just told you about.

I pick up the switchblade. It's been cleaned. When I pop the blade out it shines like silver.

A soft rustle of cloth from behind me. I don't turn around. I only look in the mirror. Without any surprise I see it's Maria, sitting on the foot of our bed, still robed and cowled and veiled.

She lifts back the cowl. Her black hair is matted and stringy. Then the veil.

That face stares back me, the face I loved and destroyed.

Hooking a thumbnail under the skin, she reopens the wound I made and peels off her face so it hangs down from one side like a half-masted flag. My penance begins; I nod slowly and raise the knife, and begin the long, long task of making my face the mirror of hers.

LITTLE DEATH
Lauren Halkon

My tribe calls me Little Death. It is a name that means many things. Sleep Giver, Dream Healer, Mercy Bringer. There is so much pain in the world that sometimes my talents are needed so that people can see the beauty again.

My name may seem strange to you. Morbid even. You may wonder why I keep it. To us Little Death is the death that comes with sleep; it is nothing to be feared. Some wiser members of my tribe say that the Big Death is not to be feared either. Myself, I am curiously ambivalent towards it, my continual dance with its smaller cousin means I am intertwined beyond conscious desire and sometimes my own sleep is restless with thoughts of what it would be to never wake up again. Lately, because of him, the Big Death haunts me more than usual . . .

But I must not think of such things now, it is early morning and the sun is risen outside. It looks like a stream rippling across the canvas and it reminds me of something I'd almost forgotten. Past days, forbidden times, laughing by a stream, dancing in the waves, holding close and being held. For a moment my eyes mist, longing overcomes me, sadness like a fever. I feel that I will surely faint. Then it is gone and I push the door aside and walk out to greet my tribe on this new day.

'Little Death.' Mayu Running Water bows before me and I can tell from the slight wrinkle in her otherwise smooth forehead that she is worried for her son. We are an unemotional people, we honour calm and do not let our troubles reach our face. That Mayu shows such concern is a bad sign.

'What is it, Daughter of Running Water?' I ask, giving her permission to speak further with me.

'It is my son, Lightseed.'

I nod my head slightly. It is as I thought. He has never been . . . normal . . . since birth. 'Go on,' I gently encouraged. I saw that she was on the verge of tears, and, though I should not, I pitied her this.

'Oh Little Death, I fear for him, his face is not his own and his eyes are blank. He looks at me and he does not see me though he acts at one with the world. There is something wrong with his soul, Dream Healer, he needs the gift to help him, please.'

I bow my head for a moment in contemplation, though already I am decided. Her plea has moved me. Despite our ways I am young and not immune to the crying of the heart.

'I will come, Daughter of Running Water. Though it be early in the day, the night has but lately released her power and so I will use the gift as I can on your son.'

I lay my hand on her shoulder. A small shiver goes through her body. The touch of Little Death is both revered and feared. The last to carry my name enjoyed this power. I do not; sometimes it seems to me that it makes me old before my time.

She puts her hand over mine and leads the way to her tent. Inside it is dark, all openings drawn against the light of day. Somewhere smokesticks burn, though the fragrance, unusually, is unfamiliar to me. It puts me in mind of moonless nights and, looking at the boy, I decide this is fitting.

His face is pale and covered in a thin film of sweat so that his skin looks false and unnatural. The muscles seem strangely mobile beneath the skin; his jaw is working though no sounds come out other than a low stream of nonsense, as would a three-year-old make. His eyes trouble me most. They are large and dark when I know that they should be blue. All our tribe has blue eyes, save me and my gifted green, it is one way the Great Spirit chose to set us apart from the rest, told us that we, of all the tribes, saw things as no other. Or at least that once we did. I remember an old old tale that told of a great love the families once bore for one another, that this love was shown freely, that couples embraced and parents smiled upon children. Just like my beloved and I before the evil struck him down. Oh Great Spirit, was it a punishment? Was it a curse on the love we showed? But only in secret, why then . . . ?

'Little Death, can you help him? My son? Can you?'

Mayu's voice brings me back to the moment and I am surprised to find that tears stand in my eyes. I quickly turn my head away so that she will not see them.

Lightseed's eyes are dark, a black so deep it burns me. For a moment I want to tell his mother to throw the tent open to the sun. I am so tired of working always in the dark. Yet I know my gift will not work in the light and so I keep what peace I have.

'Dream Healer, are you all right?'

I feel a brave hand snake onto my shoulder once more. No need for it now, the ritual of Leading to the Home is over, by all of our ways she should not touch me. But I feel comfort in that hand. And after all she has gone through. I cannot turn her away.

'I am fine, Mayu.' I feel a slight shock run through her at the use of her child-name, but she controls it well. The hand, however, still stays. 'I can heal your son if you will let me.'

'A mother's consent is yours, Little Death.' She steps away though I know it hurts her to leave her son with me. The sound of her passing from the tent is echoed by a small dance of sunlight across his face and then we are alone he and I.

For a moment his nonsense ceases and we merely stare at one another. The bed he lies on is drenched in sweat, the animal skins heaped and bunched from many nights tossing and turning. I wonder how long it is since he has had a full night's sleep.

His huge black eyes burn into mine. I see a longing in there, but one so long gone unheeded that it is unconscious, misunderstood, may always be so.

'What do you see with those eyes, little one?' I ask him. 'Is it a world none other can see?'

He looks at me for a long time.

'I have blackouts,' he says suddenly. Then silence. Then . . . 'I don't know what I do or see.'

His word shock me, for there have been many strange things happening in the camp that none could explain. Dogs disappearing, tents slashed, work destroyed and worse. Much worse. The tribe has blamed an evil spirit, perhaps the same evil spirit that has so ruined my beloved.

'Lightseed,' I say to him now, for if spirit he harbours he is no more guilty than you or I. 'Will you allow me to give you sleep? Will you allow me to enter your dreams?'

For a moment something not him flares behind his eyes, his small body tenses, his arm flails out, hits me hard in the face, causes tears to blur my vision. Afraid but determined I grab his arm, reach for the hand, fold my fingers around his. At my touch the entity whimpers and he relaxes. His fingers convulse around mine and I see bewilderment in his gaze.

'Yes.' It is all he can manage but it is enough and already I am on my way. I watch his nerveless face for a moment and think how truly sleep is akin to death. Then the scent of the moonless night leads me on and soon my breathing is one with his. We drift down a purple-edged tunnel and out into the land of dreams.

There is a landscape of deep green trees, almost black in the night. The steep face of a mountain falls away behind them. Somewhere a light shines, but it is very faint. Trees have never scared me before but they do now. These trees seem to hold all in life that humans have ever feared. They scream of loss and betrayal, disease and death. Endless loneliness and despair.

'Oh Great Spirit,' I sob, for each and every one of these trees stands for a member of my tribe. 'How did they come to be this way?'

I feel Lightseed's dream shift slightly around me, the trees flatten and distort so that I feel sick and disorientated. I know that somewhere in the real world he is feeling my distress and his mortal body coils and curls, as does his dreamworld.

'Lightseed, where are you?' I run towards the trees, though finding safe ground for my feet is nigh on impossible. The very land seeks to hurl me away from my goal. But I must find the tree that is his, I must.

The light I had seen earlier grows stronger and I turn towards it, as is only natural. It leads me onwards when my step would otherwise falter. A scent as of sweet violets surrounds me and the overwhelming feeling of evil fades momentarily. In the light I see three trees grouped close together. One I know immediately is Lightseed, it is so hunched over and twisted, almost to the ground, I can see the evil in it, I can see the lust to hurt and destroy and I know that if I can just uproot this one I can save all.

I fasten my will upon it and begin to pull its dream-being apart. The leaves come first, dried and husk-like, then the smaller, thinner branches, twirling up into the night sky like wisps of smoke from an old fire. The light grows brighter still as I do this and it is then that I catch my first true sight of the other trees in the huddle.

These two trees grow together, roots and branches both entwined. One of these trees is so gnarled with growths that I cry to see it bowed so. The other has long slender branches with diamond shaped leaves, so much like tears that I realise it is me, it cries with me, with all the tears unshed for my beloved. And he is intertwined with me in a way I had never imagined. My love for him breaks full force over me then, I cast my blazing eyes on the tree that contains the evil spirit, the spirit that has so broken so many of us. I rip it out of the ground, roots trailing, screeching to be so violently torn.

I have no pity, I cast it into the light, feeding it with my anger and love and soon it is burnt so that it never was.

All the trees around me sigh with relief. I sigh, too. I sigh for something else.

Moonless night guides me back and in the blink of an eye I am staring once more into a young face. A face whose eyes are brightest blue, tormented no longer, but with so much still to learn.

'Mayu.' I call his mother back in. I can feel the relief stream from her the moment her eyes alight on the child. She cannot keep it from her face this time and I cannot help it, I take my sister-in-law into my arms and hold her tight as she sobs her joy into my breast.

'Oh thank you, Little Death,' she cries, 'Thank you so much.'

I hold her close and this means so much to me that I let my own tears come. Behind us Lightseed gains unsteady feet and joins us. I feel small arms slip around us and a memory of seeing another hold this child as I do now makes the tears burn hotter. Never did my beloved look more beautiful than when he held the children he could never have.

It was the evil spirit that had caused this, that had taken this child, that had been here for time eternal and slowly poisoned the love out of all of us. I pulled Lightseed closer. 'It's not too late, little one,' I whispered to him. 'Teach them how.'

He backs away from me and his face tries on a smile. He reaches for his mother's hand. 'Little Death has to go now, Mother,' he says and she looks down at him. I see new light in her gaze and feel hope for what I must now do.

'Mayu,' I say and that is all that is needed, she simply nods and I am on my way.

Out of her tent I make my way to my own. People call out in greeting but I barely hear them. One more root needs healing and it is the most important of all. To me.

In my tent all is dark, as befits one with the gift. But I do not want the dark now. I want to be able to see. I light candles, as many of them as I can find, and set them around him. The tent flickers and dances with their light, a million gentle spirits caress his face and he wakes for just one moment.

I am caught by the purest of blue eyes, the soul that shines within despite the pain that racks a body that is being eaten away.

He sees me and smiles. I am lost. I reach out to touch him but he is gone again. Something tugs at my heart but I know what I must do.

By the light of the candles I watch him. His sleep is not a true sleep but one caused by the illness that has taken him so far away from me. Taken him but not the love we shared. Something even the evil spirit could not drive away completely. For a long time I sit, lost in the wonder that is him. The dark slant of his brows, the long lashes that sit on his cheek, the gentle smile, even in sleep. For me alone.

I work my magic and feel his sleep deepen; his very breath is precious to me now. I reach out to touch his forehead and wonder if he can feel me. Strange how we touch people in sleep the way we never do while awake.

His hand lies on the pillow beside him, half-uncurled. I fit my own to it. The touch of his fingers makes me want to cry and so I do.

I will stay like this for a while, I need this much. Then I will join him in the Little Death. The root I know is too far-gone for my gift to touch, but for love of him I will keep us asleep until one grows who can cure him.

ECHOES
William P. Simmons

Paul Sanderson didn't want to go home, so he took his time walking the dimly lit halls after his shift at the plant. A few heads nodded briefly in passing, obscured by the dim overhead lights. As he brushed shoulders with the glum people he spent nine hours each day trying to ignore, reading condemnation in their eyes, he wondered if the smiles knotting shadowed faces were mock shows of false cheer or malicious, knowing frowns. He was glad to leave them behind and gulp the fresh, cool air.

Squeezing his collar closer around his unshaven chin, he sensed Harper's Mill crouched around him, a predatory animal waiting for him to relax. No worry there; he couldn't recall a time when The Mill hadn't made him feel trapped. Shivering, he hurried down the industrial drive, across wilted grass, and took to the sidewalk, kicking dead leaves blown viciously by a rising gust of wind.

The pale bulge that might have been a face fled when he stared down the alley to his left.

Can't keep this up.

The guilt, the fear, a dog-tired job he hated, waiting all day knowing there was no where to go but . . .

Home?

When had it actually felt like a home, living with Nora?

Fog cloaked the limp branches lining Depot Street, bent yellowed backs over the brick skin of *Miller's Café* and *Betty's Hair Your Way*. Paul watched the yellow, sickly blanket spill noiselessly over peeling park benches and a row of potted plants that kids hadn't gotten around to smashing. It choked a ratty stray dog whose eyes stared too intelligently, swallowed a pole light before dissolving against a wiry old lady whose parched, nervous lips drizzled a low cackling sob. The crone muttered to herself and beat her walking stick into the night, and he couldn't tell if she looked afraid or eager to find something hidden ahead of her. He saw it again.

Movement.

Eyes.

He could breathe when he realized they were only bottle caps catching a passing car's headlights.

'It's worse after dark,' Nora had told him once, eyes wide and wet and sincere, grasping her hands nervously, looking to him for a kind word, a loving touch—all the things he'd outgrown, all the things he was unwilling to tell her. Afraid even to admit the problem to himself. Afraid how she would take it.

He stopped below a cracked wooden sign with shaky black lines announcing GARY'S SPOON, and peered through the wide, clear windows of the diner at bobbing heads and waving hands that didn't quite seem real. Wondering how long he dared to dally, he hurried in.

Warmth from sizzling meat hit him first. Next, the sight of a half dozen grotesques huddled over plates, eyes staring inward as their mouths chewed.

Since the waitress didn't notice him, Paul took a seat at the counter where he could stare at the glass-encased rows of sickly looking pies and bagels. He savored the deep-fat scent coating the muggy room and, suddenly, the memories were back, threatening to pull him down—the good times when Nora had still been able to leave the house; the bad times that he'd been too blind

. . . Too damned selfish, you bastard—

to appreciate, barely noticing the change before he came to find her holding herself in the corner, hiding something he hadn't needed to see.

He'd taken Nora, back when they'd still talked and openly flirted, and simply being together had been a reprieve from a world unable to affect them. She loved the house burgers, served with fresh lettuce leaves and mounds of crisp fries heaped in wicker baskets and lined with oily paper.

How many times had he sat right here, watching her play with her fries, waiting for him to finish as she asked him about his day, hinted that he was working too hard and that she needed help.

I get lonely, Paul. It's too quiet in the house.

Why don't you get a hobby? A job, maybe?

You know I can't do that. You know how I feel around other people.

Then do things to occupy your mind, honey. Christ, watch television, read a book!

Why don't you love me anymore?

I do love you.

I'm losing myself, Paul.

Oh, why do you have to be so Goddamned dramatic?

It's not . . . nonsense. I can hear myself withering. . .

Here, have more coffee.

I don't want coffee; I want you.

You've got me, babe.

I want you like before.

Do you know what you want?

Don't yell, please. You scare me when you get like this.

If it weren't me, it'd be something else.

It's everything . . .

Nora—

I am. I'm losing me, Paul.

'What is it, fella?'

Paul jumped.

It wasn't Gary, but a balding, big-bellied man whose fat rolled over a soiled apron while his arms, muscled and decorated with lush, tropical hairs, twitched impatiently.

He made his order, and wondered when he'd lost the ability to even feel sad. After three cups of coffee and waving at one of his co-workers who quickly looked away, Paul flinched beneath the shadow of a sullen counter man who dropped his plate down and belched.

Classy.

He went to work on a forest of peas and dark canal of gravy, barely noticing the curious glances from a mother sitting a few stools down, hushing two giggling boys who kicked each other with gleeful abandon. She herded her brood to one of the tables behind him, staring a challenge until

Paul went back to work on what might have passed for mashed potatoes in a starving country.

You're still doing it.

Paul mashed some crumbs in his fork.

Making her wait.

An oblong overhead light hummed and reflected off rows of filthy coffee cups as he thumbed through his wallet for money to pay his bill. Stuffing the cracked leather back into his jeans, a mustard stain reminded him he hadn't done any laundry in the last few weeks. Listening to the muffled whispers of cars dividing the night with low head-beams, he hurried through the blustery streets.

How could he have known it, the desperation he'd made of her life?

Unable to balance overtime and night classes with a wife who didn't understand the long hours it took for a man to fight his way from the poverty they'd both been born into, he just couldn't find the time or energy she required.

How was it that he hadn't noticed the depression until after they married?

His house stood amongst a wall of shrubbery, a blistered face of brick and shingles and dull, peeling wood. Behind the living room glow, a shadow paced back and forth. The face, when it peered expectantly from between parted curtains, didn't blink.

He turned away so he wouldn't have to face her yet, circled the block a second time, torn with conflicting pangs of guilt and self hatred and the sharp, ruthless pang of responsibility.

Wiping his face, he slowly crossed the yard, shivered against an angry gust of wind which blew last year's leaves over the concrete drive he'd put in at Nora's insistence.

Once upon a time . . .

When they'd eaten by candlelight and still enjoyed teasing each other's bodies, lingering in the soothing melody of relaxed breathing afterwards.

He grabbed in his coat, fumbled past gum wrappers and a pack of mints. Found the keys, lost them. Saw her stare out between the drapes before dropping back like a patient surrendering to the sick bed. Found the keys again.

Heard a crash from his kitchen.

Jabbed at the lock.

Missed.

Tried again.

Slipped because his hand was sweaty.

Heard the small, final click of the lock turning.

And stood against a wall of darkness lit slightly from a wave of dull light from the living room.

'Paul?'

He cringed, seeing the toll her anxiety had taken on her face. Pity wrestled revulsion as she closed the distance between them. And all he could think was that, somehow, a creased rubber Halloween mask had fixed its way to her face.

'You're late.'

He wished he could see if she was smiling or frowning when she spoke. Not that it mattered.

'You look tired,' she said wearily, letting her head tilt and stay against her shoulder. 'Why do you do it, Paul? What do you hate so much about me?'

He wanted to talk, but nothing but lies would come of it.

'Why do you wear yourself down: why wear me down?'

The wet nightgown stuck to her hips, and before he could move away, she drew the razor over the old, crusted rents across her wrists and belly and neck.

The tears, when they came, felt hot and useless down Paul's cheek. 'I never wanted this,' he said; moved by the sudden urge to grab her, hold her, smell the lilac in her hair, feel the soft, rosy heat of her skin. Instead, he tried to push by her, shivering at the dry crackling feel of her skin.

'I'm going to bed, okay? Just for tonight . . .'

An old argument.

An old life.

An old memory, growling between clenched teeth as she tittered, fell, and both her life and eyes faded—old paper shredded—coming apart and spilling what resembled red ashes.

He waited for her to finish, shaking, wanting to turn away again, but rooted to the spot by obligation. She drew herself up.

The same questions, the same need and confusion and hurt as she told him it was his fault but that she still loved him so very much—would always love him.

And cut.

He begged her to stop.

Her dead, cold eyes no longer saw him.

She'd be waiting for him tomorrow and the night after and the night after that.

'I'm losing myself, Paul.'

Echoes.

And Paul slumped against the wall because she was right. She was coming apart, and God, Oh Sweet Jesus; all he could do was keep coming home to watch it . . .

FEEDING THE BEAST
Ken Goldman

On their first date he told her she was the most beautiful woman he had ever seen. Blushing, she managed to feign modesty. One evening over wine she told him she loved him. Later in bed he told her he loved her.

For the wedding she insisted on writing their own vows.

During the ceremony she said she looked forward to growing old with him, adding a cute remark about keeping adjoining 'his' and 'hers' jars in the bathroom for their teeth. That one got a few laughs.

Then her pledge turned serious, and she promised to remain by his side no matter what obstacles life threw into their path. Many present cried.

When his turn arrived, he told friends and family that his world had been empty before she came into it. He vowed he would die for her, and at the time he meant it.

On their wedding day he didn't have to actually do it.

*

Wesley and his young bride would make Honolulu International in another two hours, plenty of time for what he had in mind. He focused his attention from the Piper's control panel to where it really mattered.

'"`A`ohe lokomaika`i i nele i ke pâna`i.' How's that for a Harvard man?'

'Another of your legal terms, Counsellor?'

'It's Hawaiian for 'No kind deed ever lacks its reward.' Sort of like 'quid pro quo,' but it sounds prettier.'

Charlotte smiled. 'Is this your way of asking for a blow job?'

Wesley smiled too. 'See how easy it is to master the ancient tongues?'

He snapped on the autopilot and unzipped his jeans, a guy who had the world by the balls. As one of Seattle's select divorce lawyers Wesley had managed that trick one gonad at a time.

Charlotte examined the goods, grinning even as she went down on him. The woman's tongue became hot wired, and Wesley leaned back in his seat to savor the moment. Once started, Charlotte could probably bob her head straight into Waikiki.

The manbeast within responded.

Eat it, babe. That's it, bitch. That's real good. Eat it all up . . .

Although Wesley had never met a blowjob he did not like, there was a serious downside to his bride's initiation into his mile high club. Getting sucked off at thirty thousand feet had taken his attention from the Piper's fuel gauge whose indicator had accelerated its movement towards 'E'.

Spuk-Spukka-SpukSpuk . . .

'What the—?'

'Sorry, baby. Got a little bicuspid into my work.'

'Shh . . .!'

The Super Cub's engine burped again, and Wesley stared at the blinking red fuel light unable to do more than gape like an idiot while his bone-on quickly shrivelled. Somehow gasoline from the Cub's tank was not making it through to the single engine, and he was rapidly dropping fuel. Considering the plane's altitude the whys and what-fors didn't matter much once the needle fell to 'Empty' and the front propeller turned arthritic. Pulling herself upright Charlotte saw the warning light too, and for one terrible instant the couple exchanged glances with a dim comprehension that they had shared the all-time mother of bad timing.

Spukka-Spukka . . .

'Wes, is everything all . . .?'

. . . *SpukSpukSpuk* . . .

'Put your belt on.'

'What?'

'Just do it. Okay?'

Her groom's eyes said it all. One thousand miles from the mainland his rebuilt Piper was coughing fumes like a consumptive hag. Wesley flicked his thumb at the fuel gauge because he could think of nothing else to do. He tried telling himself that maybe the indicator was damaged, maybe the vortex generator was on the fritz and the sputtering didn't really mean any—

The engine choked and the Cub took a mean dip as the bottom dropped out of the world.

Wesley had enough time only to mutter 'Oh, Jesus—' before the small plane dipped again, pulling the steering column from his hands. The engine managed one powerful fart before it went dead. The law of inertia kept the Piper airborne for an uncertain moment, long enough for Wesley to swap a last uneasy stare with his wife.

'Shit . . .'

The plane plummeted like a sack towards the Pacific. Wesley's stomach and heart mashed into one organ as the horizon became vertical and spun wildly, the entire vista of heaven and earth unravelling as if on a huge spool. The Piper corkscrewed while some distant part of Wesley's brain registered Charlotte's screams.

'OmiGod, Wes! OhGodOhGod!!'

God wasn't listening. The plane tumbled into a dizzying death spiral. A man plunging several hundred feet per second has little time to weigh alternatives. He has time only to scream his throat raw for his own sorry ass, time only to hope that death, when it comes, will be quick.

The Piper struck the water balls-to-the-sky, catching a huge cresting wave at the peak of its swell. Its bizarre angle of impact made for an intriguing lesson in physics that defied the laws of probability. Both seats tore through the cabin doors just before the floor and ceiling of the fuselage crunched into a chunk of tangled metal. The twin cushions skittered along the water's surface like skimming stones, catapulting the couple yards from the Piper's debris. Surrounded by open sea the plane's explosion seemed more of a loud thud. What remained of the cabin burst into flames.

A large area of metal detritus heaved among the waves, the misshapen globs of tortured steel gradually sinking piecemeal. A gnarled section of the plane's extended flap briefly stayed afloat, and a hundred feet from that a twenty-six inch Tundra tire and some Gucci luggage bobbed alongside the swells. One bag had sprung open and women's clothing rode the waves like a floating yard sale.

The primitive manbeast caged inside Wesley's brain kicked into action, although later he would remember little of what he did. Charlotte remained buckled to her seat, and both had somehow been thrown clear of the wreckage. Now his wife's seat rolled on the waves maybe a good hundred feet from her husband. Somewhere out there was a float kit, but that might just as well have been back in Seattle now. The Piper's cushion was no flotation device, and the plush leather pad could not remain adrift for very long. Strapped in, Charlotte would soon be going under with it.

If his legs were still working it wouldn't be a difficult swim to recover her. On his own automatic pilot, Wesley didn't consider that when he reached his woman he might be unbuckling a corpse. He knew only that he did not want to die alone.

He swam towards the red leather seat cushions, but Charlotte was not moving.

Her forehead's nasty gash was bleeding badly, and he ripped his sleeve to apply a makeshift tourniquet to the wound. Exhausted and shivering Wesley pulled himself alongside her, draping his arms around his wife with no idea what to do next. Already the leather pad had taken on too much water, and it would be going under any minute. He had managed to escape the plunge from thirty thousand feet only to come to this. The Pacific owned both of them now, and he could do nothing as he waited for the ocean to claim what belonged to her.

A remnant of the Piper's wreckage floated among the rainbow of Charlotte's strewn wardrobe. It thumped against the side of the padded seat, and at first Wesley saw only a blur in the sunlight reflected off the waves. He reached for the large box as if to assure himself it was real.

Three Person Sea CloudModel #417-B
Max Weight 510 lb
Pull Cord to Inflate
USE CAUTION WHEN INFLATING

Part of the flotation kit had broken free. Maybe God had one good ear after all. Wesley tore at the Styrofoam and found the cord, tugging at it like a madman. The heavy-duty blue and yellow vinyl inside did its thing and with a hiss the box fell apart.

The life raft fully inflated the same moment the saturated red leather cushion slipped below the surface. Charlotte had gone as limp as a rag doll, but Wesley managed to unbuckle her and pulled the two of them on board. He tried mouth-to-mouth, managing to get her to spit up a bellyful of seawater. Exhausted, he had enough strength to yarf his own breakfast before passing out.

The sun already had headed west, and the air developed a cold bite. It was 5:37, and regaining consciousness Wesley had the disjointed thought that Rolex made one hell of a watch. The timepiece was still kicking, but he didn't feel as certain about himself. When reason returned another thought occurred, this one unsettling. Soon darkness would come.

He held Charlotte close. Her pulse was weak but she was breathing. The long gash had stopped bleeding, but a grotesque Rorschach of dried blood still caked most of her face. Splashing some seawater on her, he could manage only a whisper.

'Charlotte? Can you hear me?'

Nothing.

'You okay?'

Her eyes opened. 'Are we dead?'

'Not yet.'

She took a moment to consider that.

'Then we're all right?'

'Not yet.'

She considered that too.

'Jesus, Wes. What happened?'

'Must've ruptured the fuel line somehow, maybe during take-off. It's a moot point now.'

She moved closer. 'I'm cold. And I could use a drink.'

'Room service is about five hundred miles that way.'

Charlotte watched the bleeding sunset and managed a weak moan.

'What happens now?'

'We survive,' he told her, trying to believe it. The Pacific was a monotonous heaving mass, and if land were anywhere near, the ocean gave no hint where to find it. Help would come, he told her, someone would realize the Piper never arrived at its destination. But the plane had sunk too far at sea for wreckage to wash on shore. Worse, from the air the bobbing Sea Cloud raft would appear a speck to anyone searching for them, even with optimal weather conditions.

'Maybe we should've fished some of your things from those Guccis,' Wesley suggested. 'Might've kept you from the whole 'Lord of The Flies' fashion statement. And it's going to get damned cold.'

Charlotte managed a twitching smile. 'A girl wants to look her best when she's eaten by barracuda.' She warmed herself against Wesley's chest and watched the sun drift below the horizon. 'Ordinarily I'd think this is one beautiful sunset.'

'It still is. Someone will find us. I'm sure of it. It just won't happen tonight.' He offered a wet stick of gum and took the last one for himself. Wesley spent the next minute wondering if their final meal would be a salt watered wad of Juicy Fruit.

They waited in silence for over an hour until full darkness came. Near the raft some invisible thing went *splunk*. Maybe another section of the plane's wreckage had popped back to the surface to say howdy. Wesley hoped that's all it was. He was in no mood for surprises.

Beneath a pale moon a dorsal fin sliced the water's surface about thirty feet from the raft. Wesley spotted it circling like a shadowy scout, and a moment later half a dozen more closed in. He pointed for Charlotte to see. Each time the couple turned there were others, some drifting along the waves in tandem until fins appeared on all sides. They slid closer, tightening their orbit like an advancing war party, dark floating lumps dissecting the water. Wesley slid a paddle from its neoprene sheath, holding it before him like a battering ram.

'Wes, there's too many of—'

One bumped against the life raft. Charlotte almost toppled over the side, but Wesley managed to pull her back. He felt something churning the water just below the surface.

'They're under us . . .'

In dark committees the sharks were manoeuvring for position. Murky clusters surged toward the raft, hammering it from all sides as if one might fling itself on board like a dead weight. Sprays of seawater rained on the couple while they performed a lunatic balancing act to keep the raft from capsizing. Charlotte clung to her husband as he poked the paddle at the invading snouts. Winking in and out of the moonlight the fins kept coming. Charlotte's fingers tore twisted tracks into Wesley's chest so she would not be pulled from him, but she lost her grip and tumbled over the side into the dark waters. Mouths open, the sharks were waiting.

'Wes—!!!'

Her shrieks filled the night. From the agitated seawater Wesley heard what sounded like a crunch of dried wood. He dropped the paddle, slamming fists to his ears, but Charlotte's screams wouldn't stop.

[I would die for you, Charlotte . . .]

He crouched in a foetal position.

'Wesley! Oh God, Wesley! Help—!'

'Jesus, no! Charlotte, I can't! I can't!'

[. . . *Die for you . . .*]

He mashed his ears, but the shrieks went on.

' . . . can't . . .'

'Wessss-leeeeee . . . !'

The manbeast heard. Wesley grabbed the oar again, battering the dark thrashing forms, blindly smashing at whatever moved. One of the sharks sank its teeth into the thick paddle, and Wesley played a useless tug-of-war with the fish. He stared dumbly at the worthless stump of plastic he pulled from the water.

'Motherfuckers! Shit eating cock suckers!!'

And then it ended. Charlotte's cries stopped as if an electric cord had been pulled from its plug. Their hunger sated, the sharks disappeared, gone like a magician's trick beneath the surface with their catch of the day. The ocean lapped at the raft's side as if the incident never happened. Wesley crouched waiting for an encore, but it didn't come.

The whole thing had lasted maybe six minutes, but it proved time enough to total his life with Charlotte. Wesley needed significantly more time for clear thinking to return. Assessing his circumstances he came up empty. Even if the sharks didn't reappear, he knew he remained in ten thousand fathoms of deep shit. Maybe Charlotte had been the lucky one.

Charlotte was somewhere down there now.

Or what was left of her.

Charlotte . . .

'*Sorry . . . I'm so sorry . . .*'

The gum had lost its flavor and he spit it out. It was an absurd thought to occur at this moment, but easier than recalling his woman's final cries for help before the sharks took her down, cries he could not find inside himself to answer. And easier than contemplating what might come next.

Plenty of water, but not a drop to drink.

Water water everyfuckingwhere . .

Charlotte was dead. He could do nothing about that. But he had to consider his survival now, and he knew that in forty-eight hours dehydration would turn his insides to wood shavings. Wesley remembered some Discovery Channel program about castaways who wound up drinking their own piss. In another day swilling pee would be like polishing off a daiquiri. Right about now his bride and he should have been dining on Kalua pork and sipping Mai Tais at The Royal Hawaiian. But it didn't appear he would be chowing down on solid food anytime soon.

The wind kicked up. Wesley was cold and wet. Worse, he was scared.

He slapped himself hard.

'Can't lose it . . . can't lose it . . .'

And then he almost did.

A weak pounding came from against the side of the raft. Some object had tangled itself in the mooring line, but darkness made it difficult to see the shape clearly. Wesley tugged the rope until a thin pale mass emerged, dripping of seawater and cold to his touch as he pulled it on board. Holding it to the moonlight he noticed the large pear-shaped diamond ring first. The realization took a moment. He had hauled Charlotte's arm from the ocean, gnawed clean above the elbow.

He dropped the slab of shorn flesh and bone, backing off from it as from some diseased thing. Sobbing like a child, shivering and moaning, he crouched in the corner of the raft, swearing to himself that he would not move until rescuers or death found him. He didn't give a shit that might arrive first.

At night a shivering sleep came only with complete exhaustion. During the following day his flesh seared in the heat like over-fried bacon.

Searching for a plane he saw nothing but a burning sun. Inside himself he felt a burning too. This was hunger, but it was also fear.

He was alone, more alone than any man could be.

Throughout the second night he shivered but did not sleep much.

When day again arrived he knew it would be his last.

Hunger hammered Wesley's gut in dull thunderbolts, and he did not feel like opening his eyes. Instead he lay with the morning sun warming his face. In another hour the sun would not be so hospitable.

The sharks had not returned, but there had been no rescue party either. He didn't have much fluid left inside to pull off that piss-drinking stratagem much longer. The Discovery Channel hadn't covered that part.

So many thoughts. Too many. Better to clear his head. Better not to think at all if he wanted to stay sane.

'Wesley . . . ?'

'Unghh. . .'

'Wake up, Wesley. Talk to me.'

In the brilliant sunlight he squinted. Someone—it was a woman—came into focus, but he was seeing her through gauze. He recognized the voice before he saw her face clearly. Clumps of sopping hair lay in mottled ringlets. The woman stank of seawater.

'Charlotte?'

Wesley no longer trusted his own senses. His bride's corpse rested on the ocean floor with the local marine life, that much he knew. The sharks had done one bitchin' job on her, and she wasn't coming back.

[Try to keep an open mind. Take a good look before you decide what's true. Just hold on . . . hold on . . .]

It certainly looked like Charlotte although much of her was gone. The stub of what remained of her upper arm dangled like a fleshy windsock, and tattered skin hung from her face in thick lunchmeat shavings. A portion of her skull had split, and tufts of blood-spattered curls spilled over a spongy mass that must have been the woman's brain. Sunlight peeking through an empty eye socket made her resemble a rotted jack-o'-lantern. Not much remained of her face, or her torso.

She held the severed arm Wesley had fished from the water.

'I didn't want you to see me like this, but I had no choice when you broke your vow. We have to set this right, Wesley. For both of us.'

[She wasn't there. She couldn't be there. It was too soon for this lunatic horseshit to be happening.]

'You're dead!'

'I'm not certain, but I think so.'

She tugged the tatters of silk that had been her blouse, trying to conceal the exposed flap of breast sagging from her chest like a tornsleeve. Thick strands of cheeze-like goo hung from it.

'I'm sorry, Wes. I know how bad I look.'

The saltwater crazies had finally arrived. It hadn't taken long.

[If I close my eyes you'll go away . . .]

She didn't go away, only smiled and moved closer.

'Touch me, Wesley. Feel for yourself.'

He didn't have to. Her ear dropped into his lap. She tried cramming it back into its cavity, but it wouldn't hold.

'Oh, Christ, Charlotte. Don't do this to me.'

'You're not crazy, Wes. But you're hungry, aren't you? You would do anything to eat. *Anything.*'

She didn't need to tell him. The gnawing punishment inside his belly reminded him every second.

'I can help,' she told him. 'I think maybe we can help each other.'

'You can get me out of this place?'

'No, I can't do that. But I can do this . . . '

She held her own severed arm out to him.

'Eat me,' she said.

'What?'

'Start with my arm. It isn't a part of me any more, so it won't be difficult. Eat me, Wesley. I know there isn't much left, but do it for us. I want you to.'

He felt his innards kick box, but there was nothing left inside his stomach to woof up.

'I can't do that!'

'Start with my ear, then. Maybe that will be easier.'

'Oh Jesus! Go away! Just let me die!' Wesley's breathing became labored. 'I tried to save you, Charlotte! You know I tried! There were too many—'

'—You broke your vow, Wesley. Help me keep mine.'

If solid nourishment didn't get inside him soon Wesley would starve. This wasn't rocket science, and the babbling corpse was probably some guilt-soaked brainfart anyway, a figment of an encumbered mind baked to a crisp. He was sane enough to know he was probably losing it. But if he were hungry enough to believe himself talking to his dead wife, then maybe he could convince himself he was just scarfing down some fast food.

He took the ear and gnawed. It was crunchier than he expected. The salt water helped a little, even added flavor, and he ate the whole thing. It wasn't all that bad, and it piqued his appetite.

'Tastes like chicken,' he said, licking his fingers. He even smiled.

She handed him the severed arm, and he sank his teeth into the fleshiest part of the upper segment like a man working over a rack of ribs. Charlotte's daily weight training at the spa had paid off because the meat was firm and there was very little fat. Hell, this tasted too damned fine to be a concoction of his imagination. Wesley made certain to remove the engagement ring before he started on her fingers.

Waiting until he finished, the woman held out her remaining arm to him.

'Are you sure?' he asked.

'The ring means something to me, Wesley. I'd like to keep it. I'm still your wife.'

The thought had not really occurred to him, and he felt shamed that the idea sickened him. Maybe it was better not to go there, better not to let the revulsion show.

Nothing out of line here, babe. Not a damned thing.

Wesley slipped the diamond upon the third finger of the hand attached to Charlotte's remaining arm. She moved closer.

Charlotte's lips felt cold against his. Still, they were surprisingly sweet.

She parted them a little as she always had done, and her tongue found its way into Wesley's mouth. There was no other manner to describe the sensation. He was not disgusted or repulsed. He was hungry.

. . . and here was the corned beef special.

[Too damned fine not to be real. Human flesh, the other white meat.]

The manbeast couldn't help itself. It nibbled the fleshy gobbet and felt its appetite grow.

She pulled herself from him. Wesley couldn't be positive with so much of Charlotte's face gone, but it appeared she was smiling.

'Quid pro quo?' She uttered, her uncertain expression still there.

She slid towards the shredded fabric remaining of Wesley's pants, unzipping his jeans with her teeth. First offering soft butterfly kisses with her tongue; with an audible gulp she took all of him into her throat. The feel of her mouth was waxy as if one lip might loosen and tear clear off, but she managed to get seriously down to business. His response amazed him as he felt himself grow erect.

['Eat it, bitch. That's it, eat it all up . . . ']

The woman stopped cold, her one remaining eye seeming to look through him, seeming to accuse him.

[Yes, she's got you where she wants you now . . .]

Sensing danger, the beast stirred, but too late.

Charlotte sank her teeth into Wesley's cock, attaching herself like some rabid pit bull refusing to let go. She swung her head to strengthen her grip, and the pain ricocheted straight into his brain. He twitched and kicked like a man caught in a bear trap, the crotch of his jeans darkening in an expanding smear. When finally she released him he felt the limp wad of his manhood slap low against his thigh as if roadkill dangled between his legs. He stared at the butchered member that seemed no longer to belong to him.

'Look at what you've done to me! Oh, Jesus, Charlotte . . .'

'I eat flesh too, Wesley! What did you expect? It's what the dead do!' She lunged between his legs again to finish her work.

Now the manbeast awakened completely, commandeering Wesley's brain. The jagged paddle stump lay within reach and he went for it, ramming it through the soft flesh beneath the woman's cheekbone. He twisted until he felt the delicate bone inside splinter and crunch, grinding the plastic stub into her skull until he could force it no further. She turned to face him, her remaining eye dribbling from its orbit like a ruined puppet's.

'I don't think this marriage is working for me, Wesley!'

'You tried to bite off my dick!'

'The tribe has spoken! I'm voting you off this island!'

She was on him again, ripping flesh from his face with her nails and teeth, and she kept coming back. He pushed her away in time to see a sun baked flap of his skin disappear into her mouth. But the struggles had weakened her. He grabbed the woman and twisted her in a half nelson against his chest. The easiest thing to go for was her nose, although he couldn't get a firm grip. Wesley tried three times before he managed to chew it off.

Charlotte writhed like a wounded animal and pulled herself free. She backed off from him, covering the gaping cavern in her face with her remaining hand.

The beast found a voice, and now it roared. 'The new nose was nice to look at, babe, but for eating I would have preferred the old one!' Panting heavily, Wesley spit the thin proboscis bone at her. The rest he chewed into peanut-like fragments. He swallowed, sneering at his crippled adversary.

'Say 'goodbye' to your balls, Wesley!' Charlotte growled.

'Tit for tat, Charlotte! Now say 'goodbye' to your tit!' He swiped a haymaker at her, grabbing her limp breast. With one yank he tore it free. His tongue flicked the nipple he held, licking it on all sides. 'Does this feel good, cunt? You used to love when I did this.'

Shoving the fleshy sack into his mouth he chewed, smiling as meaty chunks of pulp spurt from it. Charlotte fingered the lumpy guano inside the deep crater of her chest. With her eyes gone her face revealed almost nothing, but her body shook in violent spasms. Wesley could not tell whether she felt despair or pain. Maybe she wasn't capable of either, but he didn't care. The battle had gone beyond self-serving survival. Now it was about betrayal and humiliation, and this was much worse.

'You're a bastard, Wesley, a real bastard!'

The beast and its host came together as one.

'I'm helping you keep your vow, babe. You're always going to be with me, Charlotte, just like you promised! Right here inside my belly!'

Rallying with renewed strength she threw herself on him, biting and chewing.

Wesley slammed his Rolex against the plastic stub that protruded from Charlotte's face, removing a large jagged slab of crystal. He slashed the shard through the woman's neck, yanking a lengthy strip of meat from it and biting the rest free. In a frenzy of fresh assaults each clawed skin divots from the other, stuffing into mouths whatever shredded flesh they could snatch before going at it again. The stakes had been raised, and if there had been nothing fair in love, then perhaps the scales might balance in war.

Wesley had once vowed that he would die for Charlotte, but he had failed to live up to his promise the first time.

He wasn't going to let that happen again.

His beast would see to that.

*

Brothers Pete and Zack Mulraney were among the several rescue teams dispatched from Maui. The two usually shuttled tourists who flew among the islands, and the pilots knew a thing or two about the area and its surrounding waters. On their third day out they located a small patch of yellow and blue that, on closer inspection, proved a life raft. Seen through a binocular lens from the low flying Cessna there wasn't anything moving on board. Pete brought the small seaplane down to have a look.

A week had passed since the Piper Cub carrying Wesley and Charlotte Donner had been overdue at Honolulu International. News stations ran the heartbreaking wedding video of the pair's moving exchange of vows, and many viewers around the nation had themselves a good cry. After the fifth day the media issued the statement that all hope had been lost for the handsome attorney and his beautiful young bride. The couple's families needed closure, and in deference the search for the two continued.

From the Cessna Pete watched as Zack boarded the raft. At first he didn't quite understand his brother's bizarre signalling gesture that he viewed from the plane's cabin. The man was flailing his arms, beckoning the pilot to join him. Pete decided to check out what was going on.

He disembarked the small plane, climbing on board the life raft to discover that Zack was vomiting.

THE SERVANT
Beth Lewis

He stepped from the shadows, blood of his last release dripping from his fingers. Her smell was still upon him, peach, and strawberry. He savoured her taste, of her hair, of her blood; he relished the moment when the red liquid dropped into his mouth from his hand. Its metallic taste stayed on his tongue long after he'd drunk her life away.

The girl's heart was in his left hand; he tilted his head back and raised the hand above his head. His hand tightened into a fist and blood dropped freely into his open mouth—a second taste. Some of the liquid missed his mouth and fell onto the ground. He lowered his hand, the remaining blood falling onto his black clothes and melting into his body. He threw the heart behind him and wiped his mouth with his sleeve, leaving a smear of red across his face. More blood was needed; his thirst for life had not yet been sated.

Then he saw her, a perfect being of light and innocence; the best kind. The golden curls of her hair tantalizing him; how he wanted to touch the blonde ringlets, how he wanted to be close enough to smell her, her body, her fear.

She looked around and he retreated into the shadows. She looked where he stood for a moment, entranced. A sound; a cat knocking over a dustbin. She looked away. He stepped from the shadows again and looked at her walking away from him; she had a limp, something he didn't expect.

He thought of all the girls he'd tasted, all the cries and screams for help turning quickly to pleas for mercy. He thought of how it felt to put them out of their misery, to stop their pain, their suffering. He wasn't a bad person, he was their saviour; he was their way out, their way to another world, free from pain and heartbreak. Yet their hearts were already broken, already shattered with broken promises and broken dreams; he was there to stop it all. He'd released two people that night, four the previous night and three the night before. With thirst for life, he took other people's to rebuild his own, but it would never be whole again, never be one. He was destined to wander the earth by himself, unable to feel love or hate, an emotionless vessel, a deliverer from evil. Needing the life of others to sustain his own existence. He was not a vampire; he had seen *them* before, unhappy souls unable to see the light of day. He was different; even though he didn't know *what* he was anymore.

His thoughts turned to his past, a life of servitude, of isolation, of fire and of fiends. His master had become dissatisfied with him so cast him from the pits of fire to the world above, not caring for the consequences.

They were dire; he—the outcast—rained chaos on the world for four centuries, leaving a trail of blood and carnage in his wake; he massacred innocent souls and fed on their lifeblood, and he did all this with a smile on his face and a song in his heart. His old master became angry and wrenched the servant from the above world back down to the fiery depths of Hell. The servant was brought before the master, eyes wild and fists clenched.

'Thou art an abomination!' The master had yelled, his deep guttural voice reverberating through the halls of fire.

'Thou art a hypocrite!' The servant shot back, mocking his style of speech. A murmur of surprise rose from the assembled crowd. He struggled to break free of the horned demons that held him, but his efforts were futile and their grips became tighter.

The master eyed the servant. 'How?' He inquired, a smile flickering across his red lips.

'You bring death where there is life yet you cannot accept that another being can kill.' The servant answered, the murmur getting louder. 'Lucifer, Prince of Darkness, you do not deserve those titles. Prince of Flowers! Lord of Daisies more like! I can kill, you cannot, accept it, Devil!' He screamed, beads of sweat running down his forehead. Immediately he regretted it but he knew apologies would do nothing to save his already damned soul.

The master looked at him for a moment, then he stood; the throne behind him, made from bones and blood, slid backwards as its master willed it, shrieking on the polished stage.

'You want to kill?' He said softly, the smile on his face growing wider. He watched his servant nod. 'I'll let you kill,' the smile grew into a maniacal grin.

The servant became wary; not often, if ever, did the master 'let' anyone do anything. The master stepped off his plateau and the whispering crowd fell silent. He walked to the servant and without words ordered the demons to release him. The servant stood his ground and looked at the master. Cold steely glare of the Devil himself did not make the servant yield; it made him hesitant, but that was momentary and soon he regained his confidence.

The smile fell from the master's lips and he raised a clawed hand above the servant's head. He slammed it down on the servant and blood began to pour down his brow and drip onto his bare upper torso. The Devil pulled the servant closer to him and whispered a verse of old scripture:

It is the human soul
The soul of honesty
The soul of purity
The soul of innocence
And the soul of corruption
On these you must feast.

The servant felt his power and confidence drain from him, his limbs became weak and his face became pale. The grin on Beelzebub's face returned, his deed was done.

'You are cast out, but Malek, betray my words and return to the damned,' he said, his deep voice booming around the cavernous halls.

Malek hadn't moved. The blood still running down his face, he looked up to see a shaft of light pouring through a portal in the ceiling of the cavern. The light hit his face and his wounds healed, but the words of Lucifer bound him with immortal strength. His consciousness melted away as the light entered his body, the bright tendrils creeping around inside his being, probing his mind with their perfection. His body soon became completely embraced by the light and it started to devour him, taking it piece by piece. He suddenly became alert; the light had lost its control over his consciousness, and the pain came in waves, easing for a moment then intensifying. He could see nothing but the light and it didn't hurt his eyes. He felt himself disappearing, his legs, and then his hands hanging lifeless by his sides, finally his eyes closed, and the pain stopped.

His eyes opened to a sight his brain had not anticipated; he couldn't see colour, only different shades of grey. His eyes soon became accustomed to the light and the grey shapes came into focus. They were large blocks, buildings? No, the buildings he remembered were small with thatched roofs. How long was I down there? He asked himself, no answers, only questions, so many questions.

Words.

Native words.

Asking for the time. It was the girl he'd seen with the limp, perfect, pure, innocent; his next release. He broke from his memories in time to glance as his wristwatch; it had stopped at six-thirty the previous day.

'Two-forty five am,' he lied. 'Very late for such a pretty thing like you to be out,' he said to her, the metallic rasp of his seldom-used voice echoing around the darkened streets.

She looked at him for a moment, his colourless eyes mesmerizing her, keeping her still, keeping her pure. She blinked, mumbled a few words of thanks, and began to walk away.

He remembered the words of Lucifer, the pure and innocent; that was her. She was perfection itself apart from the limp, a minor setback, but something that wouldn't affect the process. Her limp slowed her down and gave him time to think; this one was the purest, and she would be his last.

The hunger came; he could feel it moving through his body, commanding his limbs and nerves to do its bidding. The hunger was like a separate being, dwelling in the back of his mind for days, sometimes weeks until he saw purity, then the hunger would arise and take over his senses, demanding his hands to tear and his mouth to drink.

The girl wasn't far from him, maybe ten to fifteen metres. He stepped forward, edging closer. She moved very slowly and even when moving stealthily, weaving in and out of the shadows, he closed the gap between them. He stood behind her, mirroring her movements so he could not be seen. His icy breath fell on the nape of her neck and a shiver swept down her spine.

She looked around. Nothing. When she turned back her face hit his, his gaunt, emaciated face, the hollow cheeks emphasized by the moonlight bouncing from his stretched skin. The dark pools of his eyes, seen many a celestial battle, probed her, searching inside her with his mind, looking for some kind of corruption so a release was unnecessary. He found none; this one was perfect.

She turned away from him and took her first step. He slid a sinewy arm around her neck and pulled her tight to his chest. He clamped his other hand tightly on the girl's mouth, stifling her screams. His cold breath fell on her shuddering form and he tightened his grip.

'This is your release,' he whispered, his once demure voice turned harsh over centuries of silence.

He slowly removed his hand from her mouth, ' . . . please . . . don't . . . ' she pleaded through sobs and shuddering breaths.

His hand went to her mouth again and he felt the wetness of her tears. The time had come. He stroked her face and hair, his raw eyes looking into her mind, probing her inner self, and looking for an excuse. Again he found nothing; he had a soul pieced together by others' pain; she would complete his puzzle and return his soul to humanity's wing.

'Don't scream, this won't take long,' he mumbled dreamily, revelling in the reality of his own release.

Still with his hand over her mouth he walked her into the shadows. She heard a creak and a rectangle of orange candlelight hit the cold stone pavement, warming it for a moment before the door was slammed shut behind the couple. The pavement, cold again, waited for the noises. It could hear them, through the ground, through the air.

The light came from nearly two hundred white candles dotted sporadically about the abandoned warehouse. It was empty apart from the candles and a large stone slab in the centre. Atop the slab were many varied implements of ruthless torture; she saw them and tried to scream, but his strong hands muffled her voice.

'Don't scream,' he repeated.

He bent down and picked up a piece of long black rope and bound her hands behind her back. He took his hand from her mouth momentarily before gagging her with a black handkerchief.

He pushed her to the hard, grey floor and went to the stone table. He cleared it, pushing the knives, cleavers, saws, and maces to the ground. He held one knife in his hand, its hilt adorned with moonstones. Cradling it as if it were a baby placed it gently on the slab. He went to the girl, her face was red, and her cries were loud, only muffled by the thin black cloth. He stared into her puffy eyes, small red lines, like creepers edging closer to her irises, asphyxiating her pupils.

He grabbed her golden hair and pulled her to her feet. He dragged her roughly to the table, her legs flailing in the air. He moved away and looked at her, she was trembling, and her hair was in disarray; her tear soaked face pleaded to him without words. She was perfect.

He went to her, embracing her, leaned in to her, his nose touching hers; she looked away and he breathed in her ear. 'This is it. Your final moments, make them glorious.'

His breath came in short bursts. He was laughing. The tears welled in her eyes as his laughs got louder. Then he stopped and looked back at her, an expression of disgust on his face. He ran a clammy hand through her hair not caring about knots or tangles. He pushed her onto the table and clasped a hand around his knife. He lifted the weapon to his mouth and ran his tongue along the silver blade, tasting its perfection, gave a shudder of pleasure.

The girl struggled, edging closer to the side of the table. He saw her and dropped his hand to his side. She was on her stomach and by the time he reached her, her head was over the slab, facing the ground. He curled his lip and ran his hand over her underside; he stopped at her belly, pushing his hand into her. She tipped over onto her back to the centre of the slab. Her eyes were red but the tears kept coming.

He cocked his head to one side, looking at her, then to the other side; he gave a grunt of approval and lifted the knife to her leg. The knife ran along her milky white skin, a line of red left in its wake. He untied her hands and parted them; he re-tied them to two steel rings fastened to each side of the slab and did the same with her legs. Spread-eagled and held chaste on the cold, stone slab, her body, convulsed with sobs, strained against the shackles that bound her. The cut he'd made on her leg bled onto her skirt, staining the pure white forever. The top button of her blouse was undone; he looked at it then sliced the other buttons off. As he pulled the blouse apart exposing her breasts, his eyes widened. He looked at her for a moment before raising the knife above his head.

She closed her eyes, the tears had stopped; she had given up. Her body stopped moving and she lay still on the slab, her chest heaving, but her body calmed. She didn't want to see the satisfaction on his face when her eyes clouded over; she clamped her eyelids shut, urging him to continue, urging him to get it over with.

As if reading her thoughts he plunged the knife into her mid-section. Her eyes sprung open and the muscles in her stomach contracted, leaving her sitting up, her arms pinned to the table and blood pouring from the open wound; she tried to scream. Her muscles relaxed and she slumped back onto the table. The blood welled in the centre of her stomach, a pool of red creating rivulets as it ran down her sides onto the slab, joining the blood from her leg.

He stood, admiring his handiwork; lifted the knife to his mouth and licked the blood from its blade as the helpless girl lay bleeding to death. He placed the knife on the slab and climbed up; straddled the girl and arched his back so his mouth was level with the blood that spilled freely from her trembling stomach. Lapped up the liquid, leaving the wound clean; he locked his mouth to the cut and drank at her life. Stopping he straightened his back, raised his arms to the air and mumbled a few obscure words, followed by a roar of delight. He looked back at her, eyes wild, face dripping with her blood. He'd slaked his thirst and now he could enjoy her release.

Still with his knees either side of her, he put the tip of the knife to her throat and dragged it down between her breasts to meet the wound at her belly. A thin red trail of her blood ran down her body. A few muffled screams escaped the gag as the moments to her death became less and less. He leaned over her again, his tongue dancing along the cut. She was still alive, but for how much longer was up to him.

Climbing down from the slab and taking the knife in his left hand, he went to her feet. He gazed up between her legs, held entranced by the wondrous sight. The girl had been menstruating; this was even better. As he slid the knife up the side of her thigh; a rough scratch was etched in the perfect, untouched skin. He slid the knife higher, stopped, then thrust the bloodstained blade into her body; torrents of crimson liquid came forth; he left the knife in place. He dipped his fingers in the blood; tasting it, he shivered. This was the pure lifeblood, something he had been searching for decades.

Her eyes lifeless, her body still. She had lost too much blood and would be dead in a few minutes. The line he'd drawn with the knife had stopped bleeding. He reached behind him and yanked the blade from the flesh that held it, spilling more blood. Her life was seeping away; he held the knife on high again and drove it into her throat, pulling it down the cut on her chest. Red froth poured from her mouth. A last gurgle and her eyes rolled back, her head lolled to one side. He licked the blood from around and inside her mouth. Saliva goes well with the scarlet liquid.

He drank the blood from her upper torso, leaving a clean red line. He drank the blood from between her legs, shuddering with every mouthful.

After he licked her clean, he clasped the moonstone-encrusted hilt of the bloodied knife. He carved a runic symbol in her stomach. His mark to make sure Satan was watching.

Then he heard the sirens and saw the red and blue flashing lights through the dirty window. The door he and the girl had entered started splintering under the weight of the police battering ram, then came from its hinges in a cloud of shards and dust as he slipped silently through the back.

As the police came flooding through the shattered remains of the door they saw the girl and the blood splattered slab. They found the stained knife but no fingerprints. Fuzzy radio reports sounded throughout the warehouse, muffled words from detective to detective stating the obvious. The girl had been murdered; the girl was young; her name, age, and a list of other victims. Long grey trench coats huddled around the table poking at the girl and lifting the discarded weapons from the floor, placing them in plastic bags for future evidence. It was all too routine, too familiar, too rehearsed. The trench coats muttered something and vacated the warehouse. A forensic team was brought in to analyse blood samples. Everything was normal.

Malek, he, the servant, walked silently down the alley behind the warehouse, a smile on his lips and a smear of blood across his face.

'Thou art an abomination!' The master had yelled, his deep guttural voice reverberating through the halls of fire.

It is the human soul
The soul of honesty
The soul of purity
The soul of innocence
And the soul of corruption
On these you must feast.

The Master had bound him to an earthly life devouring the spirits of the pure and the gentle. Sated now on the last of these, Malek, who had been the servant, now felt ready to plunge again into the true world of his master.

The centuries of penury were at an end, and now at last he could return until the next generation of innocence was born.

PEARLS FOR TEARS
Ian Harding

When he was alive he'd been called Billy. Now the old lady was gone there was no one to call him anything at all.

He watched the door from the shadows at the top of the staircase, the dust settling through him, wearing the stillness of the house like tailored clothes. He'd been standing at the top of the stairs for the better part of a week. Down the flight, past the mottled mirror in the lower hall, was the front door.

People were coming; sooner or later people always came.

The key rattled in the lock and he crouched back behind the banister and listened. Now he couldn't see the door—only the ribcage of light and shadow on the landing wall. Slats of sunlight and shade fell over his face. The shadow was warm and soft, like duck-down. The light—what little there was left in the day—burned him like frost. He held one of the uprights to steady himself. The wood was still alive, though barely, and if he listened hard enough he could hear it whispering in a green, teeming voice.

The door opened and he tasted outside air almost immediately. In it flooded carrying unexpected scents, like the day had breathed into the house. He smelled dry leaves and gutter mould. Dustbins. A fox. The reek of sweat and perfume mixed.

Then there were voices, two of them, thundering up through the hallway spaces. Billy listened with dread and fascination. Recently there had been the voices of the doctor and the undertaker. Before that, nothing but Eleanor's voice for twenty years or more.

'I thought she died in hospital,' a man said idly.

'No, she died in her bedroom upstairs,' a woman replied.

'Heart, was it?'

'Yes—she had angina for years. It was the cream. She had a weakness for it—said she couldn't help herself.'

The woman's voice was difficult to listen to. It was all secrets and mockery. It made him think of long white fingers that pinch hard; rooks at dusk.

The man again, tired and distracted: 'I'd like a drink. How about you?'

'If you like,' she said vaguely, her attention elsewhere.

'Did she keep any drink in this place?' the man asked.

'How should I know? There's the kitchen. Go and see.'

Footfalls moved away. Then after a time: ' . . . nothing in the fridge but mould.'

'Then try the cupboards.'

The first stair creaked as someone eased their weight onto it. Billy's attention snapped back to the woman: she was coming. His heart galloped. He felt like breathing himself into the air, disappearing behind the dust. Perhaps he could find some cobwebby corner where he'd never be found. Anywhere would do; anything to escape this woman's presence.

The man came back to the foot of the stairs. His voice was close again.

'Nothing there at all,' he said. He sounded truculent, like a child. 'Dry as bones.'

'Have you tried the living-room?' the woman suggested. 'Could be a drinks cabinet in there. Maybe she kept something medicinal stashed away for those winter evenings.' Her falsetto laugh slit the air.

The man went away again. A door opened; closed.

The woman moved on up the stairs. Billy could hear her heart churning heavily in her chest, the cartilage in her knees creaking.

She reached the half-landing and negotiated the turn of the stairs. There was a small round window here where the flight doglegged back on itself before rising again. There was a clear October sky beyond the glass—like someone had hung a blue plate against the wallpaper. The woman's profile passed the window and her shadow flickered over the upper landing, like a blink after a clap.

Billy saw the dome of her head—gloss of black hair tight against the scalp, the light lying over it like a shard of rainbow. Another step and he could see her bone-pale face, her eyes painted peacock-bright. Her suit was an uncertain tan and ash colour, like lichen on a church wall. Her shoulder bag was the colour of sunburn.

Seeing her was too much; the spell holding Billy broke, and he fled.

She stopped and frowned. 'Hello?'

There was nothing but the deep hush of the old house; still air in the empty upper rooms.

She adjusted her bag strap with a quick shrug. 'Hello?' she said again, and waited.

Billy was hiding under the teak table against the wall. Had she seen him dive for cover? A smear of movement in the dust or a stirring in the nap of the rug? He peered out between the spindly table legs at the gloss on her shoes.

She opened the door to a room that smelled of the elderly, and her face withered in disgust: lavender water and slippers with an aroma like fried fish skins and a mattress gone bad with age and denture cream.

She'd found it: the room where the old woman had died.

The man's voice came up from below: 'You there, Katryn?'

'I'm here,' she replied, pausing in the doorway. She was standing in the light but peering into gloom. She picked out the shapes of bed, wardrobe, dresser. There was a picture above the bed, but she couldn't make out the detail.

The man was climbing the stairs now. Billy watched him come. He was stout and bullish, and everything about him was the colour of coffee and nicotine: hair, skin, jacket. He was carrying two glasses, one in each hand, with dark liquid rolling around in them.

Billy smelt Eleanor's rum and felt a wrench of loss. She used to drink three capfuls before bed every night. He shut his eyes and saw her in her nightgown, her hair brushed out long and plush. She'd uncork the bottle and carefully drip out a measure—told him it brought her sound slumbers and sweet dreams.

'Drink?' the man said, holding out the glass.

It was like she hadn't heard him; like she didn't know he was there. Her attention was lost in the bedroom gloom. It held her in thrall, her face greedy.

'Katryn? Hello?'

'What can you smell?' she asked suddenly.

Mindful of the drinks, he leaned in through the doorway and took a theatrical sniff.

'Perfume and piss,' he said flatly.

'I smell opportunity.' She nodded, still infatuated with the gloom. 'Don't you? Opportunity.'

He repeated his performance: leaned forward, sniffed.

'Still piss,' he sighed. 'You want your drink or not?'

She pirouetted to face him, anger giving her deadly speed. There was anger in her thin mouth; anger in her fists.

'Why are you here, Nathan?' she breathed. 'Why are you here when you've nothing interesting to say? Remind me, please. I think I've forgotten.'

Her anger caught him by surprise. His shoulders sagged. He stepped past her into the room, hoping to escape her attention.

'Well?'

He looked back at her, couldn't withstand her gaze, and looked away again.

'You asked me to come, remember? Said you were looking for something.'

She sighed. 'Stupid of me—thinking you'd be helpful.'

'Helpful?'

'There's treasure here, Nathan.'

He looked puzzled. 'What are you talking about now?'

'I'm talking about a family rumour.'

'You mean the old woman, don't you?' he asked.

'Smart boy,' she said, rewarding him with a smile.

'What have you heard?' he went on. There was something new in his voice. An eagerness.

'Like I said—a rumour.'

'Such as?'

She surfaced from her thoughts and stretched out a hand.

'I'd like that drink now—if you wouldn't mind.'

He pushed the glass through the air and the liquid plopped.

'You will help me, won't you?' she said, taking the drink.

'You want me to look for something? What is it? Money?'

'You're warm,' she said, playing an old game now.

'Jewellery?'

'Much warmer.'

'Stones?'

'Pearls,' she said, with some hunger. 'The finest you've ever seen.'

*

A light went on. Billy looked up and saw the strangers were now in Eleanor's bedroom, straying where they shouldn't. He could smell their greed; it was there in the sweat behind their knees, in the crooks of their elbows.

He went to the door and looked in. They were quietly and methodically taking the old lady's room apart. He watched their bent backs. The man was over by the bed, stripping back the sheets, pulling the pillows away. The woman was at the dresser, lifting little bottles and sniffing at them before dropping them into the wicker wastebasket.

He couldn't bear the sight of it and had to look away. He saw the round window above the half-landing. The sky was darkening outside. Evening was coming on.

Good. He was stronger at night.

*

They began searching the bedroom.

Katryn saw Nathan wrenching at bed linen, his spine a determined arch.

She went to the dresser and pulled open the first of four drawers. Bed socks. Pop socks. Emery boards. She pawed impatiently past the irrelevant items and then checked herself, knowing it would be too easy to miss something. The plunging sensation in her belly was dread of failure. Less speed more haste. She started again from the beginning.

She slid the drawer free of the dresser and set it on the floor. This time she searched more methodically. She used both hands: exploring, testing, moving on. She began to enjoy the act of revealing so many little stowed and stashed things.

Nothing in the first drawer, or the second, or the third. In the fourth she found a nest of ivory-coloured jewellery boxes under a layer of folded silk scarves and thought the search was over.

She opened the boxes one by one, pinching away tufts of cotton wool to reveal cheap trinkets, gaudy broaches, clumsy rings, three-for-a-quid market bargains. God, some of it was even plastic. She tasted the ashes of defeat and her search grew frantic. Where had the old fool hidden them?

In the last box she found a small key that she lifted into the light. It was old and short in the barrel, with a flange like a notched tooth. She would have cast it aside if it hadn't been for the chain it was threaded on. A fine gold chain with a good clasp; the most valuable item she'd found so far.

She was weighing the key and chain in her palm when Nathan began to chuckle.

He was down on his knees by the bed. 'Jackpot!' he said, moving aside to show her what he'd found.

It was a suitcase. Inside it was a sea of photographs. Countless moments taken from the old woman's life and stored in the dark under the bed. A life Katryn knew nothing about. She saw familiar faces and the faces of strangers. Here was her grandfather, immaculate in his regimental uniform. Here he was again, this time with *her*, his hot new flame—the woman he'd left her mother for. Katryn supposed she'd been attractive once, in a dark gypsy-wild way.

But it wasn't the photographs Nathan was excited about. It was the money. In among the snaps there were notes, and plenty of them.

'How much?' she asked. He had notes in his fists—wads thick as card decks.

'Couple of grand so far.' He gave her a toothy leer. 'There's a lot more here.'

The next moment, something changed in the room—a widening quiet. They looked up and hooked each other's startled gaze.

The clock over by the door had stopped. The pendulum twitched and was still.

'No one to wind it,' Nathan commented, half to himself, and went back to counting the money.

Katryn nodded, eyeing the clock.

'What was the old woman's name?' Nathan asked. The photographs had piqued his curiosity.

'Eleanor Crosses.'

'Did you know her well?'

'Know her? I never talked to her, not in all those years. Why would I want to?' She fell silent, then found she had more to say. Bits of history; bits of opinion. She let it come. 'After Dad left my mother, he tried to bring the Crosses woman into the family, but no one wanted to know. Mother kept us away, said the woman was bad news. She was absolute about it.'

Nathan, counting the notes and whispering figures, nodded for her to go on.

'When Dad moved in with her, my mother and her sisters made a sort of protective circle, with all us cousins in the middle, safe. They were outraged, I supposed. They wanted to make her an outsider, freeze her out, hoped she'd disappear.

'But she and Dad grew strong instead. He told me once they were like two old trees—they had different roots, but their branches were entwined.'

Nathan pondered this. 'Did they ever marry, your dad and this Crosses woman?'

'Apparently.' She hesitated. 'The marriage certificate's in the drawer there. I had no idea.'

Nathan rocked back on his heels. Counting cash had made his eyes bright.

'Four and a half exactly,' he announced, his knees popping as he stood up. There were handsome towers of notes at his feet. 'I think this deserves a little celebration,' he grinned. 'Fancy another drink?'

She mirrored his grin. He gathered the empty glasses and left for the stairs.

When the quiet had settled again, Katryn stood up and crossed the room to the clock. There she stood, face to face with it.

*

The boy was standing in the doorway of Eleanor's bedroom. The day was dying outside the landing window. Dust settled through him and through the darkening air.

There was Eleanor's bed in the corner, rucked and all awry—like a storm had unmade it. Billy made the bed again from his memories, smoothing out the counterpane and folding it down, plumping the pillow and placing on it the cotton lavender-bag shaped like a heart.

This woman—this *Katryn*—was holding Eleanor's key in her hand. He could hear it inside her fist, scratching like a cricket against its chain. He was shocked that she'd found it with such apparent ease. And now she'd turned her attention to the clock.

The shaded bulb threw a circle of light on the carpet. He moved into the brightness and watched her. But it wasn't the stranger he saw: it was Eleanor. His memory was at play again, stacking up the details of her face, her clothes, her hands, until she moved in front of him again, and spoke.

'Child,' she said to him—but how long ago? Ten years? Twenty? 'I'm an old lady now. It's a peculiar place to find yourself, at the end of your given time, and it's a peculiar road that brings you there.' She was at the window, the sun behind her head. 'One day soon I'm going to walk the last staircase to the great gates and there I'm going to put my soul into the hands of the Keeper. Because, child, my soul is precious. Did you know that there's a story behind every precious thing? It's the story that makes them precious. Come here. Let me show you something . . .'

She slid open a drawer of the dresser. In the drawer was a box. From this she took a key on a chain and threaded it into the lock of the clock on the wall.

'I was fourteen when my father took our family to Africa. He was the kind of stern preacher you don't hear about in this country any more—always in his robes, even in that terrible heat.

'God had shown him a place in a dream—a harsh and beautiful place by the sea. A place to start a mission and do the good work. Within two months we were living in a village called Owayla-sula by the bluest ocean I have ever seen—and, my child, I was as lonely as the last star in the sky.

'I fell in love with a boy from the village called Dwabiliba from the first moment I saw him. Child, he put hummingbird's wings in my heart and they fluttered every time he came near. He didn't speak any English and I'd only just arrived—I didn't know any of the singsong wild words of the village. We talked by drawing pictures in the dust with sticks. It was like he'd stepped out of a dream. Sometimes he does that now, you know—steps out of my dreams.

'He took me down to the shore where his father was making a fishing boat from *hsaula* grass. He showed me his family's most valuable possession: the fishing net drying in the sun. He pointed to the ring of deep holes under his father's arm and drew a shark in the sand. Then he sat me down by the high-tide line among the shells and the sharp seaweed and ran into the sea.

'Out he swam and the sea was alive with light. He swam so far that I got to thinking bad things—the sight of all that endless water, and his precious body rising and falling in it.

'Then he was gone. He wasn't there at all. It was dreadful—to think I'd lost him to the sea. But no. There he was up again, splashing and waving.

'He came out of the water with a shell. I don't know how he opened it, but he did—and he put a pearl in my hand. I remember we both looked at it for a long time. I couldn't breathe. Then he was up and off again, back into the sea.

'Ten times he swam out and came back with a shell, sometimes two of them, opening them and putting pearls in my hand. Then he'd go back to the sea again. Eventually it got dark and we went back to the village. But we returned the next day, and the day after that, and each time he brought me pearls until, by the end of the week, there were enough. I had to cup both my hands to hold them all.

'One day he took all the pearls and just walked away—wouldn't let me follow. I waited all morning and on into the afternoon, hour after hour.

'He came back at sundown, the sky all gold and red with evening. When

I'm alone, child, and the house is quiet, I think about that evening. Words aren't enough. I can't tell you how magical it was.

'He kissed me twice, here and here, on my temples. His hands were together like this, and I swear they looked like they were filled with moonlight.'

Eleanor took something from the suede pouch. Her hands were cupped secretively at her breast.

'Here, child. Look.'

The boy stepped closer and saw a string of pearls like beads of silver moonlight.

'He brought them out of the ocean for me,' she said, and sighed. 'Then we came back to England and my Dwabiliba was gone behind me. I have never wept so deeply or for so long. These are pearls for my tears, child.'

*

Katryn had found the pearls. She could barely believe her luck. The pearls! She hid the pouch back inside the clock and took Eleanor's pearls over to the shaded bulb to study them. The light was thin and unglamorous, but still the beauty of them silvered the air. She was holding in her hand the stuff of family legend. As a child she'd heard her mother and her aunts talking about the Crosses woman's secret pearls. How the tramp had come by them, damn her. How beautiful they were, damn her. How priceless they were, damn her again.

And here they were in her hand. Her hand!

She jumped like a cat when Nathan shouldered open the door and came in with the drinks.

'Ah, there you are,' she purred, recovering quickly. Her hand moved behind her back.

'You found them, didn't you?' he said, watching her face.

'No,' she said, her voice tragic, and dropped the pearls into her bag. 'I don't think they're here at all.'

'If they're as fine as you say they are, we have to keep looking.'

She nodded; shrugged; looked away.

'You can't possibly know they're *not* here?' he went on.

He was right, of course. She couldn't know that; stupid to pretend it. She stepped past him and out onto the landing.

'Where are you going?' he wanted to know.

In front of her was a door; one she hadn't tried yet. She turned the handle and pushed, but the door resisted. She wanted to be out of Nathan's presence; he was watching her, she could feel it, putting his awkward questions together.

It was a spare room. Inside was a mini mountain of junk. A threadbare couch; a disembowelled pouffe. Pictures slumped in their frames. Boxes leaked papers. Carrier bags spilled bric-a-brac. There were dried flowers scattered over the floor. A dusty birdcage lay by a heap of shoes. A tailor's dummy with a feather boa around its shoulders reclined on a mattress of old gas bills.

Nathan joined her in the doorway. They surveyed the chaos together.

'What are you thinking about?' he asked.

'Fire,' she replied softly. 'Let's burn her memory out of this place, Nathan.'

He was quick to catch on. 'Burn her things?' he said. 'But we shouldn't. That would be—'

'Nathan,' she said, turning to him. 'She's dead and gone and past caring.' Her attention went back into the room, skipping from box to bag to bloom. 'Imagine it, cleansing the family of her name. Burning out those bad memories. Why don't we do what mother and her sisters never could?'

He studied her in the growing shadows. 'I've never heard you speak like this before,' he said.

'I've never felt like this before.' She leaned close, like she meant to kiss him. Instead he got a whisper. 'You will help me, won't you?'

*

Billy was sitting on the sill of the round window halfway up the stairs, his heart churning with grief and anger. Night inked the glass. His tears ran in abundance, dry as dust.

Katryn and Nathan were removing Eleanor's belongings from the lumber-room and bringing them down the stairs box by box. Candles lit their labours now; the bulbs in the hallway's light fitting were dead. The stairs and landing and hallway danced with a dozen points of light, making the house seem only half real—like the place was asleep and dreaming of itself. One of the candles flickered on the windowsill next to Billy's elbow.

Minutes ago the electricity supply had clicked off. Nathan found the meter under the stairs, but had no change to get the current going again—and Katryn didn't carry cash.

Billy watched Nathan emerge backwards from the room. He was hefting a box stuffed with papers and files—a difficult weight, almost too much for him. The muscles of his forearms and thighs were quivering and the sweat on his brow looked like beads of mercury in the candlelight.

He went to the head of the stairs and started down the flight one unsteady step at a time, painstakingly cautious, peering over the top of the box to check his route.

Billy watched Nathan come closer. He negotiated the turn of the stairs. The man was already panting like a dog in the sun.

There was a moment of pure panic when he came within touching distance. Billy's thoughts flew apart and took wing like gulls. With his head full of bedlam, he lashed out with all his meagre will . . . and the candle burning under his knee went out.

Darkness; a grunt of surprise. There was a beat of silence—then the box hit the stairs with enough force to send a bass-note through the whole house. The contents exploded in an avalanche. A sea of old papers and letters, pamphlets and documents tumbled down the stairs and fetched up on the parquet tiles of the hallway.

A short while later a light flickered and Katryn appeared at the foot of the stairs. She was holding a wineglass in which a stub of red candle burned. She raised the glass and toasted his clumsiness, eyed the devastation. She didn't say a word, just lowered her glass again and stepped out of sight.

Billy left the window and followed Katryn to the open back door where the night was pressing in. A breeze moved through him into the house, carrying an aroma of damp bricks and wild growing things. He could hear leaves stirring; a dog barked, miles away.

Katryn was out there somewhere, busy in the darkness. He could sense the hatred that lent urgency to her work. What was she doing, out there in the night?

Curiosity overcame him—he had to see. But he lingered on the threshold for a long time.

He'd not stepped out of the house since the evening the plane had fallen howling out of the sky and demolished the Methodist Chapel on Momus Road. He'd stood with Eleanor in the crowd at the edge of the smoking pit and pointed at the swastikas on the broken wings.

*

Katryn was building a bonfire by the fence at the end of the garden. For fuel she was using Eleanor's belongings. A bed of letters under a layer of shoes; the tailor's dummy crowning the pyre, still in its boa. The fire wasn't lit but the time for burning was close.

Standing in the oblong of light spilling from the back door, Billy watched her at work—a dark figure bending to her task, her face a pale smear. She looked like a wraith. The autumn night was doing nothing to cool her passion.

Watching her made Billy angry like nothing he'd known before—a cruel anger that scorched and maddened. Iridescence moved through him in waves the colour of salmon jumping in sunlight. He'd lost his fingers; in their place, ribbons of substance bled from his hands and corkscrewed away into the night. The light of the stars scorched his brow and chirruped in his head like insects.

His fury was undoing him.

At that moment, Nathan emerged from the house with another box. He picked and grunted his way across the yard and the garden to the fire, where he let his load fall. He and Katryn didn't speak. He turned and made his way back into the house for more combustibles.

Billy had observed their greed and their casual hatred long enough. His fury ignited. He went back through the kitchen, through the light and shadow to the foot of the stairs. How could he flush these thieves out of Eleanor's house for good? His ambition made him seethe with dark excitement. But how to do it? He moved listlessly up the stairs, not knowing how to put his will to work.

Eleanor's room still held the silence that had settled in after her last breath. He looked at her empty bed, and thought about her laughter and her songs and the stories she told him after dark. Silence didn't belong here.

He saw Katryn's shoulder bag slung from the door handle—and he saw what he had to do and how he would do it.

Nathan was back at work in the lumber-room across the landing. He was thumping around, gathering items to burn, grinding things underfoot. His grim animal reek had curdled the upstairs air.

Billy set himself to work. He bowed his head and raked in his thoughts and pressed them into smaller and smaller space until they shone bright and powerful.

He took hold of Katryn's bag and felt its horrible weight. He was sure the task was beyond him and thought about abandoning it. But Eleanor chose that moment of doubt to show him her beautiful smile and her brittle hands.

He thought about the sheer quantity of time that they'd spent together, the days falling around them like pollen, the stack of years. She'd opened up her life, invited him inside, shared her sights—and what greater gift was there to give? What greater, deeper gift?

Katryn's bag seemed to unhitch itself from the handle and climb the gloomy air. He hauled it higher and up it went until it hung among the ceiling shadows. He kept it there, hanging on his thought, and marvelled at how easy this was, how effortless, now he had the trick of it.

Then he let the bag go, and down it dropped. It struck the carpet with a thump and lay there like a dead thing.

But it was enough. The sound of Nathan's labours stopped.

'Katryn?' came his call from across the landing. 'That you?'

Billy delved into the bag, past a purse and a pack of paper handkerchiefs, sunglasses, cigarettes, car-keys. He made as much noise as he could, rummaging, spilling things. He sensed Nathan's presence looming behind him as he found the pearls.

From the doorway now, a whisper: 'Katryn?'

Billy tugged the string of pearls out of hiding and arranged them on the carpet to make them obvious. Just as Nathan came round the door, he retreated.

The man stopped, looking down. Frowning, he lowered himself to his haunches and plucked the pearls from among the other items. He held them in his palm and tested their weight. He looked from the pearls to the bag and back again. His frown deepened and decorated his forehead like the lashes of a whip.

When he stood up his frown had gone—replaced by a look of dawning understanding.

Billy flew. Out the door he went and down the stairs. He threaded himself through the banisters in his joy. He reached the lower hallway and arrowed into the kitchen. There in the open doorway, at the edge of the night, he stopped.

The yard was alive with firelight. Katryn had lit the bonfire and the flames were growing great, flinging their light across the garden and against the back of the house. Every brick and leaf danced.

Seeing the flames pained him, actually *pained* him. They were spitting sparks high into the heavens where they seemed to join the stars. Katryn's face was demented with glee, daubed all in flickering orange.

Behind Billy, Nathan voiced his fury: 'Katryn!'

It was a huge shout, almost unnatural, like the house itself had spoken.

Her reverie broke and she glanced back at the doorway.

There was a child standing in the yard, not twenty feet from where the fire burned. A little boy of eight or nine and naked as a newborn. His skin was grey as ashes. She gaped at the tips of his fingers and the crown of his head where the stuff of him, the substance, was bleeding away into the night.

They looked at each other through the tips of the flames. Then the boy turned away and walked into the house, trailing his mysteries, and he was gone. Katryn blinked. The flames hissed and rose. She moved cautiously around the perimeter of the fire and, without taking her eyes from the door, started after him.

Nathan was waiting for her at the top of the stairs. His face was pure fury. He dangled Eleanor's pearls in front of her face.

'I found these,' he said with dreadful patience.

She glanced at the pearls but didn't really see them. He face was dead, like her voice.

'Did you see . . .?' she began, then ran out of words.

He made the pearls dance. 'They were in your bag, Katryn.'

'No. Listen. I saw—'

'No, *you* listen. You thought you'd hide them from me, didn't you? Keep them hidden. You damned deceitful—'

'I followed him in. Did you see him?'

'Such a bitch of a liar.'

'The strangest thing I've ever seen, Nathan.'

But Nathan was no longer seeing her. It was the pearls that held his gaze.

'I trusted you,' he told her. 'How can anything be the same again?'

*

Back out in the night, Billy stepped into the bonfire. It wasn't heat he felt, but a wonderful coolness—autumn after a sultry summer. The flames touched and soothed him like running water. He knew that if he lingered too long he'd be lulled to sleep by the flap of the flames, and that wouldn't do. He had a task now.

He cast his thoughts around him, scooping together burning items. Every piece of blackening paper. Every smoking shoe. The bubbling remains of the tailor's dummy. The bright embers. He raked them all together and held them in his mind until he was dressed in fire from crown to toe. The effort of it made him sob.

He started back across the garden to the house.

The fire walked through the open doorway into Eleanor's kitchen. Linoleum blistered where it trod. The ceiling blackened above it. Curtains burst into flame at the windows. So did the embroidered cloth spread over the breakfast table. The apron hung on the back of the door. Little withstood the heat for long, and soon the kitchen was spectacularly ablaze.

Billy came to the foot of the stairs and went no further. His strength was gone. With a last lash of his will he burst the fire in all directions, showering flame over carpets and walls and furniture. The flames took hold wherever they fell, feasting with astonishing greed, and the hallway became a blinding kiln of heat.

Billy turned his back on the flames and went to the front door. Behind him the fire swelled with a sound like a high wind in trees. Perhaps those were shouts he heard in the din; perhaps not. And what did it matter now, anyway? Just noise within noise and nothing more.

He teased himself through the hair-fine cracks in the door and poured himself through the keyhole, and found himself standing on a path leading to a gate and beyond.

Behind him, the lower windows were filling up with what looked like lantern light. Ahead there was nothing but the wide night, vast and fabulous enough to hold every dream and memory.

What possible places were out there, waiting to be found? What possible haunts?

He said good-bye to Eleanor, and went to greet them.

THE VENETIAN BLIND
Pierre Louys

'Well, here is my secret,' she said to me, at last. 'As you seem so anxious to know, my dear, I will enlighten you, this evening, as to the reason I have never wished to marry.

'Your question shows more affection than the silence of others, into which I read sometimes so many injurious reservations. It is a fact that every one knows of the wealth of my family in all its branches; and when a rich girl does not marry it is always because she is vain, ambitious, ugly, or immoral: people are at perfect liberty to assume one or other of these suppositions in order to pass judgment on my life, if they do not, in their charity, adopt all four at once.

'Believe me, I did not refuse my suitors on their own account. It was the mere husband, the male, the official or unofficial lover, whom I shunned with a sort of terror which is only just beginning to subside now that my fortieth year has me in its safe keeping . . . Don't make any guesses yet; my story is not one of an unfortunate love-affair; no, no, I have never loved; I grew old too soon, one evening, when I was seventeen . . .

'Listen. The tale will not be long.

'After all . . . perhaps you will hardly understand why an event so trite, so much a matter of common knowledge, robbed my life of all the pleasures I might have experienced in days. It was such an incident as is reported in newspaper paragraphs: you can read of such things on the third page of every paper, and it is not even the case that I took part in the scene which I am going to describe to you. If in my solitary existence I have shuddered over it for so long, that is because I saw the thing happen with my own eyes, within a yard of me. You, who will hear it as an anecdote, will feel nothing of what I felt.'

*

Mademoiselle N. leaned her forehead upon her hand and began as follows, her eyes fixed upon the ground, without once looking up at me:

'Twenty-five years ago my mother and myself were living in an old-fashioned private house in the shadow of Saint-Sulpice. It was quite an ordinary house: no courtyard or out-buildings; all the windows looked out onto the street, which was, however, as quiet as a path in a forest.

'One midsummer night it was stiflingly hot in my room, and I could not sleep. I did not dare to open my window for fear of waking my mother. After an hour of insomnia, I got up, put on my slippers, and, in only my nightgown, went down the great staircase to the drawing-room on the ground floor.

'Here . . . but you must clearly understand the situation of the drawing-room. The house had once had a garden which also ran parallel with the street. This property had been sold to builders, and the Council had taken over part of it for roadwidening purposes. Accordingly, one window of the drawingroom opened upon a dark corner, in a recess, a mysterious and gloomy spot where the rays of the street-lamps did not penetrate.

'On entering the room I observed that this window had not been shut. The venetian blinds only had been closed. Faint with the heat and nearly suffocating I climbed up on the ledge, held on to the slanting laths of the blind with the tips of my fingers, and inhaled the delicious freshness of the night air with the whole of my body, from head to foot.

'That was the last moment of unalloyed pleasure I have ever had.

'I had not been there a minute when a couple appeared on the other side of the street.

'The man drew the girl into the secret shadows of the corner. He was a sham workman, one of those who work three weeks and loaf six months for the reason that their good looks enable them to despise honest labour. Her I recognized at once. She was a girl of fifteen to whom my mother had been very kind, and who was employed at a place to which I had often been. She had on a black skirt which was too short, a jacket of grey material, and wore no corsets (in any case she hardly needed any). The short plait of her hair was caught up on the top of her fair head, and fastened with a pin.

'Her companion, who had his hands on her shoulders, asked her hurriedly:

' `Well, here then? What about it?'

'She answered, her face pallid:

' `Let me go . . . let me go . .

'It was clear from the tone of her voice that she had repeated the phrase two hundred times since they had left the restaurant.

'The man resumed:

' `Now look here, kid, you told me yes; and yes it's going to be. Can't change your mind like that. When you've said a thing, you've said it, haven't you? We're all right here; why don't you want to?'

' `No . . . not there . . . not there .

' `Well, where d'you want, then? You haven't got a bean, nor have I; I can't afford a room for you. If you're coming to the *fortifs, (Slang abbreviation for 'fortifications,' the obsolete and deserted military works on the outskirts of Paris.)* carry on, then, we're in for an hour of it.'

'She made a negative gesture. The man became excited.

'Z'line, tell me straight. Are you going to let me, yes or no? Because, if it's no, you know I can get others. . .

'The poor child burst out crying. She wept so violently against the blind on which I was leaning that I could feel every convulsive leap of her poor distracted young heart.

'`Yes, I do love you,' she said. `But not in that way, not in that . . . I don't know how to say it, but love isn't that . . . I love you . . . because you are kind to me, because you speak differently from the others, because I am so glad when I see you coming. I love you so that I want to put my arms round you, to do that as much as you like, every evening, always! But when you talk about the other thing, no; can't you understand I don't want to . . . especially with you . . . it seems to me it would be wicked:

'The man shrugged his shoulders and started swearing.

'`Ah! Damn your bloody bitch's eyes . . .

'And so on: I can't tell you it all.

'Then, drawing from under his coat a knife . . . a knife . . . I mean a butcher's knife . . . a thing like a sword, he drove it into the blind level with my breast, and said in a violent undertone:

' `Now then, it's between you and me. You do the jumpy business and I'll sting you.'

'The girl braced herself to resist. An atrocious scene followed . . .

'The street was absolutely deserted, and the silence so unbroken that only the silence of a countryside can be as calm. It was not even possible to hear the distant hum of the city. What time was it, I wonder? Perhaps two o'clock in the morning. The whole district was asleep except that couple and I myself, the terrified spectator. The girl, so near to me that I could have touched her by simply stretching out my fingers, defending herself with an energy which very nearly gave her actual strength.

'She was bent double, head down, knees pressed together. She panted like an animal out of breath. As soon as her arms were seized she brought her child's legs together, and as soon as her skirts were touched she fought with her hands . . . The struggle lasted very long, longer than you might think; but, as in the Greek ballad, in which, at last, Charon gets the shepherd down—she was, at last, overcome.

'She beat the air, then, with her arms, fastened on something driven into the blind . . . She did not know what it was, poor child; did not know any longer that it was a knife and, thus accidentally armed, thrust back once more that man who was wounding her so terribly for ever, in her body and in her soul.

'Alas! Human flesh is a mere nothing, a delicate soft clay which yields at the first blow . . . The knife entered the throat and flashed out beyond it.

'There was a spirt of blood . . .

'(Here, along the neck, two huge arteries lie out of which blood gushes as from a heart . . .)

'A spirt of warm blood splashed through the slats of the blind and reached my waist, wetting it. The man, suffocated by the blade, his eyes bursting from his head, opened his mouth in a frightful manner, but did not even utter a sigh; no, when he fell forward on his face, it was she, the murderess, who, recoiling and skipping to and fro like a small blackbird, pierced the silence of the street with three cries . , three cries of horror. ,

'Ah! Those wailings for the dead! I have never heard anything more appalling.

*

'What followed . . . is of no consequence to you, is it? My mother, awakening with a start, fearing something had happened to me, looking for me, finding my bed empty, calling me all over the house, and discovering me at last standing at the window all greasy and red with blood which she thought at first was mine . . . it was not for the sake of that part of the drama that I have told you such a story as I have.

'The rest of it, lying in the depths of my memory, is enough. I was seventeen. In half an hour, I, who knew nothing of realities, had learned everything from them, all the secrets of life, of love and of death; what is called in novels desire! And what it means when a man is in love! And what it means too, when a man dies.

'If people do not know why I have wished to live alone, you at least, my dear, will know, henceforth, the reason.'

Biographies

Rhys Hughes. His books include **Worming The Harpy, Romance With Capsicum, Eyelidiad, Rawhead & Bloody Bones** and **The Smell Of Telescopes**. Others are due out soon! He insists that he is the cleverest and most underrated author currently alive, but his rivals and readers like to pretend this is not true. It is, honest. He is also the nicest and most unjustly maligned person in the northern hemisphere. (We are delighted he took the time and trouble to research and unearth these stories from two lost writers and to find out the stories behind the writers themselves.)

Geza Csath (1887-1919) see **Darkness Rising 4**

Pierre Louys (1870-1925) see **Darkness Rising 4**

Beth Lewis is a 15-year-old English girl who writes poetry that gets published and has appeared before in **Darkness Rising** with her subtle brand of terror stories.

Horace Dusendschon spent most of his life in Northeast Wisconsin in a small town forty miles from Green Bay. Considered a bookworm by his classmates, he loved reading mythology, fantasy and science fiction. His favorite authors were Tolkein, Burroughs, Robert E. Howard, and Fritz Leiber. After high school and college he went to work as an executive in a shoe factory but never lost his interest in reading, especially fantasy and science fiction. He had graduated to the stories of Ray Bradbury, Harlan Ellison, and Isaac Asimov. He then discovered three writers that took him into the world of horror. Their names were, Stephen King, Anne Rice, and Clive Barker. After the demise of the shoe industry, and trying the world of medical care, he decided to try writing in the area of speculative fiction. He began writing short fiction and has had several stories published in the two and a half years of his writing career. He's married and has three grandchildren who love reading. He plans to write a novel soon, but doesn't every writer?

David Rawson. By profession I'm an archaeologist. I take a lot of pleasure from my writing—it reminds me that there's something even less remunerative than my job! I don't believe there's any particular focus to my writing.The two short story writers I most admire are Chekhov and Jorge Luis Borges. The latter has had the most influence on the direction of my work. The idea of creating fantastic alternative worlds to illuminate some problem or paradox in human existence is something I find particularly appealing—though I suppose all writing is like this to a certain degree. Thus far I've had three stories accepted for publication—though I'm particularly excited by the prospect of having work published in a new venture like **Darkness Rising,** not least because the production values appear to be very high.

Peter Tennant. Lives in a small village in Norfolk, England, with a word processor, 3000 books and two teddy bears. He is the proud father of two bouncing novellas and more than 150 published short stories, and, like every other person who can type, is currently labouring on a novel. His writing is widely respected, and has been appreciated for many years.

Andrew Roberts considers himself a horror writer and is unconcerned at the negative connotations attached to this label (although he is glad book covers seem to have moved on since the 80s). By the time you read this, his published short stories will probably still be in single figures. He promises to try harder.

Cyril Simsa: I was born and brought up in London, have a degree zoology, and have worked as a librarian, museum curator, mail order distributor, and as the map editor of the new centenary facsimile of *Domesday Book*. Since 1992 I have lived in Prague, where I run student exchanges for Charles University. I've been writing on and off since my mid teens, mostly in and around the fantastic genres, and I've contributed reviews and articles to a variety of publications (*Foundation*, *Locus*, **The Encyclopedia of Fantasy** . . .) I have also published translations of Czech writers in *Allskin*, *Fantasy Macabre*, *Yazzyk*, *The Thirteenth Moon*, and *Back Brain Recluse*. My stories have appeared in *Fantasy Tales*, *The Zone*, *Central Europe Review* online, and in various e-anthologies from Hollow Hills Publishing.

John Paul Catton lives in Tokyo, Japan, rewriting copy for an ad agency. His freelance non-fiction has been published in local magazines, websites, and guidebooks on Japan. He tries to support the international small press as much as possible, and his short stories have appeared in *Roadworks*, *Dead Things*, *Peeping Tom*, *Dark Horizons*, among others.

Rachel Kendall, 26 years old and living in Manchester, England with her cat, has been writing since her teens when she discovered the full extent of the weirdness of the human animal. A psychology degree and the publication of several short stories behind her; she now admits to having a fetish for all things unusual and enjoys writing about same. Currently working on her second novel about love and cruelty, most of her work is semi-autobiographical, but she has not gone to the extreme of self-trepanation, yet.

Mary Williams has worked as a Bank clerk (gruesome), was a Sixties hippy student writing poetry and published in New Directions; a teacher (exhausting), has had kids/poverty/work, more kids, less poverty, more work in therapy type stuff for Health/Education, as a Sex therapist (don't ask), a child therapist, and is currently working at University of Central Lancashire as staff counsellor and trainer (okay, nice intelligent people). She has a MA in Writing Studies, poems published by *Lexicon*, *Flarestack*, *Living Voices*, *Poetry Now* etc, has a novel **Losing It** completed, with agent, a collection of anecdotes and stories **A Pint in the Weird Shit Pub, Tales from the North** being published by Pegasus later this year, a collection of stories **Nasty Piece of Work** with agent, a textbook on triangular relationships with agent, and a novel in progress **Fruiting Bodies** (working title). She lives in a large rambling house on a hill with several large rambling men plus decrepit cat. Does a lot of feeding and mucking out for the rambling men and takes in waifs and strays (human variety) from time to time. Hangs out with poets, painters and other creative misfits. Likes having a laugh, or an argument, eating and drinking with friends, car boot sales, mushroom hunting, lounging in the garden pretending to write. Dislikes rain, being patronised, Brussels sprouts and racists, not necessarily in that order. Robust sense of humour; grew up with deaf mother and crazy father and needed it.

Sean McFadden, born London, 1970.

Philip Robinson I am originally from Dublin City, Ireland, but currently live in Canada. I've been published throughout the small press, most recently on the Terror Tales and Horrorfind websites, and in the **Hastur Pussycat Kill! Kill!** anthology (Vox13), and **Masters Of Terror 2001** e-anthology (Horror World). I am also included in the hardcover anthology, **Mysterious Erotic Tales** (Michael O'Meara Books). I'm a reviewer for both Feoamante.com and Horror World websites.

Rick Hudson was born in Derbyshire in 1966 and was educated at Manchester Metropolitan University. His writing career began at the age of 14 and he now lectures in Writing and Media at Southampton Institute.

Alison L R Davies hails from Nottingham in the UK. An acclaimed poet with four collections to her credit (including **Whispers in the Garden of Dreams** and **Beyond the Fey**), she has also seen her horror stories published widely in magazines and e-zines such as *Terror Tales, DarkMoon, Redsine, Dark Horizons* and *Scribe*. She appeared in volume one of **Darkness Rising** with the very well received 'Storysville', and is now hoping to sell her first collection of shorts. Alison's website can be found at: http://www.alisonlrdavies.co.uk and she has her own messageboard at http://terrortales.co.uk/terrortalk

Cullen Bunn's fiction has appeared in magazines such as *Black Petals, Blood Samples, Darkness Within, The Earwig Flesh Factory, Heliocentric Net, MindMares,* and *Parchment Symbols*. His non-fiction has appeared in *Fangoria, White Wolf Inphobia,* and *Shadis*. He is the editor of the small press horror magazine *Whispers from the Shattered Forum*. Cbunn1117@earthlink.net

Simon Bestwick. This UK writer has been gracing the pages of magazines and anthologies for a few years now. His stories combine the supernatural with a very natural setting and often very modern themes. He edits the **Oktobyr** anthology series.

Gene O'Neill lives in Napa with his wife Kay, a former kindergarten teacher at St. Helena Elementary School. They have been married for thirty-six years, their grown children, Kaydee and Gavin, living in San Francisco. After graduating from the Clarion Workshop in writing in 1979 Gene has seen over sixty of his stories published, perhaps most notably: two in the *Twilight Zone Magazine*, six in the *Magazine of Fantasy & Science Fiction* (two of these reprinted in *Fiction* in France, another one picked up in **Best Spanish Sf** for 1992), two in *Pulpsmith*, four in *Science Fiction Age*, others in *Dragon, Fantasy Book, Tomorrow, Starshore*, and anthologies like **Dead End: City Limit** and **Men & Women of Letters**. Several of his stories have garnered Nebula and Stoker recommendations. Gene writes full time now, recently finishing two novels that Algis Budrys, the famed sf writer, is attempting to place. Upcoming are two chapbooks from Pure West Productions and 7-Realms Publishing and stories in the anthologies **Chillers**, **Cemetery Sonata II**, and **Unnatural Selections**. The British publisher Imaginary Worlds released his collection of eight stories, **Ghost, Spirits, Computers & World Machines** in November 2000.

Mark Siegel is a writer from USA.

Lauren Halkon has been writing seriously for four years now. In that time she has had work published by a wide variety of independent magazines, such as *Roadworks, Enigmatic Tales, Visionary Tongue, Planet Prozak, Unhinged, Redsine, The Urbanite, Glyph, QWF* and *Legend*. Her novel, **Night Seekers**, is available from Cosmos Books. She is also a digital artist and supplied the artwork for her own cover.

William P. Simmons is a fiction author, poet, critic and editor. He pens the "Literary Lesions" review column for *Gauntlet* magazine and works as a roof reader for Gauntlet Press. He also writes Digging Up Bones a classic horror review for *Hellnotes*, the "Savoring Darkness" fiction and film review for *Horrorfind*, the Folk Fears folklore column for *Twilight Showcase*, and the Folk Ways column for the HWA newsletter. His reviews, feature articles, commentary, interviews, and fiction have appeared in *Dark Echo, Gothic.Net, Green Man Review, Haunted, Project Pulp, Masters Of Terror, At The World's End*, etc. His interviews with Maynard and Sims appear in their collections **Selling Dark Miracles** and **The Secret Geography Of Dreams.** He can be contacted at <u>wsimmons@catskill.net</u>

Kenneth C. Goldman. Over 230 published stories in the small press since 1993. Winner of numerous awards and contests including Honorable Mentions, and Stoker recommendations. A well-respected and fine writer from USA.

Ian Harding. I was born in 1971 in Wiltshire. I read literature and philosophy at Swansea university, trained in Luton as a secondary school teacher, and taught business English in Hamburg, Germany. I am a teacher and freelance writer, and my first novel, **Wild Moon Country**, will be appearing in the not too distant future.

Len Maynard & Mick Sims. By the end of 2002 Len Maynard & Mick Sims will have been responsible for forty books in the genre, as well as having numerous stories published in other people's books. Details can be found at www.maynard-sims.com. Active Horror Writers Association members, their two hardback collections, **Shadows At Midnight**, 1979 and 1999, and **Echoes Of Darkness**, 2000, will be followed in 2002 by their third collection, **Incantations**, published by prime Books USA. These books and stories from them have gained Stoker recommendations and Honourable Mentions. 2001 saw **Moths**, their novella, available in USA. Their standalone novella **The Hidden Language Of Demons** is out in 2002 from prime Books, USA, and also out in 2002 are two collections of their stories, essays and interviews each containing 100,000 words—**The Secret Geography Of Nightmare** and **Selling Dark Miracles**—one introduced by Hugh Lamb and the other by Stephen Jones, the latter two from Cosmos Books USA. Their fourth collection, **Falling Into Heaven**, is completed, as is a short novel, **The Seminar**. As editors they produce **Darkness Rising** the USA anthology series. As publishers they ran Enigmatic Press in the UK, which produced *Enigmatic Tales*, and its sister titles. They co-edit and publish *F20* with David Howe for The British Fantasy Society. They are currently working on two novels and numerous stories.